# Destiny Unlimited

A Novel By
**Vanessa Davis Griggs**
proudly presented to you by...
Free To Soar

*Destiny Unlimited* ™

Copyright © 1999 by Vanessa Davis Griggs

**All rights reserved.** No part of this book may be reproduced or transmitted in any form or by any means, electronic or mechanical, including photocopying, recording or by any information storage and retrieval system without written permission from the author, except for the inclusion of brief quotations in a review.

Published by:
**Free To Soar**
P. O. Box 101328
Birmingham, Alabama 35210-1328

Library of Congress Catalog Card Number: **99-90622**

**ISBN 0-9673003-0-4**

**First Printing
September 1999**

Printed in the United States of America by
Morris Publishing
3212 E. Hwy. 30
Kearney, NE 68847
(800) 650-7888

This book is Dedicated to You...
One of many Valuable Treasures.
May you always continue and strive to Be,
The best you, that You
Were meant To
Be!

# Acknowledgments

*"No man is an island unto himself."* First, I am always honored and careful to give praises to an Almighty and Awesome God. I pray I have done justice with what He has given me to share with you.

To my mother, Josephine Lee Davis who has always believed in me while teaching me--by example--what true love is! To my father, James Davis (Jr.), who taught me what it means to have a true "father." To Jeffery, my husband and friend...words aren't enough to express how much you mean to me. Thank you for believing in me and my purpose!

To my children; Jeffery Marques, Jeremy Dewayne, and Johnathan LeDavis Griggs...you are true blessings!

To my sisters and brothers: Danette Dial, Terence Davis, Arlinda Davis, and Emmanuel Davis, thank you for the part you have played in my life. To Robert Dial who always appeared impressed I was writing; Cameron Davis for always expecting a "good word" on my progress. To Reverend and Mrs. James Frazier...thanks for always being wonderful and supportive, even after I moved away.

To all my friends, but especially Rosetta Moore, Bonita Chaney, Pamela Hardy, Loretta Griffith, Elizabeth DeRamus, Shirley Walker, and Ella Wells for believing. To Dr. Phillis Varnado, Dr. Marilyn Williford, Barry Allen, and Seleta Randle-Frelix for the early feedback. To "fred" Maurice Plemmons and Mary Hope--angels here on earth--what else is left to be said?! To all who have been kind or offered me encouraging words (as well as those who didn't)...I thank you! I am *"the sum of all my parts."*

Last but not least, to my publisher "A company with a message." Yes, **I am...Free To Soar!**

"The soul is dyed the color of its thoughts.
Think only on those things
that are in line with your principles
and can bear the full light of day.

The content of your character is your choice.
Day by day, what you choose,
what you think and what you do
is who you become.

Your integrity is your destiny…
it is the light that guides your way."

Heraclitus Greek Poet, Philosopher

*Destiny Unlimited*™

# ONE

"It's dark...cold," eleven-year-old Amethyst Price said. An old woman came and pulled a satin and velvety patched quilt close around the little girl's shivering chin.

The old woman shook her head. "You *still* cold, Child?"

Amethyst, with fluttering eyes, tossed and managed to mumble, "It's like a chill...that won't warm. Grandma say...a chill means...somebody's walking...on your grave. It's cold..."

"She did say that, didn't she?" the old woman whispered to herself. Concern crept over her face as she religiously massaged Amethyst's forehead with long and purposeful strokes. "So much to do...so little time to do it."

"Too soon," Amethyst said like most folks say, 'good night' before she cried out to the blackness, "Mama..." then a quieter, "Why is it so dark?"

The old woman tucked the quilt tighter and began to rock Amethyst while humming a tune, "*Two wings to veil my feet...two wings to fly away...*" She stopped. "Tell me Child, about your family. Your mama...your daddy...those two older sisters of yours...and that fine younger brother--"

"Michael? He doesn't believe me. He thinks I make things up. But I don't. I *don't*! I tell him the truth, but he doesn't believe me. It's so dark...so cold here. Oh why is it so cold?"

"All right, Child...tell me about your parents instead."

Amethyst tossed even more as a pain-like frown came over her face. "They're making fun of my mama and daddy... putting them down. Somebody make them stop. Stop it! Stop it I say! They are *so* good parents! Dark...so dark...and so cold."

# Vanessa Davis Griggs

"Not what others say, what you know. Tell me what you know is true. The happy things. Yes, of course...tell me your happy thoughts."

Amethyst stopped tossing and began speaking easier, not to the woman, she didn't even realize she was there. Amethyst talked about her mother. How she was always there for them...always...with a caring listening ear. Taking...no--making time for precious moments. How she worked at the hospital--long backbreaking hours--before coming home to the same. Not allowing herself to be sick or tired let alone sick and tired. Filling their home with love and understanding as she took care of what was needed for the family. Her family.

Amethyst muttered on about her father, when he wasn't working hard out somewhere, how he could be found working hard around the house. Telling about Valentine's Day and how he would--without fail--bring each child their own little box of candy. How when they needed money for school, trips, or the likes; if he hadn't given them the money when they first asked, they would leave a note next to his metal lunch box to remind him. How he managed to scrape together the dollar...or two...or three--in change, always in change...always. And he never forgot. Not once. On she went about him working sunup to sundown six days a week, never complaining when they raced and jumped up on him as he dragged his exhausted body through the door. A man who more than any thing or any body loved and cherished his wife and children. His family.

She spoke fondly of Sunday mornings...Mama and Christine's grand breakfast...her and Charlene's table setting. Amethyst told how they would all sit around a tiny table; Daddy asking for grace causing them to be even more grateful for "what they were about to receive." Then to Sunday School and Church they'd go. Mama waving her hands in the Spirit with a little "shout out" to God for all His blessings of the past

### Destiny Unlimited

week. Daddy, turning and catching them talking...tilting and nodding his head in Mama's direction--assuring them she wasn't *that* much in the Spirit not to notice them misbehaving.

Mama's magic after church with Sunday dinner as she turned white stale spongy dough into fresh golden baked bread. And the smell! Oh the smell screaming, "*Come and get me!*" Then around the tiny table again, each taking their places... telling what they were most grateful for "on this...another day."

Amethyst's shaking seemed to quiet. Suddenly, she opened her eyes wide and practically looked through that old woman having charge over her. "The light," she said, "...it's so bright! So white and bright!"

"What light, Child? What do you mean bright?" The old woman kneeled down...her eyes fixed on Amethyst's stare. "Listen to me," she said. "Child, listen to me...hear me." Then the old woman began to pray the way elders pray.

Amethyst sat up and opened her arms. "The light," she said before hearing a voice...a familiar one...that caused the light to dim. "What's happening to the light? Where has the light gone? Yet it's not so dark...not as cold."

The old woman breathed a sigh of relief. "Good," she said, "*that* darkness...*that* light has passed." She stood to her feet. "For now anyway. For now." She nodded towards a drifting Amethyst. "Light and darkness cannot occupy the same place, Child. Remember that. Where there is light, darkness cannot exist. Where there is love, hate cannot persist. Where there is joy, sadness cannot take hold." She patted Amethyst's hand through the quilt. "Rest now, Child. Rest. You're yet a long way from home...a mighty long way."

And Amethyst--baffled by the voice that seemed to be speaking inside her head--faintly thought she heard, "And where there is life, there can be no death." *Strange* are life's callings. Strange indeed.

## TWO

"What street is your house on, dear?" Mrs. Dexter said to Amethyst who sat quietly alone in the back seat of the white Mercedes trimmed in gold; her own daughter Erica now sitting in the front seat...a sharp contrast to the way this day had begun. Erica looked back at her "friend" and grinned.

For Amethyst, things began changing the day after she won those two school trophies. That was the day Erica Dexter, a rather popular student, came and practically begged her to become friends. Amethyst couldn't help but think she'd gotten vanilla ice-cream on top of her hot apple pie. Everyone at Fairmont Middle School, knowing Erica had no use for "commoners" like Amethyst, was stunned. That's when the whispering began as all wondered what fourteen-year-old Erica was up to...this time. And if she really *was* sincere, then what had changed her?

The one thing everyone linked to Erica's incredible "heartfelt response" was Amethyst's receipt of the coveted *Most Outstanding Student* and *Most Likely To Succeed* trophies. Awards Erica months ago had faithfully rehearsed to accept, practicing everything from her look of surprise when her name was called, down to her walk across the stage. But instead of her name, Erica found herself pre-empted by "some *no-name label* wearing, darker-skinned country girl" who--of all things-- brought her lunch from home three out of five days to school.

Miraculously however, in only two short weeks, she and Amethyst were somehow now "the best of friends." And the next to the last day of school, Erica waltzed in with "grand" news.

# Destiny Unlimited

"Amethyst," she said, "Mommie's picking me up from school on tomorrow in our brand new Benz, and she and I both thought it would be fabulous if you could come home with me. We can play video games, hang out by the pool, have lunch on the terrace...things like that. We can even watch movies down in the theater room. What do you say?"

Amethyst's eyes lit up. "Really? You want *me* to come?"

"Yes...you. Really! Also, Mommie said she would be happy to take you home afterwards. That way you won't have to worry about getting someone to come pick you up."

"Wow Erica, I don't believe this! You really have a pool?"

"Of course! You don't expect me to go dipping in one of those public things do you?" Erica remembered this was Amethyst she was talking to...her mother had warned her about her tone. "What I mean is my daddy won't hear of it. I'm his little peach you know."

Amethyst couldn't wait to get home and tell everyone. Yes she, Amethyst D. Price, had been invited as a guest to a real live mansion. Erica, her new friend no less, had asked. Oh life!

"Mama, you just gotta say yes! You just got to!" Amethyst said.

"Oh I do, do I?" Her mother smiled while moving one gray curl from her face. "I don't know about this Amethyst. You know how I feel about you going to people's houses when I haven't met their parents yet." It was then the telephone rang...Erica calling to see what Amethyst's folks had said about her coming tomorrow. Amethyst explained what her mother had said and the two mothers spoke briefly. Judith Price looked in her daughter's saucer-like awaiting eyes.

"Amethyst," she said, "to be honest...I really don't feel good about this--"

"Oh please Mama! I promise I'll be home before it gets late. It's only for one day. This could be a reward for my being

## Vanessa Davis Griggs

picked Most Likely To Succeed," she said, saving the other award for another time. Amethyst's mother sighed, looked past the pleading only to see the joy that engulfed her child's face.

"Okay...I suppose you can go. Now Mrs. Dexter said she would bring you home but I--"

"Erica says she just got a brand-spanking new Benz."

"Is that right?" Mama smiled slightly. "Well, looks like my baby's gonna taste all kinds of fine things. That's good--you should taste them. Find out what you like and what doesn't set so well on your stomach." She believed in her daughter, believed that all children should be given a chance...no matter the color...no matter the creed.

Amethyst kissed her mother on the cheek, then raced to call Erica. She could hardly fall asleep.

When school dismissed, Erica and Amethyst strolled casually to a white Mercedes Benz with gold letters. Amethyst couldn't help but think how beautiful Erica's mother was--slim and a light golden brown...like Erica. Her hair, streaked with burgundy over a light auburn tint, was swept around like a roller coaster.

"Amethyst, it's so nice to meet you, dear," Mrs. Dexter said. "Now hop in you two; we've got a big day planned. Amethyst, your mother made me promise to take good care of you." She smiled as she adjusted her Ray Ban sunglasses.

The two girls exchanged looks, giggled, then jumped into the back seats. Amethyst sucked in a deep deep breath. Aah, the smell! Even the *back* was nice!

Erica was right. Amethyst was in for a grand time. She couldn't believe how huge this house was compared to hers--not that she was comparing the two. Her house had a special magic of its own. Where this house was spacious, hers was filled with love and sweet memories. Still she had to admit, this was the largest house she'd ever set foot in...having only on occasion ridden by houses so grand...left only to imagine what lay on the other side of their grandiose leaded glass doors.

The floors in the house--mostly hardwood and marble with only the bedrooms carpeted--were pleasant on the eyes, though Amethyst wasn't convinced she'd care to walk barefoot on marble in the winter time. The front terrace was outlined with limestone columns and balustrades. *Why, the landscape in that area alone had to have cost a fortune!*

Erica floated down the curved staircase with its custom-made wrought iron as though she were rehearsing for her wedding. Mrs. Dexter had personally shown Amethyst every room, exquisitely and meticulously furnished--including the master bedroom with its double hand painted dome and three tier chandelier hanging in the center. The master bath contained *two* separate showers--Amethyst's entire house had only one and it shared space with the *only* bathtub. Her eyes widened. Hushed, raised under a skylight, was a black oval pearl Jacuzzi!

Mrs. Dexter and Erica's tour ended back in the kitchen with its fancy gas stove and griddle, an indoor grill, and *two* ovens set inside a stucco alcove surrounded by oval shaped and hand painted grape arbor tiles. The sun cast a natural warmth inside the nook area as it flooded through a laced decorated five-sided bay window.

"Now this is a dream house!" Amethyst said smiling.

Just the reaction Mrs. Dexter and Erica had hoped for. "Yes, it is a *dream*," Mrs. Dexter said. "A dream very few people ever attain, too...dear."

Amethyst smiled. "Yeah, but my mother says you can have anything if you dream big enough. I've always been a big dreamer, but I see I have room for improvement." She looked around the room with reverence as she sat down.

Erica leaned forward in her chair, propping her chin up on both palms. "Your mother said that? So what does she do for a living?"

"Works at the hospital," Amethyst said proudly.

Mrs. Dexter walked over and sat down two glasses of soda, one next to each girl. "And what exactly does your mother do at the hospital, dear?"

Erica took a sip and watched Amethyst almost without blinking. "Yeah. What *exactly* does your mother *do* at the hospital?" she said, breaking the word hospital into three pieces.

Amethyst swallowed hard the sip she had taken, careful not to spill any on the glass table. "Makes sure that it's kept clean," she said, smiling.

"*Oh?*" Mrs. Dexter said with a frown. "How...nice."

"Yes ma'am, it is nice! You see you can't have germs running loose in a place where people go to get well. Mama takes pride in what she does. Her job is just as important as the doctors and nurses." Amethyst gulped and beamed her own approval. "This soda is good!" Sodas came few and far between at her house.

Erica and Mrs. Dexter exchanged a glance and a smile. "Dear, I don't mean to put what your mother does down--I'm sure it helps you to think her job is equivalent to that of higher ranking personnel at the hospital. But what your mother does is far from equal. So tell me--what does your *father* do?"

Amethyst hesitated. *Had she given Mrs. Dexter ammunition to rip her mother apart? Was she planning on tearing her father down too?* She could make up something to tell her. Not because she was ashamed, on the contrary, she was proud of what her father did. Nobody could fix things like him. *Mr. Fix It* is what everybody calls him. "He's a handy man technician," she finally said, then repeated his favorite phrase, "An honorable day's work for an honorable day's pay."

"A handy man *and* a cleaning woman," Mrs. Dexter said. "How...*quaint*." She turned to Erica. "You know Erica, we should keep that in mind the next time we need some help around here."

"Why, Mommie? Maria cleans just fine. But maybe if Amethyst's mother finds herself in need of extra funds, she could give you a call. I know you'd be able to find something for her to do." Erica smiled and sipped her drink. "Oh, and there is that nail that's backing out...on the deck. I almost snagged my Tommy's the other day." Erica stretched to look down at Amethyst's worn out jeans with her extra long belt that had to be threaded twice through the loops. "Amethyst, do you think your father could bring his thing-a-ma-jig and fix it?"

"That thing-a-ma-jig's called a hammer," Amethyst said lowering her eyes. This wasn't fun. *They're making fun of us.* Looking Mrs. Dexter's in her eyes...*'Always look folks in their eyes,'* Mama always said. "I'm ready to go," Amethyst said.

"Why? What in heaven's name for? We didn't do anything to upset you did we Amethyst?" Mrs. Dexter patted and primped at her still faultless hair.

"No," Amethyst said sharp and blunt before hearing her mother's voice again and adding, "...ma'am. I'm just ready to go home now if you don't mind."

Mrs. Dexter stood up and walked back to the counter. "Well mercy! You kids today are so touchy. People try to impart a little knowledge and wisdom and you just tuck tail and run." She turned back and looked at Amethyst. "Amethyst, all I wanted was to impress upon you that winning some, say cheap little trophy, like *Most Outstanding Student* or *Most Likely To Succeed*, is *not* declaration that a person such as yourself really can succeed." Mrs. Dexter tore off a piece of plastic and

## Vanessa Davis Griggs

wrapped one of the sandwiches she'd prepared for lunch. "Here," she said handing the wrapped sandwich to Amethyst, "I made this for you. Wouldn't want to take you back home hungry now, would I?"

"We have food at home," Amethyst said with a bitter tone and a look to match.

"Oh dear, cheer up! Believe me, you'll thank me for this some day. It'll save you a lot of heartache later. Someone like yourself just doesn't have what it takes to be successful. You're what folks call...disadvantaged. Do you understand?"

The tears wouldn't stay put as they rolled their way down Amethyst's face.

"Look dear, it's not your fault." Mrs. Dexter took a napkin from the holder and handed it to Amethyst. "Now you stop that. You can't help it your folks don't have much to offer you. I just can't stand to see anyone get their hopes up for nothing, that's all. I'm just a little softy I suppose. To think you could possibly be successful--it just doesn't work that way. That's all I'm saying. People who succeed are the exception, not the rule." She looked at Erica. "Am I right baby or what?"

"Oh yes, Mommie; you are right! You're always right. See Amethyst, success is about what you have, live in, wear, eat, and drive--to name a few."

"And dear, being black, and a poor black, I hope *that* doesn't offend you, but you do realize that fact alone doesn't help your case in the least. It doesn't matter how smart you are, when people look at you, just what do you suppose they see first?" Mrs. Dexter waited expecting Amethyst to answer. Seeing that she wasn't, she continued. "Your color of course! You have to be the right kind of person to overcome these type **dis**-advantages. You need the right breeding, rearing...the way you talk matters...what you wear...the way you carry yourself-- all these things matter. Please don't misunderstand me--I'm not putting your people down if that's what it sounds like. I'm sure your parents are good honest folks doing the best they can with what they have to work with. I just don't want you getting your hopes up. That's all. Do you understand now?"

Amethyst gently picked up the sandwich, located her backpack, and slowly headed for the door. "Yes ma'am. I understand perfectly. I'll just wait outside."

Mrs. Dexter let out a sigh. "Oh Amethyst? Dear? I just had a thought. Might you be interested in selling the trophies you won? I could pay much more than they're worth. I'm sure the money would be more useful than those silly things."

Amethyst stood with her hand on the door knob and shook her head. "*No*? Are you sure?" Amethyst nodded. "In that case...I'll get my purse and take you home. Just don't ever say no one tried to tell you. Aim high all you want. But know this, it's a longer way back down when you fall!" She smiled at Erica who was admiring her own polished nails. "Erica dear, am I right or what?"

"Oh Mommie--you're always right." She lowered her hands. "That's why I know I'm destined for success! You see Amethyst, a person like me...can't...miss!" Erica smiled. "Some folks have it, some folks don't. I happen to have it."

Amethyst continued to look at the black and white diamond-shaped marbled floor before stepping outside onto the rough concrete. She quietly shut the door behind her and looked up at the indigo painted sky. "Why are *you* so blue?" she said to the sky. "It's me and my family they just trashed." She sat on the steps, stuck the sandwich inside her backpack, and waited for the two of them to fly her home in their high tech, newly designed, automatic...broomstick.

"Dear? I asked what street is your house on?" Mrs. Dexter said again, snapping Amethyst back to the reality of what seemed to be a long ride home.

## Vanessa Davis Griggs

Amethyst thought a minute longer. *Wasn't it enough they cut me and my family down; must they trash our house too?* She cleared her throat. "You can just drop me off at the park. It's this next exit...Kelly Avenue."

Mrs. Dexter glanced over at Erica. "What did she say? She talks so low I can barely hear her."

Erica turned around and grinned at Amethyst. "You *need* to open your mouth! Mommie can *barely* hear you talk."

"I said," Amethyst almost yelled, "you can drop me off at the park."

Mrs. Dexter turned sharply to Amethyst. "The park? Why, I can't drop you off at any such place. I'm sure not even your mother would appreciate me doing that. Not in the least."

"My mother won't mind. The park is a few blocks from my house," Amethyst said. "If you take me home, I'll just walk over there anyway," she lied.

Mrs. Dexter glanced from Amethyst to Erica. "I don't know about this..." Still, she decided it would save her some time since apparently the park was closer. "Are you sure you'll be all right here alone?" she asked.

"I'll be fine," Amethyst mumbled as she walked away dragging both feet.

"Amethyst?" Mrs. Dexter said from her rolled down window.

Amethyst turned around.

"You know dear...it's only good manners to thank a person once you've been invited as a guest into their home. I do realize you may never have been taught this...or maybe you just forgot?"

Amethyst stood wondering if this woman could possibly be for real. "Thanks," she mumbled and continued on.

"You're welcome," Mrs. Dexter said. "Maybe we can do this again."

### Destiny Unlimited

*Yeah. Right,* Amethyst thought without bothering to look back.

Mrs. Dexter and Erica waved good-bye. Amethyst slung her backpack containing three books, a straight A report card, the sandwich Mrs. Dexter had given her, an empty notebook, and oh yes!...Charlene's three-year-old bathing suit she had hoped, but didn't get to wear today, onto her left shoulder.

The past hours with Mrs. Dexter and Erica had struck a true nerve with Amethyst. All of her life she had watched people...some who had, but most who did not. So why were some people successful while others doomed to struggle forever? Despite what Mrs. Dexter had said, Amethyst still believed that people ultimately had a hand in their own future. They were the ones who had the power to cause things to happen...or not. Destined...Destiny? Destiny too. And if destiny was the mother of success then she didn't mind being her child.

"Listen," a quiet voice whispered.

She immediately looked around figuring someone to be playing a joke on her. She saw no one. Shrugging it off to the wind, she continued on.

All types of "elements" were at the park, and her mother--who wouldn't have approved--had no idea she was there. Amethyst decided she'd search for the keys to success and making things happen since she was out. Then she could go home and wouldn't have to talk about her day with the Dexters. What could she tell her family anyway that wouldn't upset them or worse...cause her mama to "...lose her religion!"

## THREE

Amethyst noticed an older man dressed in fine threads starting from his head down to his spit-shined leather shoes. His burgundy double-breasted suit reminded her of the streak in Mrs. Dexter's hair. The hat he wore with the black band encircling it, held tight a feather for the wind to tickle. The man talked to the birds while tossing bread pieces. Amethyst thought, *Maybe there is something to learn from him*, so she stopped to listen.

"My tongue is the pen of a ready writer. My tongue is the pen of a ready writer," he said continuous and deliberate. He sounded like a preacher and the pigeons? His faithful flock pecking hungrily to devour his every word.

"Excuse me," Amethyst said. He turned and looked up. "Forgive me, but I heard you talking to the birds as you were feeding them. What exactly do you mean by...your tongue is the pen of a ready writer?"

His face was hard...he did not smile. Some might have pegged him mean...grumpy even. "What?" he said snapping at her. "Young Lady, get this straight, I was not talking to any such birds. I was merely meditating on a present financial dilemma. Words usually assist me while I'm in deep thought."

"Meditating? Are you in deep thought a lot Mister?"

He looked at her. "Well...now...I've never really considered it. But I suppose one could say that I am." He sat back against the bench. "So little pecan with the sandy hair, what are you doing here? With a book bag at that?"

She thought long before answering him. She didn't want to tell him about school and how she had helped the teacher clean out the closet. She didn't want to tell him how the teacher had given her some books to read over the summer so she wouldn't be bored. She didn't want to tell him about Mrs. Dexter and Erica (who turned out not to be her friend after all) or the words that had cut her heart like a knife but fortunately not her vision for life. No, she didn't want to tell him any of these things. What did they matter anyway? She alone could choose what she said or didn't.

"I'm on a quest," she said as her eyes twinkled with pride. She couldn't control the smile that automatically appeared on her face.

"A quest, huh? Well Young Lady, you look much too young for something so grown up. Shouldn't you be in school or something today?" He cracked his mouth to a half-smile; his face appearing softer when he did.

"I'm eleven," Amethyst said, "going on twelve. And in case you haven't noticed, I'm not the only kid here. School's out." Maybe she had made a mistake stopping to talk to him after all. What could he possibly know about success? He didn't even know school was out.

He laughed as though he had read her mind. "Eleven going on twelve, eh?" he said. "Well now...that does make all the difference in the world. Only someone old enough to be on a special quest would say eleven going on twelve as opposed to eleven-and-a-half."

"Are you making fun of me?"

He smiled. "No, Young Lady. I most certainly am not. And I'm sorry if I have offended you by mistaking you for someone younger. But trust me, it will be one of your greatest compliments later in life."

Amethyst thought about what he was saying. He *was* right about that age thing though. All her mother's friends seemed so excited whenever a cashier at the store would ask them for some form of ID on the occasions they purchased "stuff they didn't have any business with anyway" as they always put it should she happen to be in hearing range.

As if to draw her attention, the man cleared his throat. "Back to this quest you're on. What sort of a quest is it? That's if you don't mind my prying."

She twisted and frowned. "Well, I'm searching for the key...or keys to success. I want to know how to make things happen," she said smiling.

He twisted his mouth; deep rows like those in gardens furrowed across his head. "Keys? To making things happen?"

"Yes."

"Hmmm. Maybe you should begin with something not so challenging." He tried--unsuccessfully--not to smile. "I think that's going to be tough one."

"It's not going to be tough. And if there is such a key, I'm going to find it!"

"Calm down," he said pulling back from the force of her words. "I didn't mean anything by it. Seems like you've made up your mind, so please...don't mind me. Tell me though, what makes you think there is such a key to find?"

Amethyst sensed she had hooked his attention. "Or keys," she said. "It's like when you go in search of treasures, there might be a map, a special key. Say, wouldn't it be something if it turns out to be a real magic lamp? Yeah, a magic lamp...with a genie inside."

"A genie too, huh?" He smiled. "Look, I think what you're doing is quite honorable. But if there was such a key, a magic lamp, a genie out there that was responsible for making things happen, don't you think somebody would have discovered it by now?" Without warning, a strong gush of wind came and blew his hat right off his balding head. It tumbled like a weed as he chased it several yards before finally cornering it against a nearby bench.

## Destiny Unlimited

As he brushed the dirt from his hat, Amethyst heard a sweet voice inside the wind.

The man came and sat back down while brushing his burgundy pants leg and pinching downward his razor-like crease. "Now, where were we?" he said stroking his thinly trimmed beard. "Oh yes! A genie and a key. Now--are you referring to a genie like the ones told in those Aladdin tales?"

Amethyst wasn't listening as much to him as she was trying to hear what the voice in the wind was saying. "Mister, do you hear that?" She cocked her head to one side.

He looked around at the few children who were running towards the sand box. Other than them, no one else was even close. "Hear what?" he said.

"The wind? Do you hear the wind?"

He laughed. "Of course I hear the wind--as much as hearing wind goes. It's starting to die down now I do believe although I smell a storm brewing, over yonder way." He pointed in the vicinity of Amethyst's house.

"No. I meant did you hear what the wind was saying? You see, there's this voice...it's seems to be hiding in the wind."

He laughed again. "A voice in the wind, huh?" He looked around before lowering his voice. "And what exactly is this voice saying, Young Lady?"

"I'm serious." She stopped and listened again. "Faster, please," she began to whisper out loud. "I can't make out the last part." She was quiet, listened, smiled, then turned back to the man. "No. It's not exactly like the genie in those stories. That's been the problem...people mixing up the truth with fairy tales. There is a genie; it's invisible. It's spelled G-i-n-e."

The man smiled and patted her on her shoulder. "That's not quite the way you spell genie," he said smiling.

"I know how to spell Mister! G-e-n-i-e. But this genie is spelled G-i-n-e."

"You're smart for eleven," he said. Then the expression on her face caused him to add, "...going on twelve."

Amethyst smiled. "You think I'm making this up?"

"No, Young Lady. If you say you heard a voice...then I believe you. You know the Lord does work in mysterious ways. At least, that's what I've been told." He smiled. "Just so we won't be strangers...name's Fuller." He extended his hand.

"Amethyst!" she replied while shaking his hand with a quick pump. She had totally forgotten he was a stranger.

"Amethyst? What an unusual name. Well, it's a pleasure to meet you, Miss Amethyst."

She remembered the reason she had stopped in the first place; he had yet to answer her question. "Mr. Fuller?"

"Yes ma'am."

"The words you were speaking when I walked up...about your tongue being the pen of a ready writer-- where'd you get that saying from? And why were you repeating it over and over?" she asked.

Fuller laughed. "You must have thought I was crazy; I assure you I'm not. I had an uncle once who talked to birds. Mostly because he was in the spirits..." he whispered, "of the bottle that is. Yep, Uncle Bubba talked to any and every thing." Fuller threw out pieces of bread then handed Amethyst some.

"I didn't think you were crazy. Not really anyway. Else I wouldn't have even stopped." She tore off pieces of the bread he had given her, and tossed it.

He smiled. "To be honest, I got that saying from my father. You see, my father was a preacher. He pulled that scripture straight from the Bible. He told me--I think I was just about your age at the time--he said, 'Here boy. Learn this here verse. Come out of Psalm 45 and one. It'll take you far in this life.' Now one thing you have to understand about my father is, when he told you to do something, that was pretty much all there was to any meaningful discussion." Fuller looked at Amethyst and smiled. "He told, you did it."

"So why do you think your father believed you needed to memorize that verse?"

"It's funny," he said with a laugh. "I had really never thought about it; just figured he was slightly crazy, you know, a bit too much religion. But sitting here talking with you about it, I see what my father was really doing. He was making me aware of my words...didn't want me talking wrong I suppose."

"Talking wrong?"

"Yeah, talking wrong. He must have figured I needed to be more aware of the importance of my tongue and the role it would forever play in my life."

"You mean the words you speak?"

He nodded. "Yes, I suppose that must have been it."

"So that's really saying our tongues are like pens. And a pen is what we use when we want to write things down."

"Yeah," Fuller said. "Sounds good to me."

Amethyst became more excited with every word she spoke. "And when something is written down, it is no longer invisible but now visible."

"Yes. Exactly." He took his hat off and began to scratch his head. "Well I'll be. You know what else my father would say? That the tongue could bring life or death to a situation. One could heal or kill with just the tongue."

Amethyst scrounged her hand around in her backpack, pulling out her notebook then hoping...wishing...searching diligently for a pen she knew wasn't there. "Sort of like a two-edged sword?" she said still searching.

"Precisely!" Fuller said laughing--a laugh more animated now than at any time since Amethyst had sat down beside him. "That's what my Daddy said. A tongue can cut both ways if you're not careful." He reached inside his jacket and handed her a pen. She wrote feverishly. "So what you got there?" he said.

"Oh this?" She held up her notebook. "I'm writing all this down. Keeping an account...so I don't forget anything."

"Then you need to hang on to that pen for later." He grinned and shook his head. "Smart, little thing! How old did you say you were? Sixty-two?" She laughed. "Well I'll be dang if you don't look a day over eleven...going on twelve," he said.

Amethyst smiled, closed the notebook, stuck the pen in the spiral part, and stood up. "It was nice meeting you."

He held out his hand. "No, Young Lady...the pleasure's been all mine." She shook his hand as he bowed politely while tipping his hat. "Mine indeed."

Amethyst felt like a princess. "Mr. Fuller? May I ask you just *one* more question?" she said.

"You Miss Amethyst, may ask me anything. Anything your heart desires."

"How do you manage to dress in such fine clothing...if I'm not being too forward," she said with a smile. "What I mean is...what do you do different from others who may never know the feel of such fine threads as those?"

"Threads?" he said. "Oh you mean these old things?" He grinned. "Now had you asked me that question before we had this *enlightening* conversation, my answer would have been totally different. However, giving it some thought, I can see that my tongue is the pen of a ready writer. It appears the one thing I have forever let slip from these lips in regards to my *threads* as you call them has been: **I dress sharper than the lilies of the field. And that even Solomon in all his glory was not dressed as fine as one of them. Therefore, I dress sharper than Solomon ever did.**"

Amethyst opened her notebook and wrote. Turning again to Mr. Fuller she said, "Thanks Mr. Fuller. Thanks a lot!"

# Destiny Unlimited

## FOUR

Amethyst's quest in the park lead her to a man squeezed into a raggedy jacket and a pair of pants not long enough to be called floods, yet too long to be labeled Bermuda shorts.

He mumbled while searching through garbage cans, "My tongue is the pen of a ready writer! Yeah? And folks think I'm crazy. It's him that's out of his dag-blasted-cotton-picking mind!" The man turned and looked at Amethyst who stood gazing at him. "Just what are *you* staring at?" She didn't answer. "Go away I say. Gon' now! Shoo!"

Amethyst didn't budge. She took out her notebook and began to write.

"What's the matter with you? Are you deaf or just hard-of-hearing? Most likely just plain old hard-headed the way most young folks are these days." Amethyst continued to write. "Hey...you," he said, "did you not hear me? I said for you to go away!" He trapped a piece of paper that rolled on the ground from the push of a small breeze as he mumbled at it.

Amethyst stood there not sure how to take him. The words he had spoken were the exact same words Mr. Fuller had spoken minutes earlier. But something was wrong with this picture; he was shabby...and nasty-looking.

He waved his hand across her face. "Say kid...what's your problem? You never seen nobody converse with themselves before? I...am a bum. A bum. Yet my aim is not to scare anybody dumb, and I sure wouldn't hurt you, Red--"

"Don't call me Red!" Amethyst said with such force she scared her self. "My hair is sandy, a light auburn. My skin is pecan. But I am *not* red!"

He stared back at her. "So what are you doing here so early in the day? I thought all you young folks knew how to do was sleep, watch that dag-blasted-electronic-baby-sitting-device called the television, and play video games." He rubbed his face full of porcupine needle-like more salt than pepper, hair...a face that would surely draw blood if accidentally touched. The hair on his light brown head stood to attention as the red white and blue flag on the pole waved nearby.

"I don't sleep late," Amethyst said. "And I'd rather read a book any day than watch television. TV and video games can't hold a candle to what I can create. My theater mind. Mama says she doesn't believe my brain ever rests," she said.

"Aah, young folks!" He batted his hand down. "What are you even wasting your time talking to somebody like me for anyhow? Don't you know a foolish old bum when you see one? A homeless bum at that. I am Daniel Lewis, as God is my judge, but everybody calls me Lewis the Bum." He bowed then walked over to the garbage can, pulled out a hat, and grinned as if he had just discovered the wheel. "I wondered where I had put you," he said, mashing the hat on his head. "My helmet!"

The hat was every bit as ratty as its owner who was minus a tooth...or two in the front; Amethyst noticed the gap when he grinned. He dusted off a plump crust from a pizza someone had thrown away, then kissed it to the sky.

"Such a waste," he said. "Such waste. As always, Lewis to the rescue."

"Stuff like that'll kill you," Amethyst said. "It's crawling with germs."

He chewed it--using only one side of his mouth. "Is that right, Miss Smarty-pants? Well you know what they say; we all gonna die from something!" He licked his fingers. "I'd rather my death not be from starvation." He stopped smacking long enough to look in her eyes. "So, what's your name, R--...kid?"

## Destiny Unlimited

"Amethyst," she said squeezing down her eyebrows as she turned up her nose.

"So why are you still hanging around? It should be obvious by now--even to a blind man--I don't have nothing to offer you. I'm barely making it myself." He reached inside his jacket and pulled out a bottle stuffed inside a brown paper bag. "Juice," he said holding it up to his own face for approval. "What's a healthy lunch without a little juice to wash it down." He turned up the bottle and staggered backwards. "Aaaah! Now that hit the spot!" He smiled. "If you really want to know what's gonna be the death of me, then this is where you might start looking. If I were smart, I'd give this mess up and get my life together."

Amethyst sat on the bench. "Then why don't you?"

He looked stunned. "Why don't I what?"

"Why don't you give it up and get your life together?"

He snickered. "Oh you're a funny one I see. Little Miss Smarty. Probably from all those books you read huh? Look kid, you're young so I'll forgive you for seeing the world through sunglasses." He took another swig before flopping next to her.

"You could change things you know," Amethyst said.

He laughed, except this time, it was different. Not as lively as before; more reflective with a pinch of attitude. "Look at me, kid. I mean *really* look at me. I'm the classic loser. I was born a loser, and I'll most likely die a loser." He sighed. "There are two classes of people in this world...the haves and the have nots. It's the law of the jungle. The bigger ones annihilating the smaller ones. It's not a pretty site, but it is what it is."

"I don't believe that," Amethyst said.

He pulled back and looked at her. "You don't believe it? What's not to believe?"

"I don't believe there are only two kinds of people. And as for that size thing, I've heard how elephants are afraid of little bitty mice. Did you know that as small as a spider is, it can kill a grown man? And a bunch of ants attacking something can also kill. You know, there was this one time I got bit by a red ant...it hurt...and itched for days."

Mr. Lewis took another swallow of juice. "I don't mean to hurry you along kid, but is there a point to this or something? I mean I do have things to do. Contrary to what you've been told, food doesn't fall from the sky. Unless of course, you happen to be Moses leading people to the promised land."

Amethyst remembered the sandwich Mrs. Dexter had given her. She pulled the sandwich out, tore it, and handed him half while she examined the other half. "My point is, there are those who try regardless of their size. They try regardless of the circumstances in which they were born."

He nodded thanks as he practically swallowed his half in one bite. "Kid, I remember when I thought the same way. I tried. The Lord knows I tried. I did all the right things, or so I thought. Said all the right words--but look at me. I'm a bum. I'm a 56 year-old man who looks closer to 86. I'm what many call a natural born loser. It just wasn't in my cards." He began to twirl his hat. "Oh yeah, I had a good job once--twenty-nine years of dedicated on-time service. And do you know how they rewarded me? Sent me packing. Called it downsizing, but just like that, turned me out on the street then hired some younger person to come in and take my place." He laughed. "I took what money I had; tried my hand at investing. What I didn't lose, creditors took. All I have left, sits right here before you now."

"Yes, but Mr. Fuller said--"

"Fuller? Fuller? You talking about Fuller who be down on the other end talking to those stupid pigeons? The Mr. Fuller who tries to act like he's Donald Trump...*that* Mr. Fuller?"

## Destiny Unlimited

Amethyst nodded. "Yes, Mr. Fuller. Except he's not talking to the birds, he's meditating. Anyway, he says--"

"Look, I don't want to hear nothing that man's has to say. Donald Trump, he ain't. More like Donald Duck. Around there quacking about your tongue being some kind of a pen. What's that you say? He's meditating? Meditating my foot! He's just out of his cotton-picking-mind is what he is!"

"But--"

"But nothing! Kid, look...all I know is what I know. I know that I'm never gonna win no matter how I try. I know speaking all that mumbo jumbo stuff Mr. Fuller go around spouting don't do one thing for me or anybody else. When I look at myself--it doesn't matter what I say--I still see a loser. You can dress me up in a fancy suit all you want. You can shave me bald and bathe me clean! You can fit me with a brand new set of teeth. But no matter what you do, somehow the bum is going to manage to shine through. You understanding anything I'm saying?"

Amethyst thought a second. She opened up her notebook and began to jot something else down.

Mr. Lewis saw how intense she was as she wrote. "You want something to put in that little book of yours? Then write this. Even before I landed here dining from this buffet of garbage cans, I saw myself here. Although I was making good money on my job, somehow I still always saw myself as the bum I truly was to be. Now that I'm here, I've just decided not to fight it. Talk all you want, speak all the right words you can think to say; but if your mind sees a thing differently from what your mouth is verbalizing then ultimately...what you **see** is what will **be**. I'm living proof of that."

Amethyst stopped after writing **What you see is What will be** and then looked up at him. "So you're saying you always saw yourself as a bum?"

He sighed hard like he was tired. "Kid, were you not paying attention to a word I said? Yes. I always saw myself as a bum! I saw myself being right here doing exactly what I'm doing right now. Even before I got here." He stood, pressed his hat down on his head and walked away without another word.

Amethyst sat thinking. She then quickly stood up. "Mr. Lewis!" she yelled. "Mr. Lewis! You succeeded then!"

He stopped and turned around. "*Excuse* me?" he said tilting his head sideways and wiggling his right ear with his hand. "What did you just say?"

She ran to catch up to him. "I said...you succeeded then! What you expected is what you got. In your mind you saw yourself right here doing exactly what you're doing and somehow--or another--your brain worked to help manifest what your mind saw. That means...you're a success!"

He looked at her even more puzzled. "You know, kid... normally I wouldn't waste my time discussing something silly like this with a child. But would you care to explain just how being a loser could possibly qualify me as a success?"

They were standing toe to toe now; she flashed him a warm smile. "You said you saw what you were, then became what you saw. The way I figure, it didn't matter that you had a job making good money. It didn't matter that you had money invested. Your vision for yourself--your life in fact--was that of a bum. Therefore, against all the things life tried to bring you that was contrary to what you believed, you still somehow managed to succeed in making your vision come true. So Mr. Lewis, you are not a failure at all...you...are a success!"

He laughed and shook his head. "Lord have mercy and folks think I'm crazy!" He staggered away though his head held higher. On occasion he glanced back and grinned as he chewed on the words and wonder of a kid who somehow believed him not a failure, but instead, one who had managed to succeed.

## FIVE

It was evening, but Amethyst wasn't ready to go home. They'd surely want to hear about the Dexters, and she hadn't figured out what to tell them just yet.

The silver slide bounced a beam of sunlight into her eyes as she walked by. Dropping her backpack to the ground, she climbed up its steel ladder before fighting the wind with her face as her body flew towards it. *Life is like a slide*, she thought. *You climb up to enjoy seconds of thrills even coming down.*

After a few more times down the slide, she went to the swing with its own up and down tendencies. Hopping onto the merry-go-round, she thought it too much like worrying...*feels like you're doing something, yet it takes you nowhere.* Finally, she glanced at the see-saw but there was no one around to balance the other end. Then seemingly out of nowhere, a woman around sixty, the color of wet pine mulch, thick gray hair with traces of black wrapped into one fat braid that trailed down her back, walked up and went to the other end.

"Get on," the woman said in a deep voice.

Amethyst hesitated. What if she fell and hurt herself?

"Folks call me *O My*. Now get on." She held the handle. "Look, if you want to ride you got to get on," she said poetically.

Amethyst did as instructed. The old woman acted more like a teenager, reminding Amethyst of her sister Christine, before Christine got so prissy.

Amethyst's mother was home beginning to worry. *Mrs. Dexter did say she would bring Amethyst home, didn't she?* Judith Price glanced again at the clock on the wall. Even with daylight savings time it would be dark soon. *What on earth could they be doing that she hadn't called or come home yet?*

Judith dialed. "Mrs. Dexter? This is Judith Price, Amethyst's mother."

"Yes, Ju-dith. What can I do for you?" Mrs. Dexter was both prim and proper.

Judith Price frowned. What an odd thing to say. "Well, actually I was wondering what time you were planning to bring Amethyst home. I don't want her wearing out her welcome on her first visit."

"Wear out her welcome?" Mrs. Dexter said as she began to motion for Erica to bring her a pad and pen. "Now how could such a dear sweet child like Amethyst *ever* wear out her welcome with us?" She shrugged her shoulders to Erica as she wrote *Amethyst is not home. Wonder where she is?*

"Now if it's any trouble or an inconvenience, it's no problem for me to run over there and pick her up. If you'll just give me directions to your house--"

"No," Mrs. Dexter said. "Oh no Mrs. Price. We were just having so much fun...we simply...lost track of time. That's all. There's no need for you to put yourself out. I tell you what...we'll finish what we're doing now...and I'll get her right on home to you. Will that suffice?"

"Why...yes. Sure. I wasn't meaning to rush you; I was just concerned when I saw it getting late. I wasn't sure whether I had misunderstood or what--"

"Oh n-o. Everything's...peachy-king! So we should see you in about...an hour we'll say?" Mrs. Dexter flinched and nibbled at her thumbnail. "Bye now."

Erica came around the counter and hung up the phone. "What is it? Little Miss Most Likely To Succeed hasn't succeeded in getting home yet?"

### Destiny Unlimited

"No she hasn't!" Mrs. Dexter said pacing in front of the kitchen sink. "And I wonder where the little brat is?! Out at this time of the evening. The little fast thing."

"She's probably still at the park."

"I hope so. I do *not* have time for this now. I should have just told her mother and been through with it. Come on--let's go find her and get her home."

Mrs. Dexter arrived at the park determined to locate Amethyst and get the h---, get out of that hole...sooner rather than later. She didn't feel safe in the daylight, and she most certainly wasn't going to be caught in that neighborhood after dark. She looked around, positive this had to be where the bad elements...the thugs came and hung out. *A bunch of lazy things.* She had no intentions of her sweet innocent daughter being exposed to this criminally infested environment.

Mrs. Dexter and Erica saw Amethyst sitting on a bench near the see-saw talking to an old woman and quickly jogged towards her.

"Amethyst!" Mrs. Dexter walked to her. "What is the meaning of this? Why are you still here? Do you know your mother is looking for you? Did you even think about that?"

Amethyst looked up. "Shoot! Mama! What time is it?"

Mrs. Dexter looked at her watch. "Almost seven now."

Amethyst turned to the old woman--not only did she not want to talk *about* the Dexters, she didn't want to talk *to* them either. "I didn't realize it was so late!"

Mrs. Dexter moved closer. "Fortunately for you, I've covered your tail. I didn't let your mother know where you really were. She believed you were still with me at my house having a grand time. And that's what we're going to let her continue to believe after you get home. Do you hear?" She folded her arms and patted her left foot. "So hurry up and get your...things; I'm taking you home myself this time."

# Vanessa Davis Griggs

Amethyst sat on the bench and continued to swing her legs. She gazed at the merry-go-round. "I'll go when I'm finished," she said with a face of stone.

Mrs. Dexter surveyed the area. There were just too many teenagers around this place for her comfort. She watched four teenage guys huddle together...talking--and on occasion-- glancing in their direction. "Erica," she said pulling her to the side, "I believe those thugs are eyeing your shoes! And what's all this jewelry around your neck? You're begging for us to be robbed. You look like--what was his name? Mr. T.! Yes, you look like a Mr. T. wannabe minus the bad haircut!" she whispered.

Erica made an attempt to hide the Prayer Box charm that dangled from her wrist. Her mother would really go ballistic if she had even an inkling she had borrowed this "jewel" from her safe box. "Mommie...why would anyone even waste time with my trifling things when they can get voo-coo for *your* **rock.**"

"Oh my God! I wasn't thinking!" She shoved her hand quickly into her pant's pocket, twisted the three carat solitaire off her finger, then leaned over and whispered, "These hoodrats probably could care less if I were only wearing a plain band. They'd probably try and steal that too. Anything for a fast buck. Now let's get this child and get out of here!"

Mrs. Dexter walked back over to Amethyst and the old woman. She pulled out a dollar bill and held it out. "Look lady, here's a dollar. Go buy yourself a nice hot meal or something." She then turned to Amethyst. "And you...I told you to get your bag and let's go. I don't like it here!"

"Well I do," Amethyst said. "You go; I can find my way home just fine."

Mrs. Dexter clenched her teeth. *You little brat!* she thought but said, "Look dear...your mother trusted me. She'll

## Destiny Unlimited

probably want to sue me if anything should happen to you--not that she'd have a case--but it would be such an inconvenience. Taking you home now will only cost me a few minutes of my time. But since my time is valuable, then I want you to get your things...and let's go! *Now!*" Mrs. Dexter noticed the old woman hadn't taken the money yet.

"Look lady," Mrs. Dexter said to her, "take this already! I don't have all day to fool with you. Either of you! And I'm certainly not planning to give you any more than this for you to drink up if that's what you're thinking!"

The old woman began to laugh. It was a presaging type of laugh. Mrs. Dexter stepped back a couple of steps...pulling Erica along with her. "What is the matter with you? Are you crazy as well?" Mrs. Dexter crammed the dollar into her pocket. "Great! Now these hoodlums know I have money too!" She noticed the four guys seemed to be coming closer, so she grabbed Amethyst by one arm. "Erica, get her knapsack! We're leaving, whether she's ready to go or not!"

Amethyst snatched her arm away. "How dare you!" she said grabbing away her backpack from Erica. "How dare you think you can treat people the way you do and get away with it! You're mean! Just plain old mean! Mean and insensitive--both of you! And were my mother to know just what kind of people you really are, she wouldn't even punish me for speaking this way!" Amethyst closed her notebook, shoved it into a slot on the outside of her backpack, and strolled away.

"Why you little--!" Mrs. Dexter began, but then stopped and sucked in a sober breath. "You will not speak to me in that tone of voice, do you hear me? Your *mother* probably won't punish you because she knows *nothing* about respect!"

Amethyst stopped in her tracks...turned...and hurried back. "My *mother* has more class and more respect in her little pinkie than you do in your whole entire body! You've insulted my family, insulted me. You even came here and insulted this feeble old lady without knowing one thing about any of us! You're just a prejudiced old goat; that's what you are! Prejudging folks without knowing them. Judging folks because they don't have what you think they should. Calling yourself defining what's normal or right by some rule you've set up in your mind. Then to think you can force people to simply bow to your standards." Amethyst took a step towards her...forcing her two steps back. "Well Mrs. Dexter, I have seen your standards and you know what? Your standards are hereby rejected!" Amethyst grinned. "And you know what else? You're not so great! But I'm not sinking to your level. My *Mama* says it's better to stand than to crawl any ol' day!"

Mrs. Dexter lunged forward. "Why you little--"

The old woman stood and caught Mrs. Dexter's arm. "Leave her be," she said in a calm deep voice.

Mrs. Dexter looked at the long wrinkled fingers that held tight her wrist. Her eyes traveled back up only to be met by the old woman's piercing stare.

"I said **leave...her...be!**" Then she released her grip and began to laugh as she reached under the bench and retrieved an old worn-out duffel bag.

Everything was bothering Mrs. Dexter now: Amethyst's words so easily spoken...the old woman's laugh...Erica's mind (which seemed to be everywhere except where her body was lately)...the teenage guys' methodical glances in their direction.

Amethyst and the old woman walked together... crossing the path of the four teenagers who appeared headed towards Mrs. Dexter. Mrs. Dexter searched her purse while keeping her eyes glued to each of their long slinky striding steps. "Come on Erica!" she said. "Who cares about that child! You and I need to get out of here. *Now* Erica!"

### Destiny Unlimited

She only relaxed when her fingers finally touched the cool pearl handle of her .38 Smith and Wesson--her license to carry it safely stashed inside her car's glove compartment. "Now let one of those little thugs try something," she said under her breath. "I'll have something they can have all right!"

Mrs. Dexter and Erica walked faster. The four teenagers stopped where the Dexters had stood. Amethyst, now alone, headed across the park. One of the teenagers began to yell after Mrs. Dexter. "Yo lady! Hold up a second!" Mrs. Dexter began to trot...dragging Erica with her. "Yo! Lady!" he yelled again, "I said, wait up!" Mrs. Dexter stopped, pulled out the gun, and turned squarely to face them...the gun systematically pointing towards each one's teenage heart.

"Stay away from us! Trust me--I know how to use this!"

All four stopped. Erica stopped. Amethyst stopped. The old woman stopped. And for a minute, time seemed to stop. Mrs. Dexter aimed the gun at them--one second for each one as she continued to move from one to the other.

"Look lady," one of them said, "we're not trying to hurt you." Another guy stuttered. "We thought we saw one of you drop something. We thought it might be important! One of you dropped something...that's all we want to say lady."

Mrs. Dexter held the gun steadfast. "You didn't see us drop a thing!" she said. "Now back away from me and my daughter and nobody gets hurt all right!"

One guy cut his eyes across to the guy standing next to him. "You see! What did I tell y'all? Let's just forget about this. This woman's crazy!" "Yeah," said the guy on the end. They backed up a few feet before turning to walk away.

Mrs. Dexter lowered the gun. Amethyst had watched in sheer disbelief.

## Vanessa Davis Griggs

Erica played with the pendant hanging from her neck chain. "Wow!" she said, "You're a regular little Dirty Harriette! I guess you showed them."

"I hope so," Mrs. Dexter said carefully placing the gun back in her purse.

It began to sprinkle. People raced for cover, leaving the park deserted in a matter of minutes. One of the teenage guys ran and caught up with Amethyst. Aljuwon...from down the street; he liked her sister Christine--a lot. Christine could do much worse.

"Amethyst?" Aljuwon said. "Would you mind doing me a little favor?"

"Depends on what little is," she said blinking back the sprinkling rain.

"It has something to do with that crazy woman you were talking to, the one who pulled the gun on us back there." He smoothed his fuzz of a mustache.

Amethyst listened as he talked, on occasion shaking her head adamantly. He drew closer to her and whispered more. Finally looking up at him with her big brown eyes, she nodded and said, "Sure--I suppose I can do that." Following his lead, she then smiled.

Not fifteen minutes later, what could have easily been mistaken as the first blast of an expectant thunder...was in actuality, the crackling explosion of a gun.

## SIX

A shot. One shot. Not one to ring around the world. Not one that would even set a small country to arms. Not one that would normally grab a news room's busy attention except were it needed to fill the void of a fifteen second spot.

"Oh my God! What have I done?" Mrs. Dexter looked at the gun before almost dropping it to the ground. She kneeled quickly beside the still body--a gunshot wound to the head. "Please don't be dead! Please don't be dead!" she said as she felt frantically for a pulse. "My God!...do you have any idea how much trouble this could cause me? Please don't be dead!"

Eleven-year old Amethyst Price's body lay motionless on the ground as Mrs. Dexter grabbed her hand...careful not to get blood on herself. "Oh *please*, don't let her be dead!"

"Mommie," Erica said as she stood beside her mother. "I hate to say this because it sounds cruel, but if she's dead, then no one would know who did it."

"What?" She looked through tears at Erica. "What did you say?"

"I'm saying, nobody has to know what really happened. Everybody knows muggings and shootings go on all the time. And in a neighborhood like this, I'm sure it isn't the first time somebody's gotten shot. It's life. It's unfortunate--"

"Erica, I can't just leave her here!" Mrs. Dexter was disoriented. "People saw us with her."

"Then call her mother and tell her mother the truth," Erica said.

"The truth?" Mrs. Dexter said trying to think what she should do now.

"Yes--the truth! Tell her she asked you to drop her off at the park which you did--that's true. Tell her you saw her talking to a few people like she knew them already--also true. Then you can tell her that Amethyst insisted she could walk home from here so you left her here. See Mommie--all true!"

Mrs. Dexter gazed into space hardly able to believe what her ears were hearing coming out of the mouth of her own daughter. "Erica, I can't just leave her here like this. The right thing is to call and get help in a hurry."

Erica gently pulled her mother's hand away from Amethyst's hand. "Let's say you call an ambulance and she pulls through...she'll tell them everything."

"Then you and I will just have to tell the truth, baby--"

"Yes--our truth, Mommie. The truth that a shot was fired after believing we were about to be robbed...possibly killed. The truth that some teenage boys had been hanging around us pretty much the whole time since we arrived here--"

Mrs. Dexter looked at her. "Those guys *were* checking us out all evening, weren't they?"

"Yes they were." Erica helped her mother to stand. "We turned, fearing for our lives, the gun was drawn, it accidentally fired, and neither one of us saw anyone so we assumed the shots had scared the culprits away," Erica said.

Mrs. Dexter stooped back down to caress Amethyst's hand. "She's just a child--a young innocent child," Mrs. Dexter said. Innocent like she had believed her own daughter to be. But here her child was plotting and scheming to cover up this...this... Oh God, and she's not even batting an eye as she's saying it. "Erica, I can't just leave her like this. No one meant for this to happen; it was an accident." Yet here Erica was planting ideas in her head as though she were the child instead of the adult. "Erica, where do you get ideas like that from?"

### Destiny Unlimited

Erica smiled, proud that her mother was interested. "I got that one from a movie I saw on TV last week. Timely, huh?"

Mrs. Dexter looked towards heaven. "My God! What have I done?" She stood and looked at Erica. Searching her face. "When did you start becoming this heartless person? Where on earth are you getting this type attitude?"

Erica stopped smiling and looked into her mother's eyes. "Why Mommie, I'm the spitting image of you! You said it yourself...the apple doesn't fall far from the tree. It's true far more than in the case of the poor people you refer to."

"You listen, I'm calling an ambulance to get this child some help--if it's not already too late." Mrs. Dexter turned away, wiped tears from her eyes, and turned back. "And *you*...you'd best pray she doesn't die!" Mrs. Dexter checked to be sure no blood was on her before hurrying Erica to the car.

She was shaking, cranked the car, pulled out of the parking place, and sped down the road...her body trembling in disbelief. "I'll call for help on my cell phone. That way they won't be able to trace it's origination."

Erica fumbled with the radio...turning it up louder. She began to bounce to one of her favorite sounds--*Responsibility* by the Ghetto Twins. Her mother quickly snapped the radio off. "You and I are going to have a long talk when we get home, young lady! Do you hear me?!"

Erica waved her hand. "What-ever," she said. "As long as you understand Mommie that I'm *destined* for greatness. Amethyst was a loser; you said as much yourself." She laughed. "In fact, you all but told her that to her sweet little face. Did you see her tears? Now how heartless is *that*, Mommie? Do you really think the world will miss her if she's suddenly not here? Her goals probably consisted of a house full of children...each by a different father."

Mrs. Dexter pulled over. "I want you to shut your mouth! Now! I mean I don't want to hear another word out of you, do you understand me child!" Her voice was stern with a look to match. "I mean it, Erica Louise Dexter!"

Erica rolled her eyes, grinned, and pretended to stop a pending laugh.

"*Now* what's so blasted funny?!" Mrs. Dexter said.

Erica pulled the laugh under control. "Oh I was just thinking. You know Mommie, that's the first time I've ever heard you truly sound black!" She burst into a loud roar. "Well get down then *Mama* with your bad self! **Say it loud...**"

Mrs. Dexter glared at her, then picked up her cellular phone. She began punching in the three digits and Erica managed to quiet down to an occasional cricket sneeze.

"9-1-1," the woman's voice said on the other end.

Mrs. Dexter disguised her voice. "Yes, I think someone may have been shot. I believe it may have been a child–"

"Are you saying a child shot someone?" she asked.

"No. A child's been shot! In the park. On Kelly Avenue. You need to hurry," Mrs. Dexter said.

"Ma'am? Are you with the child now?"

"No," she said, glancing over at Erica who had her hand clasped tightly over her mouth. Mrs. Dexter shook Erica's leg to emphasize she meant what she said about being quiet. "No. I had to locate a phone," Mrs. Dexter said to the operator. "Besides, I wouldn't have wanted to move her. Please Miss... hurry! She might die...if she hasn't already."

"She? So the child is a girl?" the operator said. Mrs. Dexter didn't say anything. "Ma'am, could I have your name, please?" Mrs. Dexter stared at the steering wheel.

"Ma'am...are you still there?"

## Destiny Unlimited

Click! Mrs. Dexter pressed the End button. She grabbed Erica by the shoulders and turned her to face her. "What is so funny Erica Dexter?" she said.

Erica stopped laughing on a dime. "The way you were sounding. That's a pretty good disguise. You'll have to teach *that* to me someday, too! Or maybe I'll just *catch* it...like I've caught other things from you. You know...*caught* not *taught.*" Then she gently wiggled from her mother's clutches, took her fingers, locked her lips, and pretended to throw away an invisible key.

Mrs. Dexter sighed and put the phone back in its cradle. "Erica, no matter what happens...you and I both know the truth. And I can tell you this much for sure, truth is like a moth. Somehow, it always manages to find its way to the light. Do you understand what I'm saying?"

Erica looked ahead and smiled only slightly. "A moth, Mommie? Now really. I much rather favor the butterfly myself. They're pretty...like me."

"Erica! This is serious! Do...you...understand?"

Erica rolled her eyes and looked out her side window. "Yes, Mommie. Whatever." Then she looked back at her mother, cocked her head, and smiled.


Erica searched the car, but it was nowhere to be found. Where had she lost it? She searched down in the seat...under the seat...on the side by the door. Even in the back. It wasn't anywhere. "Where could such a little piece of sterling be hiding anyway?"

How was she ever going to tell her mother she had lost her "precious" little Prayer Box charm off that stupid old bracelet. The only picture her mother possessed of her mother, father, and baby-self, was safely tucked inside that trinket from

Tibet. The only picture on earth of the three of them as a family. Her mother's only concrete proof of her memory of her parents. Erica knew her mother would be "perturbed" about her borrowing the bracelet without having asked; but then again, she would never have allowed her to wear it had she bothered to ask either. "Duh!"

*Oh well,* she thought as she slammed the car door shut, *Mommie probably won't even realize the old thing is gone!*

## SEVEN

"When the pupil is ready, the teacher appears," a voice in the wind whispered.

A cool breeze whipped across Amethyst's face. Standing to her feet, she undeniably felt lighter.

A woman tinted a pecan color, fifty or sixty with gray and black braids tied together like a fat rope--out of nowhere it seems--came and lorded over her. Pressing both fists in the curves of her waning hour-glass waist, the woman said with force, "Come along, Child. We have much to do but not much time to do it."

Amethyst scanned her surroundings trying to decipher first where she was then where in heaven's name this woman wanted her to go. "Where am I?" she said as she gazed at things *appearing* familiar: the swing, silver slide, the faded merry-go-round...a see-saw. *Looks like the park but it doesn't feel like it.*

"I'm sorry, but I must get home," Amethyst said. "I know my mother's worried sick by now." The old woman didn't acknowledge her. "Say? Just who are you anyway?"

The woman stared into Amethyst's eyes before displaying a beautiful set of teeth. "The question my Child is not *who* am I, but *who*...are you." She frowned, then smiled again. "The question is not so much *where* you are now but more where you are going." Soothing like a calm breeze yet warm like the sun, Amethyst was sure she knew this voice, but where...how?

"Yes!" The old woman nodded. "I am she! I come to establish you. Not to tell, but show. I am the ancient of days--keeper of examples of greatness for future generations. I am teacher--said to be wise from reflection and experience. Some say I am sage...neither male nor female--" She was so serious.

Amethyst smiled and found herself pointing at the old woman's body. "Well do forgive me for possibly being wrong, but you look like a female to me."

"Really now? Then I must thank you." She looked satisfied. "Precisely the look I was going for." She began to walk away...long strides...focused...deep on her intent (whatever her intent was). "Come along, Child," she said, looking back and seeing Amethyst was not moving. "We have much to do but not much time to do it." Still--Amethyst did not budge. The old woman stopped in mid-stride and frowned. Tilting her head slightly she said, "What is it now, Child?"

On one hand there was something about this woman that made Amethyst believe she should be afraid yet, she wasn't. Amethyst cleared her throat. "Ma'am...I've met more strangers today than I care to count. I'm not taking another step until...unless you tell me who you are and what's going on."

The woman played with her chin as though she were having trouble recalling her own name. Beads that hung from the bottom of her top and from the bottom of her skirt (occasionally sweeping the ground), dangled and bumped each other creating a faint click-clacking sound. "A storm brews," she said gazing up. "We...must get you safe. Otherwise you'll most certainly catch...your death."

Amethyst remained glued where she was.

"All right then. I am A-lura Ja-mah-ri," the old woman sang in a deep silky with a touch of an Island accented voice as she smiled and nodded twice.

Amethyst's eyes widened. "Now that's an unusual name," she said before remembering her manners and adding, "...but pretty."

# Destiny Unlimited

Miss Jamahri laughed while dusting one hand against the other. "Oh? And Amethyst Destiny Price is *not* an unusual but pretty name as well?"

Amethyst looked closer. She began to stumble backwards at the same time...stammering. "Wait a minute...I never told you my name...how do you know it? How do you know me? I must get home. Who are you? What do you want?"

Miss Jamahri smiled. Then laughed until it grew to an uncontrollable roar. "By the Wings of Soul--it is my **business** to know!" she finally said. "Now come along child! We have much to do but not much time to do it!"

Amethyst wasn't sure what was going on, but she felt-- at least for now--it was in her best interest to keep up with this...*Miss Jamahri--but* just for now. Until she located a phone.

Miss Jamahri turned around. "From here on out, I shall call you Am. For short. *Am* is such a powerful word; and you do know, there's a little *am* in all of us!" She continued with giant size steps.

Amethyst started to protest. She wanted to protest. She didn't like nick-names--never did. Still, Miss Jamahri was right; *Am* was a part of her name; a part of both their names in fact. Being called Am might be okay. For now.

Miss Jamahri looked back and grinned. "*Am* is present tense unlike *was* which is past tense, or *will be* which is always and forever in the future. I am...means now. **Pre** sent! Destiny. I Am...now. And you know, Child...the **I**, is whoever **I** is...at the time." She smiled as though what she said made *perfect tense sense*. "Can't you feel the power?" Miss Jamahri raised a fist. "The power of *I Am*!" She continued, purposeful steps onward.

Amethyst frowned. Miss Jamahri wasn't as tall as she had first thought. It must have been the height of her voice that made her such a giant in the beginning. *Am?* Amethyst was starting to believe Miss Jamahri was talking about more than some silly nickname, too. *Am* is *power? And I am Am?* she thought. All she ever wanted was to know how to make things happen...uncover a few keys to success maybe. *Okay, Miss Jamahri—let the quest begin.*

Miss Jamahri, with a smile on her face, turned and stared. "Yes, Child," she said, "Yes. By the Wings of Soul...let the quest begin." And with Amethyst's thought answered, Miss Jamahri charged ahead for now, leaving Amethyst baffled on *how* the two had come to be together. *Peculiar woman.* Indeed.

\* \* \*

Bright and early the sun streamed through the tall scenic windows. The door creaked as it slowly opened. Amethyst blinked as she carefully adjusted her eyes to the room.

"Good morning!" Miss Jamahri said, greeting her with a warm smile. The sound of her voice broke up the specks of dust gliding down the streams of sun that flooded through the window, sending them scampering quickly to regroup.

Amethyst sat up and scanned her surroundings. "Good morning," she said back. "Where am I?" Amethyst tried to piece together all she could recall. The woman stood before her as she lowered a tray with a plate of sausage, scrambled eggs, grits, homemade biscuits, strawberry preserves (spooned into a cup), and a freshly squeezed glass of pulped orange juice.

"Why, you're on my place. Land as far as the thoughts can think, sky as blue as the jay, air as clear as a morning sea breeze. I call it Enig."

"Enig? What's an Enig?"

"Enig, short for enigma. See, I figure one must enig before one can have an enigma. I'm sure some scholar would protest my word as well as my use of it, but since it belongs to me, I can attach whatever meaning I see fit." She smiled.

# Destiny Unlimited

"How did I get here?"

"Well let's see Child. What all can you recall?"

Amethyst remembered being in the park; Mrs. Dexter and Erica coming to take her home; Mrs. Dexter pulling out a gun...she and Aljuwon's little talk...gun fire. After that, she only remembered feeling light before an old woman came up saying things about I am, was, will be...school kind of stuff. No, wait...it wasn't school stuff at all. That old woman was her. This Miss Jamahri--that was Miss Jamahri talking about '*I am*' and power or something like that.

"I remember running after you," Amethyst said. "We were in the park, except it wasn't really the park at all. At least, I don't think it was. Then I followed you hoping to call home."

"And after that?"

"I remember being cold. I was so cold. After that, there's just a blank."

Miss Jamahri adjusted the tray. The food smelled good; Amethyst could hardly think of anything but eating. She was starving but wasn't quite sure why.

"Eat up, Child! I'm sure you're famished. It's been a couple of days since you've had anything solid."

"A couple of days? But I--"

"Aah, don't waste your energy trying to figure it out. It will come to you soon enough. And if it doesn't, no harm is done." Miss Jamahri walked over to the window, put her hands on her hips, and gazed out.

Amethyst bowed her head and said grace. Miss Jamahri watched from the corner of her eye occasionally nodding and smiling. Amethyst then hurried and mixed the eggs with the grits, alternating her taste buds between the egg mixture and the sausage. She glanced up at Miss Jamahri who continued to gaze out. She poured preserves onto a now clean plate--with the exception of the two warm buttered biscuits. Breaking off pieces of the biscuit, she dragged the soft, steamy light brown and white through the cool jelled strawberries. *This is so good!* she thought. Miss Jamahri continued to glance at her.

"Care for some more?" Miss Jamahri said, her hands folded together on top of her silky white apron.

Amethyst didn't want to appear greedy, though she certainly would have enjoyed at least one, maybe two more biscuits and a tad more of the preserves. She shook her head, deciding it was best to wait until she got home to pig out.

Miss Jamahri smiled as she grabbed hold of the tray. "How about I bring you a couple more of those made-from-scratch biscuits anyway and maybe just a bit more preserves to go along with them?" She looked back at Amethyst and smiled. "They're only going to waste if somebody doesn't eat them."

Amethyst smiled. "In that case, sure. Everything was great! You're a wonderful cook." Miss Jamahri's cooking tasted much like her own mother's.

"Yes, Child. Things are always better when you take time to appreciate them. You know," she said, "people take so many of the simple every day things for granted. Much too often, if you ask me. It's a shame too that we must do without sometimes before we can truthfully appreciate what we had."

Amethyst thought about what Miss Jamahri said after she disappeared. She was right. Simple everyday things. Practically every day since she could remember, she had always had sausage, eggs, grits, biscuits, and some type of preserves (strawberry being her favorite). Yet, she had eaten them like a programmed ritual. Only in not having had them it seems was she truly appreciating how great they always were. This had to be a key--*appreciating what you already have*. Surely one of the keys to success, to making things happen. Appreciation in all things. Not ever taking any thing or any one for granted. She missed her family now having never fathomed

## Destiny Unlimited

there would be a day when they wouldn't be somewhere she could greet them. Her mother, filling the place with sights, sounds, and smells as she transformed a simple house into a loving home. And though this house appeared to be very lovely, it just...wasn't...home.

She tried to remember the last time she had said thank you to her mother for a meal. Had she said thanks to her father for fixing her bed the other week when Michael used it as a trampoline? Or the time her father fixed an old typewriter just so she could turn in an A+ book report. Had she thanked God for her family (including Michael)...a home never short of love...true friends? Sure, she had mindlessly uttered the words "thanks"..."thank you," but had she ever *truly* said it with its true worth in mind? Was she applying the weight it deserved?

*Yes!* she appreciated the taste of the strawberries and the spongy insides of hot buttery biscuits baked just right, but had she ever truly been *this* grateful? Grateful for experiences... grateful for opportunities...grateful for simple pleasures?

She thought about Mr. Lewis in the park eating out of garbage cans--not having a place to call his own. Somehow (although she was unsure *what* was going on in her own life now) she wasn't scrounging for food. Was she truly grateful for the things of life? Grateful for the warmth of sunshine, the autumn colors of fall, the pastels in rainbows? Grateful for brand new days and brand new mercy...and just life itself?

Amethyst wished she had her notebook now so she could write all this down. Miss Jamahri was back in no time with the tray. "Here you go," she said almost singing the words. A glass of juice filled to the rim, three--not two--biscuits, and a whole *jar* of strawberry preserves slid as they vogued on the tray. Amethyst had received more than she had hoped for.

"A funny thing about gratitude..." Miss Jamahri said as she sat down the tray, "...marvelous things seem most attracted to those who show they are grateful for what they have already received." She smiled and pulled out something she had stuck behind her back and held by the band of her apron.

Amethyst's eyes danced. "My notebook! But where--"

"I thought you might be wanting this about now. You had it when I found you; I put it up after we arrived." Miss Jamahri headed towards the door. "Oh," she said reaching into her pocket and turning back, "here's your pen...an expensive one at that. It must have fallen out of your notebook."

Amethyst took the pen, stared at it, then recalling Mr. Fuller and the words he had spoken, she chanted, "My tongue is the pen of a ready writer. My tongue is the pen of a ready writer." She smiled. "Miss Jamahri...you're a life saver!"

Miss Jamahri cocked her head to the side and with a serious look she said, "Let us hope so Child. Let's hope so." Then she smiled.

"Thank you," Amethyst said. "And I really mean it."

"Oh Child, you're more than welcome! I will say this much, the words *thank you* have their own way of making people want to do just that much more for another. Don't ever forget that. It works across the board...in all areas of life... heaven...as well as on earth." Miss Jamahri winked as she walked towards the doorway. She turned to face Amethyst. "Am, I have a special game I'd like to play--sooner it must be rather than later. Do you think you feel up to it now?"

Amethyst looked up. "A special game...limited edition?"

"Yes. Very much a limited edition." Miss Jamahri walked back to the bed. "It is a type of card game, but quite a serious game nonetheless. It has its own special rules that must be adhered to completely. So, are you gamed?"

"A card game? I love games...it doesn't matter to me."

"Oh but it does matter. Just as long as you understand the seriousness of this game. It's called *The Game For Life*. There

## Destiny Unlimited

are three rules. I did not create them, yet I am obliged to enforce them should you decide to play. Before we begin, I will explain the rules to you. Should you agree to adhere to them, the process will automatically start from that point."

Amethyst put a piece of strawberry stained bread into her mouth. "Okay, sure--"

"But..." Miss Jamahri said holding up a finger, "should you feel you cannot agree to these rules, then the game is over. Now, have I made all of this perfectly clear thus far?"

Amethyst wondered why Miss Jamahri appeared to be so intense about everything. How serious could an old card game be anyway? As long as it's not *Old Maids*. And who ever heard of a game being over before it begins?

"Am?" Miss Jamahri said, "...the decision is entirely up to you. No one can force you to play should you choose not to. Not even I. You must decide of your own free will. As long as you know, the decision is yours and yours alone. But should you agree to these rules and decide you will indeed play, then the game from that point takes on its own life. Do you understand this as well?"

Amethyst smiled. What's the big deal? It's just a game. "Yes ma'am. I understand," she said swallowing sweet morsels melting in her mouth. "And now I must tell you something. I hope you don't mind losing because I aim to win! My parents constantly tell me...*Always aim to win.*"

"That is good to hear Child. I am so counting on that. Now...I'll be back for your tray a little later. Then we shall see exactly where you and I stand." Miss Jamahri smiled. Closing the door gently behind her, she leaned against it. "Yes Child... do aim and play to win," she whispered. "I assure you, you will have to play hard, to win this one."

49

# EIGHT

Amethyst had dozed off. How long...one, two...three hours? She hurried, putting on clothes that draped across a blue winged back chair. Staring out of the arched window, she took in the summer scene and decided to go outside this room.

This room in this single level house was spacious, yet cozy; old-fashioned, yet modern. A room she would no doubt miss upon returning home to her shared quarters with Michael. Opening the door, she glanced down the long hall before quietly stepping onto a dark stained hardwood floor. She looked inside three rooms where the doors were open, before coming to a room closed off by a set of tall walnut-stained double doors. Carefully, she cracked one of the doors open and wondered whether Miss Jamahri was in there. The floor just past the door, creaked as she stepped inside to get a closer look.

Inside was a room comparable to a small town library. Shelves filled with books as tall and as wide as the room itself. A sliding ladder leaned against a shelf--an aid to reaching higher levels. Amethyst forgot all about manners and found herself engrossed...drawn completely. This had to be heaven! Warm and cool at the same time with so many books! She scanned various titles ranging from classics to the far out--Miss Jamahri seemed a student of all type writings.

"Quite a collection I've managed to acquire wouldn't you say, Child?"

Startled, Amethyst jumped as the old woman had come up without making a sound. "Oh, yes ma'am! I was just admiring them. I-I hope it's all right. My coming in here without asking permission first. I didn't know where y--"

Miss Jamahri smiled. "Certainly, Child--it's quite all right with me. What good is having something if you can't share it with others." Miss Jamahri walked over to the ladder and grabbed a few books. "These are some of my favorites. Here, why don't you hold on to them...in case you're interested in reading them later. This book by George S. Clason...*The Richest Man in Babylon* was truly a delight. Then there's *Think and Grow Rich* by Napoleon Hill and a more updated version...*Think and Grow Rich: A Black Choice* by Dennis Kimbro and Napoleon Hill. I have another by Dennis Kimbro, *What Makes the Great Great*. I got a new book the other day you might enjoy..." she walked over to the large mahogany desk. "Here it is. " She handed her *the Gospel of Good Success* by Kirbyjon H. Caldwell. "Take it too."

Amethyst took the books. "You don't mind? I mean, I may have them a while. But I'll be sure and get them back to you when I'm finished. I promise."

"Mind? Don't be silly. I live to share knowledge like this. I've got a lot more where those came from...as you see. My *fair share* books. *Fair...Share.* Books about the mind--both the conscious and the sub; books that minister to the soul; books to make you laugh...make you cry...make you think. You're more than welcomed to any you find here...if you feel it will assist you in your journey."

Journey? Oh, she must mean my quest. But I don't remember telling her about it. "Thanks," Amethyst said. "And I promise I'll take care of them."

Miss Jamahri smiled. "So...I see you're up and around before I even got a chance to get back to you. I do apologize, but I've been feeling a little puny these last few days. An energy shortage so to speak. Old age, I suppose."

"I hope you're not coming down with something," Amethyst said as she continued to eye even more books she was interested in. "Og Mandino? Who is he?"

"You mean you've never heard of Og Mandino? Why, he wrote a wonderful set of books. Here..." Miss Jamahri came over and pulled out a few thin books, "...these three are my favorites. *The Greatest Salesman in the World* is a classic in my opinion! And this one, *The Greatest Miracle in the World* will make you feel like you're the best thing to hit the scene since sliced bread--"

Amethyst laughed. "Sliced bread?"

Miss Jamahri half-smiled." An old expression--you would have had to have been there." She handed Amethyst the last of the threesome. "This one, *The Return of the Ragpicker*, kind of wrapped up the stories."

"What about this one...*The Celestine Prophecy*? You think I'd like it?"

"Maybe. I did. But then, it's hard to find a book I haven't gotten something out of. Except maybe a book like *Bell Curves* or books that try to put or hold down a whole race of people. No, I do not encourage or support those." She grabbed a book from a lower shelf. "Here's a fine book as well. The Bible. This is one of my old Bibles. Take it...I've marked pages of many uplifting and encouraging passages. You'll find lots of good solid principles in there. Nothing new under the sun, they say." Miss Jamahri started towards the entrance. "Take whatever you like...or think you might need later. Oh yes, and don't be surprised if a few of the books don't call out to you. Vying for attention. That's how I ended up with so many myself. And as you can see, I've had to build them their own house practically...just to have somewhere for them to sleep."

Amethyst suddenly remembered no one knew where she was. Come to think of it, she didn't really know. "May I use

## Destiny Unlimited

your phone?" she said. "I need to call home and let my folks know where I am and that I'm all right."

Miss Jamahri shook her head. "Sorry. No phone here."

"Really? Well in that case I'd better get home. Mama's probably worried sick, and I'm most likely in mega-trouble. I appreciate all you've done for me though. I don't know how I'll ever repay you. Wish I could have stayed longer."

Miss Jamahri waited near the opened double doors. "Before you leave, there is the matter of that game left to be played. Hope you haven't forgotten? I made a batch of my world-famous, *Alphabet Soup for Success*. It's called alphabet because of the twenty-six ingredients that go in it. Surely you're not going to leave without at least tasting a bowl. Why, you can eat it while I explain the rules of the game."

Amethyst couldn't believe Miss Jamahri was still talking about that silly game. *What would it hurt to play—after all, she had been quite loving and caring?* Amethyst wasn't as excited about soup in summer weather. But with twenty-six ingredients, Miss Jamahri must have gone to a lot of trouble. "No ma'am I didn't forget," she said, "Your soup sounds really nice."

"Then come Child. We have much to do but not much time to do it. Follow me. Everything's already prepared." She looked at the books Amethyst held tight. "Bring those books if you like; you may find they come in handy. We must hurry though. I don't wish your mother any more worry than necessary. Yet, I believe you and this game will *both* do me some good." She hesitated. "I'll let you in on a little secret: The soup is made using a special recipe. There are a few duplicated copies but I have the one and only, penned on its original gold parchment paper. It's valuable. Valuable."

Amethyst eyes widened. "Really? May I see it?"

## Vanessa Davis Griggs

Miss Jamahri smiled. "We'll see. Later maybe. Only very special people get to taste it, let alone touch it." She indicated Amethyst should walk with her. "So we'll just have to see."

\* \* \*

"Now, do you remember what I said earlier about the three rules?" Miss Jamahri said as she dipped a ladle into the pot of soup, filling a yellow ceramic bowl to its brim.

"Sure. And I remember you said that if I decide I don't want to play, then I don't have to." Amethyst watched the steam rise from the bowl. She also noticed Miss Jamahri had only taken down one bowl to fill.

"Very good, Child. Now come...sit down...and I shall tell you these all important rules." Miss Jamahri placed the bowl in front of Amethyst, pulled out a chair, and sat directly across from her. Gazing into her eyes, she was ready to begin.

Amethyst looked down at the bowl filled to the top then back up at Miss Jamahri. "You're not having any?"

"Maybe later. But please, taste...tell me what you think."

Amethyst blew across the full spoon of liquid and chunks--watching Miss Jamahri watch her. She carefully put the stainless steel up to her mouth before looking back at the old woman. "It's good," she said, but thought it tasted much like...chicken soup.

Miss Jamahri nodded once before relaxing and sitting against the back of the chair. She folded her hands into each other and began. "The first rule to the game: A player may only use those tools granted them at the beginning of the game though exercising and adding to those tools is both permissible and highly encouraged. Upon all junctions, crossroads, and other negative situations, the player must recite three times within an allotted time the following: *Imagine--I'm a genie...I make things happen.* After reciting these words, the player

## Destiny Unlimited

should proceed and conquer if necessary. Only upon the successful conclusion of a card, may the player progress."

Miss Jamahri looked to see whether Amethyst was truly paying attention. Satisfied, she continued. "Number two: A player must adhere to the instructions printed on each card drawn without wavering, attempting to change it, to cheat, or to show any real despair under any and all challenges or circumstances.

"And third: If a challenge or circumstance doesn't kill the player, it will make that player stronger. Therefore, a player must not give in...give out...or give up. Quitting in any form or fashion is not permitted in any case, or for any reason. Should a player quit before the game has run its full course to the end, disqualification will be called and the player ultimately loses. All rights and privileges from that instant on will be revoked, and that player shall cease to be a player." Miss Jamahri sat back and waited for Amethyst's response.

"Sounds okay to me," Amethyst said. "Let's get started!"

"As you wish Child." Miss Jamahri got up from the table and came back with a pack of golden cards still secured and sealed inside cellophane. "Now, only you are allowed to break the seal that holds your cards together. After which, you must shuffle the cards without looking, and with care, choose ten cards. You are not allowed to look at any card until it is time for you to deal with it. After completion of a card, the player may then advance to the next card of the chosen stack." Miss Jamahri's hand was stern as she laid the pack of cards down on the table. "Any questions before we begin?"

"None I can think of, but if I have a question later--"

"Once the seal is broken, I am not allowed to answer any questions regarding the playing of the game. You may ultimately find yourself in tough situations and places, but you must *never* forget the three rules. These rules are double-edged;

they have potentials to cut both ways. Still, the final outcome lies in your hands and only yours. Remember...never give up."

Amethyst thought Miss Jamahri was beginning to sound a little too serious again. "Now what was that I was supposed to say three times again...if I need to?"

"Commit these words to heart, Child. Your deliverance may very well rest within them. You will see what I mean when the game commences. The words are *Imagine—I'm a genie...I make things happen*. Say it now...before we begin."

"Sounds like a silly thing to say to me—"

"No! The word *Imagine* broken down is I'm a genie—*Im a gine*. Think of this as just a way to remind you when things may become too heated for you to stop and think. There is so much power inside you, Child. Know that true genies of the world don't come in bottles or lamps. Imagination holds the keys to things that happen in life." She took both of Amethyst's hands. "Now say these words with me so you won't forget."

Amethyst dryly said, "Imagine, I'm a genie...I make things happen."

"Again."

Amethyst rolled her eyes then grinned. This was just plain silly. "Imagine—I'm a genie...I make things happen," she said a little louder.

"Good. Now once more."

"Imagine—" Amethyst said, already tired of it, "I'm a genie...I make things happen."

"Good, Child! Now I believe *you* and *I*...are ready."

Amethyst reached for the pack—the sooner she got finished, the sooner she could get home to her family. Miss Jamahri grabbed her hand and stopped her. "Remember, Child...there are forces out there that would destroy you. You must treat this game as though your life depends upon it.

### ~~D~~estiny ~~U~~nlimited

Because Am...in ways in which you have no idea--it truly does. Am I clear?"

"Yes! Miss Jamahri! You're clear!" Amethyst laughed but noticed the concern on the old woman's face. "Is there anything else you feel I should know? Something you want to say before I break the seal?" Amethyst knew her folks were past worried. She just wanted to get through and go home.

Miss Jamahri sat back against the chair. "Only that once the seal is broken, I will not be able to intervene. You must stay focused. No matter what happens, no matter who you might meet or what anyone tells you...*you must not quit* until the game has run its full course. Understand that this game must be finished completely before it is truly over. Only then you may be declared a winner--if there really is such a creature."

"O-kay," Amethyst said deciding Miss Jamahri was more than just a little strange. "By the way, about how long does this game usually take?"

"It takes as long as it takes."

"Yes, and how long is that usually? Thirty minutes? An hour? Two?"

Miss Jamahri leaned closer to Amethyst. "Child...it **takes** as long as it *takes*! Sometimes the longer, the better. You just remember...no matter what, no matter who...*you must not* stop until the final card has been played. Should you quit any time before that, the consequences could have a deathly impact."

"Don't you think you're exaggerating just a little bit--"

"No, Child! This...is...serious. If you don't feel you can see it through to the end, then you need not waste your time beginning it at all. If a student doesn't do any of the work required and receives an '*F*'; and a second student starts the work but does not finish yet also receives an '*F*'...then what difference does it make? They both made failing grades--the outcome being yet...an '*F*'."

"But in the second case, at least one of them tried where the other one didn't even make an effort."

"An 'F' Child, is *still* an 'F'! Credit is not given for beginning a thing, it is given for finishing it. The race is not given to the swift or to the strong, but to the one who endures to the end." Miss Jamahri sat back. "Dear Child, if you have not made up in your mind before you begin a thing that you intend to see it to its conclusion, then it is better--and many times more profitable--not to even begin."

Amethyst watched Miss Jamahri; she was serious. "I'll finish, okay."

"Good! Then we may proceed. Just remember, let no one turn you away from what you know to be right. No one." She nodded for Amethyst to continue.

Amethyst touched the cards and felt an electrical spark. Miss Jamahri had her so tensed--building a silly game up like this--she even found it difficult to keep her hands from shaking. Breaking the seal, she shuffled the cards, cut the deck, then handed Miss Jamahri the pack to spread out on the table. Amethyst then proceeded to choose ten cards, keeping each one face down as instructed. Miss Jamahri placed the discarded cards to the side and indicated to Amethyst she should gather up the ones she had chosen.

"Now Child...it begins from here. Turn over your first card. Just remember...no one, no matter what."

Amethyst's hands trembled even more. *It's only a game,* she repeated to herself. *A silly old game.* She smiled at Miss Jamahri who sat patiently waiting, intense as always. *And a silly old woman apparently with no one else to play with or talk to. Silly.*

Amethyst turned over the first card.

Lightning began flashing inside that little kitchen... thunder rolled, colors from rainbows crashed like glass at her feet. The books she had brought with her sailed through the

## Destiny Unlimited

air--words floating before her eyes! Books in the library called her and came flying in...swirling around her head. *Conversations With God* by James Melvin Washington, Ph.D., another *Conversations with God--Book 1...2 and 3, Dare to Win, i hear a symphony, The Positive Thinker, Phenomenal Woman, Their Eyes Were Watching God, God's Trombones.* The young, the old, the used, the new all gathering together to become one--words steadily crashing at her feet.

"Miss Jamahri!" Amethyst yelled, her hands covering her ears. She watched and heard things flashing...flying by. "Miss Jamahri, what's happening? Why aren't you doing anything! Miss Jamahri, make it stop!" She ran, looking to see if the weather was the source of this turmoil, but outdoors was calm--as still as a normal summer day. "Miss Jamahri, what kind of a game *is* this?" More thunder, lightning flashed inside. Alphabets floated around the kitchen. "Miss Jamahri! What's going on? Miss Jamahri!!! Please! Please...make it stop!" she yelled before attempting to seek shelter underneath the tiny kitchen table.

## NINE

Lightning flashed. Thunder roared, "boom," like an explosion. Intense, loud, blinding. Amethyst grabbed her notebook and held it against her chest. Things were still flying across the room. Without warning, the floor opened up and she fell through. Free, spinning downward, past the earth's core... through molten and intense heat. She tunneled out to the other side of the world and beyond into a deep dark deep, wondering where IF she would stop. Drifting rapidly towards the heavens the stars...moon, she felt a tug as a rope wrapped around her waist and halted her drift though not the buoyancy.

Amethyst's floating felt much like being in a mother's womb--the rope was her umbilical cord. Suddenly the rope began to retract as she was being drawn back towards the earth. Earth, like the pictures in books, was round. She recognized various shapes and sizes of land and water bodies. She identified countries, oceans, and lakes. All this from turning over one card?

Amethyst gazed, amazed at what she saw. Quietly, the earth began to wiggle and stretch before her. She watched it unfold from a ball-like state and stand straight. A beautiful woman of many colors--long green hair--smiled and cocked her head as she danced, before reaching to catch a falling star. "Let this be a dream; please let this all be a dream," Amethyst said closing tight her eyes.

"Well hi there," Earth said leaning for a closer look.

Amethyst blinked and paddled backwards. "H-h-hello."

Earth smiled. "Amethyst Destiny Price? I am, correct?"

## Destiny Unlimited

Amethyst stuttered more, "Yes. And you are you?"

"Oh, just call me *Mother*--everyone else does. Mother Earth!" She tilted her head to each side, the way one does to get a kink out. "Oh it feels so good to be able to do that. You know Child...the hardest thing in the world to do is to step out on nothing and to be able to stand."

Amethyst heard screams.

Mother Earth placed one hand to her lips. "Oops, I always forget. They probably think it's another earthquake. But I get so cramped up staying in the same position months on end. I'll just stand still a minute until they settle down. Why don't you come closer so I won't have to yell? I won't hurt you."

Amethyst tried to move towards Mother Earth but kept floating every way except where she wanted to be.

Mother Earth began to laugh. "That's not exactly the way to go about doing it. You're trying too hard. And on top of that, you're using the wrong method."

"Okay, so how should I do it then?"

"Close your eyes, imagine what you want, see yourself doing it, believe that it's done, give thanks...be sure to do what you need to do. That will usually about do it."

"And *that's* suppose to work?" she said more like a fact.

"Suppose? It works. It might take you a while to get the hang of it, but it works. So come...you can stand on my shoulders. They're wide enough and strong enough to hold you up."

Amethyst imagined herself standing on Mother Earth's shoulder. Mother Earth grinned. "Concentrate...now don't be half-stepping on me."

Amethyst closed her eyes tighter, concentrated harder... imagining first...then believing it to be so. When she opened her eyes this time, she was surprised to find her feet planted firmly on solid ground. "It worked. It really worked!"

# Vanessa Davis Griggs

"Of course it worked! Now don't forget to give thanks... you wouldn't want to hurt the feelings of those who've helped you. You might need their help again."

"Thanks," Amethyst said. "Are you really Mother Earth or a figment of my over-active imagination?"

"You've been told you have an over-active imagination?" she said, shaking her head. "I declare, the things that go on in this one body. Yes--I am Mother Earth. I make one sudden move, and people holler earthquake. I sneeze, they yell tornado. I get the flu, and it's hurricane somebody. A touch of indigestion and it's an erupting volcano! So when I do move, I do it slow and careful. That's how I managed to push up land that for a long time rested beneath the oceans...I made lots of mountains, too. Scientists have finally figured it out. As soon as they discovered ocean fossils on top of some of those mountains, they knew something was up!" She grinned like she had a secret. "I even rearranged a few smaller islands, snapped them together like puzzle pieces, oh yes I did!" Mother Earth laughed. "What can I say...I get bored! They look any day now for me to break California off and make it a little island."

"Are you planning to?"

"We'll see!" Mother Earth said smiling. "We'll see."

Amethyst looked at Mother Earth. "Forgive me, but do you know what's going on with me? I mean, one minute I'm playing cards with an old woman, the next minute I'm floating out here talking to *Earth?* of all things. Am I dreaming, losing my mind? *Dead*? I don't even know how I got here? Do you?"

Mother Earth nodded. Yes she knew. Mother Earth batted her long dark eyelashes. "You're not dreaming Amethyst," she said. "All of this is real." She put her hands together like in a prayer. "You're playing *The Game for Life*. Ten cards you selected being played out. And I concur, you are a

62

## Destiny Unlimited

brave young girl...full of Spirit with much to give the world. This is a truth."

Amethyst's feet were still planted on Mother Earth's shoulder. "So are you the first card or what?"

"Yes, in a matter of speaking. And you had best keep count. There are powers of darkness and principalities lurking about who would rather you lose this game."

"How do I know when a card begins?"

"By the lightning and thunder...sights and sounds--no rain. Rain signifies all is done. However, don't be fooled. Lightning and thunder both must come. Now, we must begin. There is much to accomplish in a short time."

Amethyst imagined herself being in front of Mother Earth and instantly, she was there. She whispered words of "thanks," then gazed into the face of Mother Earth. "Why is it everyone speaks so seriously about a game?"

"Because it is serious. Were you not informed that to quit or mess around and be taken out, your round would end? It's as simple as that. All your dealings will not be life or death plights, but those that are...can be fatal."

"Yeah, but it's just a game. A game."

"True. Yet who defines games?" Mother Earth was solemn. "Amethyst Price, you are charged with the task of creating your own world. There are many elements to this charge, and I have been appointed to get you started. Others will come as required." She licked her lips softly. "Any questions?"

"None that I can think of." She twirled once around Mother Earth's head. "Oh. This world I'm suppose to create... does this mean you go back to being a ball? Like before?"

"Of course. Even me, you must call forth."

"And how do I do all this?"

"Did you not read any of those books or see any of the words that flew around you before you reached this plane?"

"You mean like Genesis?"

"Yes, that would be a start. Just do me a favor--make it easy on yourself. Handle the essentials first. Don't do like this one being and be too creative. He forgot so much stuff it was pitiful. *You* try living in a world without firmament or rain for a while. Talk about dry." She smiled. "Look at me...acting like the Mississippi River--just running off at the mouth."

"So are you saying I should use Genesis to start?"

"If you like. Just speak loud; there's nothing worst than a wimpy *Let There Be!* If you're going to do big things, use a big voice. Start things off with a Bang! Let the universe know who has been charged! Comprende?"

"I understand," Amethyst said, happy she knew what comprende meant.

"Let's get started then. Hey--Let There Be," Mother Earth said. Amethyst then noticed Mother Earth and she was without form and was void.

Darkness was on the face of the deep. Amethyst's face reflected off the waters. It was hard to believe any of this could truly be happening. But if she wasn't dreaming...and she hadn't lost her mind, then she knew she had to be as serious about this as everyone else seemed to be.

Amethyst called out to the darkness...with force...with power, **"Let... there...be...light!"** And just as Genesis reported it when God had said it--*and...it...was...so!* She proceeded, careful about what she *did*--and *did not*--call forth.

"Impressive," said Mother Earth, now a normal-looking woman around thirty-five, green dress, dark brown hair. Amethyst was asleep in a green pasture beside still waters. "I

### Destiny Unlimited

see you added a few things too. It's *your* world. You created it. Rest today. Tomorrow I shall return." And then she was gone.

Bright and early and true to her word, Mother Earth's voice nudged a still sleeping Amethyst. "Come, we're due to visit a special place. Get up now."

More asleep than woke, Amethyst stretched and groaned. "Where are we going? Do we have to go now? I'm tired," Amethyst said promptly turning over.

"Quitting already? You certainly didn't last long at-tall."

Amethyst jumped to her feet. "No I'm not *quitting* already!" She splashed cold water on her face. "All right, let's go!" She reached down and picked up her notebook. Then she found a piece of leather, cut it into two straps and attached it to the notebook to create a shoulder-length-pocketbook-looking-thing. "This will be much easier to carry around."

"Good morning, God," Mother Earth said with a smile. "What have you got for me today? I want to be a part of it."

Amethyst noticed the glow when those words were spoken. Mother Earth gestured for her to try it. She did. "That was nice." Amethyst said. "Did you make that up yourself?"

"No. An Episcopal priest named Sam Shoemaker did. As an experiment. To see if it would make a difference. People call it, *the Pittsburgh Experiment.*"

Then in just a blink of the eye, Amethyst and Mother Earth were standing outside gates to a city filled with people. "Where are we?" Amethyst said.

"We are in the City of Tomorrow's Yesterday."

"That would be Today? Is that its real name?"

"As real as dirt is mud," Mother Earth said. "Now, you must be careful here. There is an energy surrounding this city where every word spoken is made manifest--if not today then in the morrow. There is no such thing as an idle thought or word in this place. Nor is there a thing as a *'figure of speech'* or *'slip of the tongue'*." She had a stern look about her. "I am clear?"

"As clear as a muddy windshield," Amethyst teased.

"Amethyst...do not play when you walk inside there. When your feet stroll past that gate, that energy will work using your words in like manner."

Amethyst sighed. "Now what's the purpose of my being here again?"

"You mean...in my opinion?"

"Yours...whoever. I don't really care."

"If I were you I'd watch what I say and my thoughts, and learn from O.P.M.--Other People's Mistakes. That's what I'd do."

Amethyst walked close behind Mother Earth into the city, watching all who came near. She heard a mother with two children squawking at an older woman.

"I'm broke I tell you!" the mother said. "Broke! And every day I wake up, it's the same old thing--broke. If I could change things, I'd change it in a heart beat! But I'm doomed to be broke! Always in need. And it's *always* something!"

Mother Earth leaned over and whispered to Amethyst, "From her mouth to God's ears. She said it today and tomorrow will wonder why it is so."

Amethyst watched a man sitting on the sidewalk, speaking to people as they passed by. "Can you help me? I'm sick. I just need a little help. Excuse me Miss...Miss, can you help me? I'm sick ma'am. I'm just the sick trying to get well. There's no more to me than what you see. Sir...sir, can you help this sick man, please? I don't expect much. I never feel well--just the same o, same o."

Mother Earth leaned over again to Amethyst. "You can guess where he'll be tomorrow and just what he'll be saying."

## Destiny Unlimited

Amethyst laughed. She couldn't believe how silly these people were. "You'd think they would realize that they're the ones creating this whole mess! Day after day on top of that."

"You would think so...wouldn't you?" Mother Earth smiled. "It's as plain as the nose on your face."

A little boy walked past Amethyst. "Mom, look at the plain nose on that girl's face. It's so plain."

Amethyst looked at Mother Earth. "I don't think my nose is that plain."

"Oh...I apologize. I must be careful around here as well."

Amethyst stopped and looked over a fence. "Now that's ridiculous! A feet trying to strangle a lady? Come on!"

Mother Earth cringed. "The classic '*My feet are killing me*' no doubt. Look over there Amethyst, that lady must have complained about her child getting on her nerves. He's stomping all over them. Goodness--that's gotta hurt!"

Amethyst tried not to laugh, but all this was just silly.

An angry customer was yelling at the manager of a store. "Why don't you just drop dead!" she said. Whereby the manager promptly fell dead right at her feet.

Mother Earth shook her head. "Oh my. There goes another one. Will people ever learn the power of the tongue?"

Mother Earth and Amethyst had been there three days. Every day, to Amethyst's disgust, she was greeted with a bowl of oatmeal for breakfast. She couldn't believe it; she'd dropped hints saying, "Oatmeal again?" but two days passed and each day, no matter how much she hoped for something different, she was greeted with oatmeal. "Oatmeal," she said "again."

Amethyst decided tomorrow if there was oatmeal, she would no longer be polite. Mother Earth wasn't eating oatmeal, why should she? Sure enough her tomorrow was the same as the previous days--one bowl of gray gooey plaster awaited her.

Amethyst sat down and stared at the bowl. "Mother Earth, I've tried not to complain. But every day now since we've been here, I have had oatmeal."

"Uh-huh. And every day since you've been here, you have said '*oatmeal again*'."

"But I've wanted sausage, eggs, grits, juice...maybe toast or a biscuit. The biscuit doesn't even have to be homemade. Still, to my disgust, I get oatmeal. And I don't even like oatmeal!"

Mother Earth smiled and sat down. "Then say that."

"What?" Amethyst relaxed her frustrated body. "Say that? What do you mean...say *that*?"

"Every day you have said oatmeal, and every day that is what you have gotten. If you want something different, then learn to speak your desire."

Amethyst was starting to understand what Mother Earth was saying. "Well what if I said, I don't want oatmeal?"

Mother Earth grinned. "Either one of two things: The only words that will be heard will be the words following **don't**, which in your case would be **want oatmeal.** Or what you don't want is known, but what you do want, still is not."

"You're kidding me, right?"

Out of nowhere a billy goat came and began nuzzling against Amethyst's legs. Mother Earth laughed. "Now Amethyst, I told you when we arrived you needed to be careful of the words you spoke. Your words create. If you don't see it today, you will see it soon enough." She giggled. "See...as in billy goat? *Kid*-ding." She laughed.

"Yeah, but--"

"But nothing! And if I were you, I'd be careful with the '*buts*' while that billy goat is hanging around." She laughed. "Now, if you want something, then my advice to you is to say *that* and only *that*! And if you don't want something, then

## Destiny Unlimited

change your thoughts...change your words...change your world. Put a watch over what you allow to come out of your mouth. It's that simple." Mother Earth took back the bowl of oatmeal and stood over the already hot stove.

"So are you saying in, real life, if I say something, it's going to manifest itself because I say it?"

"Maybe not by saying it once or twice, but if you keep saying it enough, and it gets down in your spirit and your mind gets hold of it and uses it as a blueprint to create from... then it's pretty much a done deal. At that point, you have made your pact. It's as plain and as simple as..." Mother Earth thought about what almost slipped from her mouth and decided to change it. She smiled and said, "...that."

Amethyst shook her head as she thought about how silly she herself had been--having done the same things she had witnessed others who lived in this place do. She had not learned from O.P.M...Other People's Mistakes.

"Mother Earth, it's amazing how shortsighted people truly can be."

"Eat quick," Mother Earth said sitting a plate of eggs, grits, sausage, and biscuits before Amethyst as the steam rose to the air. "It's time for us to leave this place. There is much more for you to do."

## TEN

Mother Earth looked around at the place. "This is our exercise area. There are various trainers here dedicated to serving your needs," she said.

"Now this is more like it," Amethyst said smiling as she checked out the place and the equipment with a quick eye.

"Think so?" Mother Earth walked away. "Enjoy!"

"Where are you going?" Amethyst turned, but Mother Earth was already gone.

"What's your pleasure?" a little man about four-feet-five said to Amethyst.

Amethyst could tell he was a man, though she had never met a little person in person before. He had a full beard, yet he was as tall as she.

"Well now, look what the wind blew in!" he said at a train-like pace. "You going to stand there smiling all day or were you planning on working out any?"

Amethyst jumped. His tone was mean. "Work out? So what can I use?"

He made a "psss" sound with lips closed. "Gee girl. You can use whatever equipment you feel you need to pump up what needs pumping. You have to work at making things happen. My motto is: *Wake up and smell the smoothie! There's no such animal as something for nothing!* Don't ever forget that." He grabbed her hand and walked over to the treadmill. "Now this little baby will really get those faith muscles jumping!" He pointed to the machine with weights. "That one there is good for working on your belief muscles." He flexed his thick hard steel-like biceps in her face before dragging her to the rowing

### Destiny Unlimited

machine. "Now this one helps increase expectations." He felt her calves. "Kind of puny yet, but not bad for your age. There's much potential--I can tell that."

"What are you talking about? I thought this was the exercise room?"

"It is, Sweetie. And I'm the exercise man--Big D! That stands for Big Dreams." He took her to an ab machine. "Now this machine is great for developing commitment muscles. It'll make 'em hard as a washboard." He lifted his shirt to show his abdomen. "See? Bu-yow! That's what I call commitment!"

"But--"

"You still don't get it. Look Sweetie, everybody pretty much gets the same measure when they're born. Same muscles, the same amount of faith...yadie, yadie, ya! Following me still?"

Amethyst nodded.

"Use your mouth, Sweetie. You're not some toy with a head bobbing around on a spring." He clapped. "You know?"

"Yes!" Amethyst said loud.

"Better! Now stay with me on this. We have the same number of muscles when we're born, but who do you think ends up winning Mr. or Miss Olympia? You know, those body building contests?"

"Those with bigger and more defined muscles?"

"Precisely! I can see you've been exercising those brain muscles, all 100 billion cells--give or take a million! Good, good, good--you wouldn't want underdeveloped muscles there for sure! What was I saying? Oh yes, no one is born with muscles like those that win those contests. Well, they *are* but they must be developed first; and how do you think that's achieved?"

"Exercise?"

"Right-o. Give my girl a star! Makes my job so much easier when I don't have to go over it but once. Okay, now that we're on the same page, can we move to the paragraph about faith, belief, expectation, commitment...muscles like those?"

"Sure," Amethyst said looking at him while trying not to stare. She smiled. He was so...cute! Mean sounding, but cute!

"Now! If you want them to grow bigger and better then just how do you suppose you go about doing that?"

Amethyst smiled. "Exercise," she said.

"Sweetie, I think I love you! So that's what you're here to do...exercise those things and get them pumped. Just remember this is not an overnight cure. You've got to constantly work on them. Now I'll get you started with our equipment here, but I want you to work on them on your own, too. Okay?"

Amethyst started to nod but the picture of a toy with a spring for a neck popped into her mind. "Yes...sir," she said.

"*Sir?* Sir? A sweetie with manners to boot! This must be heaven!" He smiled. "So what do you want to start with? Faith? Belief? Expectations? Commitment?"

"Faith. I'm not as pumped in that area as I'd like to be."

"Faith it is!" He pulled her to the treadmill. "You've got to have faith to stick with this! The scenery before you will oftentimes remain the same for miles and miles, but just know... something *is* happening." He laughed. "I crack myself up sometimes! But this is serious business, and I don't want you taking *me* lightly." Big D laughed even harder. "Ooops! That one slipped! Did you get it? *Taking me...lightly.*" He saw the look on her face. "Oh well, like other things in life...it will come soon enough--or not."

"How was your exercise class," Mother Earth said.

Amethyst toweled off sweat. "So you came back?"

Mother Earth smiled. "Of course. I had to be sure the state was ready for your visit."

"State? What state?"

## Destiny Unlimited

"You'll know when we get there." And in a blink, they were there. Amethyst looked around and everywhere her eyes landed, she saw nothing but people living in lack. People without the basic things in life even, like food and clean water. People working sunup to sundown making meager earnings to get by from one day to the next only for the cycle to begin again. Children ran behind whomever happened by--begging for anything people could or would spare. Some children had bloated stomachs. Malnutrition. Bugs scurried all around.

"I don't like this place, Mother Earth; I wish to leave."

"Why should you be able to turn your face when I cannot?" Mother Earth said with a somber expression. "Look upon these faces because there is no reason for this. Not in a land of plenty. Stockpiled food going to waste while these are not able to leave this state for something better. Indeed, some of this is could be their fault--yet, some is the fault of others."

"What state is this Mother Earth? Tell me so I'll be sure to never come this way again."

Mother Earth stood solemn. "This is the great State of Poverty. Population: still counting. And the State of Poverty can be located right next door to the State of Abundance. Truly places in the world just like you see here, but there are even greater States of Poverty dwelling inside the minds of more people than the world even knows. You see, if a man has in him the State of Poverty, he will always be poor no matter what another does for him. If a man has the State of Abundance within, then no matter what, he will never be truly without."

"Why is it necessary for me to see this? What can I do? I'm only a drop in a bucket."

Mother Earth smiled and in a blink, she and Amethyst were standing outside in rain which only fell into a bucket Amethyst found herself holding.

"Count the drops that fall into the bucket, Amethyst," Mother Earth said.

Amethyst watched as the rain quickly filled the bucket. "I can't count these drops! They're falling too fast. There are too many of them! This bucket is getting heavier by the second. Can't you see...it's practically full already."

"Bravo, Amethyst! Drops in the bucket can be a powerful force when united."

"That's great when it's a lot. But what if it's only one?"

"Each one can only be one. When one does its part, that is usually a beginning for others to join in."

"And if not?"

"You're just full of questions, aren't you? If you are the only drop, then at least, make a splash when you do what you do." Mother Earth squinted her eyes. "Any more questions?"

Amethyst smiled. Mother Earth looked at the sky. "Time for a shift change. It's been a delight, Amethyst."

Amethyst opened her mouth to speak, but Mother Earth was gone in the time it had taken her to blink.

\* \* \*

Amethyst waited...wondering what was next. She saw several flashes streak across the sky. *The second card?* She was responsible for keeping count. *Mother Earth said Thunder and Lightning. With all the modern technology available, you'd think they could at least provide an electronic counter, a computer or something!* she thought.

## ELEVEN

The earth moved slightly and Amethyst steadied herself.

"Time is so relative!" said a dark skinned, skyscraper of a man with a long black beard tucked loose inside his belt. "Don't you think so, Sis?" He had a flare-like strut about him. Looking her over, he smoothed down his beard. "Amethyst I presume?"

"Yes, but--"

"Stand up straight when you talk to people, Sis! I don't have time for this! I've told them time and time again but does anyone ever take the time to hear a word I say? No. Well, it's high time they start! It's time out for this! They're so far behind the times, it's not even funny. I've tried from time to time to tell them. But in good time they'll get it--believe you me. Time has a way of changing things. I've said it time and again, but I suppose it won't hurt to say it once more. What time is it anyway? What does it matter? Whatever time, it's time to go. Ooh-wee, I tell you Sis, you're in for the **t-i-m-e** of your **l-i-f-e**!"

"Let me guess, Father Time, right?" Amethyst smirked.

"Aamp! Wrong!" He squinted. "Do I look like somebody's father?"

"Well...no, but I thought--"

"First mistake. Never just think! Get the facts, acquire the correct information. Then you can think!"

"Who are you then?"

"I am the infamous, the-one-and-only, the never-has-been-never-ever-gonna-be-again...G-Time!"

Amethyst frowned. "Who?"

He smiled and shook his head. "Little Sister, first of all, you're gonna have to pay attention. I don't have time to be repeating myself. Neither do *you* have any time to be wasting. So just call me G-Time."

"Sure Mr. Time--"

"No, no, no! Don't call me Mr. Time! Do you have any idea how old-fogey that makes me sound. Little Sister...I do have an image to uphold."

"But it doesn't sound right to just call you G-Time."

"Okay, then just call me Mr. G. How about that?"

"I can do that."

"All right! Then let's get going!" He zapped out a five pointed star. "Hop on, we need to get to New York City in a flash. Sister, I'm telling you...you're in for the time of your life!"

Amethyst smiled. "We're riding on a star?"

"Yeah." He held the star upright as Amethyst got on the front part of the slant. He leaned over and whispered, "Don't tell anyone, but I was actually aiming for the moon and missed. Ended up with this star instead. That's exactly why all the manuals say to aim for the moon. Had I aimed for the stars, you and I would probably be riding on an eagle about now. I don't know if you've ever ridden an eagle before, but they can be temperamental at times. And the little smart-alecs who actually aim for eagles? Well, let's just say that riding a rock is a hard way to go." He laughed as he mounted on the star slant.

"Hold on tight, Sis. Let's head for the time of your life."

And like a flash, they were off. They arrived--a star falling from the sky--into New York City. The entire view was breathtaking! Now Amethyst stood inside a fabulous hotel room.

"Amethyst, we will be here for *one* day. And I have a gift for you too."

"You do? I don't know about accepting a gift from you."

## Destiny Unlimited

"Oh...okay. I understand. So I guess you don't want to know what it is either--"

"Okay Mr. G. What is it?"

He pulled his long black beard out and ran a brush over it as he spoke. "Your gift is the present."

"I know my gift is a present, but where is it?"

"I didn't say it was a present. I said it was **the** present! There's a difference you know."

"I don't understand."

"Your gift is *THE* present. You're opening it now. Every passing second is a brand new gift. Your gift--present--is the *present*. I tried picking something that would fit, was the right color, and would be just what you wanted."

Amethyst flopped down on the couch. "You mean my *present* is the *present*? The right now...the time that's happening even as we speak? *That* present?"

"Yes! Isn't it wonderful! Oh what better gift to receive than this. It is the only gift around that gives constantly." G-Time looked at her. "Why so sad, Sis? I know you're not going to tell me you don't like it. Do you have any idea how hard this is to come by? Do you know what the going rate for a gift like this is these days? Well let me tell you, because I happen to be in the know--it's priceless Sister! Priceless! You can't just buy this anywhere. No amount of money in the world can secure it. And if you're not careful, even when you do own it, it can slip right out of your hands...lost...gone forever! Stolen even." He snapped his fingers. "Just like that. Nada! No more to experience only to remember. S-i-s, you'd better listen to G-Time and learn to enjoy every single minute of your present. I also know, an unappreciated gift can be taken away or granted to someone who will." He leaned over and stared at her.

Amethyst laughed. "Well, if you're going to go and put it *that* way--then I guess I love it. I love my present."

"You guess? You guess!" He stood up. "You're going to have to do better than that! I'll tell you what, just give it back! That's what you can do. Give...it...back!"

Amethyst had a puzzled look on her face as she began to laugh. "What?"

"Don't be laughing. There's nothing funny! Give me my gift back. You don't want it, I'll just keep it and enjoy it myself."

Amethyst laughed. "You know I can't give it back!"

"Why not?"

"Because, well, because I already used it up. So there!"

"Oh, so you act like you don't appreciate it yet and still, you use it up all the same! Okay then give back what's left."

Amethyst was rolling with laughter now all over the couch. "No," she said defiantly.

"No? Little Sister, do you know what?"

"Let me guess. You don't have *time* for this. Right?" Amethyst sat back.

He laughed. "Oh, so you read minds too huh?"

"Mr. G?" Amethyst said. "Seriously though, thanks for the present."

He smiled, pulled her hair, and said, "Any time. Any time." The clock in the finely decorated living room began to chime. G-Time reached inside his shirt pocket and pulled out a wad of green bills. "All right, Little Sister...it's ten o'clock now. I'm going to give you this $1,440--"

She sat up straight. "One thousand, four hundred and forty *dollars*?"

"Just hold up now Little Sis! Give me time to finish what I have to say. Now--as I was *s-a-y-i-n-g* before I was so rudely interrupted, this money is yours to spend any way your heart desires. There are only a couple of rules that come with it. One is you have only one day--that's 24 hours--in which to spend it."

## Destiny Unlimited

"I can do that!"

"Bup-bup-bup-bup-bup-ba. Interrupting me again?" Amethyst shook her head and smiled. She pretended to lock her lips.

"Better. Now, may I be allowed to continue?" He looked at Amethyst, she nodded and smiled. "Okay. You must spend it in one day. It doesn't matter to me what or how you spend it, just that you spend it. Now--" he said looking to see if she was about to interrupt again. Satisfied that she wasn't, he continued. "If you do not spend all of it, what you don't spend comes back to me...no questions, no whining, no explaining, no regrets."

Her eyes widened. G-Time waved his hand to let her know it was okay for her to speak. "Mr. G, you say what I **don't** spend goes back to you?"

"That's correct. Now, anything else?"

She grinned like a yellow happy face button. "No, sir! I can't wait until tomorrow. You're going to take me out?"

"Of course. How irresponsible do you think I am? Everybody knows a child your age, and straight out of the south, Alabama, at that--shouldn't be allowed to run loose and alone in New York. That's the other rule...you can't go anywhere without me. I'm supposed to be some kind of guardian motif."

"No problem, Mr. G. No problem at all!" She smiled and hurried to her big spacious bed in this wonderful hotel. The Ritz! Who would have thought! She fell asleep quickly, dreaming about all she planned to do tomorrow.

Amethyst got up bright and early. She knocked on Mr. G's door several times, at first only lightly as not to startle him. Then her knocks became steady pounds, until finally she was screaming through the door at him. Still, he didn't stir. For two solid hours, she tried to wake him. She wondered if he was still in there. What if something had happened to him? Seconds after that thought, she heard him stirring on the other side.

"Mr. G? Are you okay?"

"Yeah," he said groggily opening the door and wiping sleep from his eyes.

"Mr. G, it's already eleven o'clock. I got up early, but I couldn't wake you. Could you hurry now? Please."

"Hurry? What for? This is the first time I've ever been able to sleep in! Little Sister, do you have *any* idea how great this feels with my busy schedule?"

"But Mr. G--"

"What have I told you about interrupting me?"

"Sorry, but Mr. G this day is getting away every minute. Can you please just get ready so we can leave? Please! I've got a lot to accomplish today."

"All right, all right! I'll get ready and then we'll go."

"Great!" Amethyst flashed a smile. "Don't be long now."

"Yeah, yeah, yeah. Save your hoorahs for the popsicle man," he mumbled. She faintly caught other words like "children" and "persistent" and "pesky."

Amethyst went back into the living room and waited. Mr. G was out and dressed in less than thirty minutes. He walked into the kitchen. Amethyst watched his every move. She couldn't believe it, he was making breakfast?

"Mr. G? What are you doing?"

"What does it look like? Fixing something to eat, Sis."

She let out a sigh and walked to the bar that separated the kitchen from the living room. "Look, I have money! I can buy you breakfast. A big breakfast...a gigantic breakfast! Let's just get out of here before it gets any later."

"Shush up, Little Sister! I'm making my own breakfast. Would it kill you to give a brother time to get his grub on for once in his life?"

## Destiny Unlimited

Amethyst flopped down on the padded bar stool, her head drooped as she looked at her swinging feet.

Mr. G sneaked a look at her and grinned. "I won't be long. Why don't you find something to do while you wait?"

"I don't want to do anything. I just want to get out of here, that's all."

G-Time finished cooking his breakfast and took his plate into the living room where he turned on the television. "Come on and watch a few cartoons with me." His eyes glazed over like he was hypnotized. "Hey--this is funny!"

"Why can't you just hurry so we can go?"

G-Time was laughing hysterically at one of the classics. "I just love that Porky the Pig guy...say--did you know the Sugar Smack Bear was black?"

"No," she said uninterested in his trivia questions.

"Look, Sis. No need of you being upset with me. Your attitude is not going to make me go any faster." Then he turned his attention back to the show and began laughing again. "Hey Amethyst, who am I? Beep-beep!" he said.

Amethyst rolled her eyes and left the room. Mr. G continued laughing at the show. Loud sometimes...like his goal was only to further aggravate her.

At one o'clock, he knocked on her door. "Are you still going, or have you changed your mind?"

Amethyst jumped up and was at the door in a flash. They went to see a show that was to start at two o'clock. After that, she had plans to hit as many stores as she could manage. G-Time took her to a toy store so she could decide which video system she wanted to buy.

"With this much money, I can buy all three and worry about which one I like best later," she said. Then she made the mistake of letting him try one of the games. It took her two hours to get him away from the thing!

# Vanessa Davis Griggs

Finally, it was time for them to go back to the hotel. Amethyst had a lot of packages. She had bought games, toys, clothes, jewelry...not as much as she had intended, but at least she had bought some things.

"So, let's see how you made out, "G-Time said at ten o'clock exactly.

Amethyst pulled out the money she had left over. "I spent $700, and it's your fault I didn't get to spend the rest." She flashed him a triumphant smile.

"Fault? Fault! You're going to blame me? Tough break, Little Sis. From my calculations, you owe me $740." He held his palm out. "So pay up. Now."

"But I'll be sure and spend it tomorrow--"

"Is that right? Well, Sister-Sis, there's only one problem with your little plan. You won't be getting this *here* money to spend tomorrow! The rule was, what you didn't spend, you lost. The rest was to come back to me."

She glared. "You did this on purpose. You wasted my time deliberately so I wouldn't be able to spend it all so that way you could get it back. What a racket--"

"Excuse me little Sis--I don't mean to argue with you, but whatever gets wasted or doesn't get done can't be blamed on anybody else. No, no! The rule was, what you didn't spend, you lost. You didn't spend it. This offer was good for one day only. So hand it over." He wiggled his fingers. "Come on."

Amethyst picked the money up from the table where she had counted and slammed it down next to him. "Here! Take it! I don't care any old way."

He had a stern look to his face. "Now Little Sis, when I gave that to you, did I give it to you that way? Did I slam it down next to you like that?"

"No," she said sullen.

### Destiny Unlimited

"Then, I don't expect *you* to give it back to *me* like you just did. I don't care how upset you are. Now you pick that up and hand it to me the right way."

Amethyst did as he said. "It's still not fair!" She folded her arms and huffed...stomping her right foot in the process while staring back at him.

"I had a horse that did that very same thing," he said as he sat on the couch. "Now come here and sit down." But Amethyst wouldn't budge. "I said come...sit *down!*"

She scrambled and flopped down on the couch.

"Little Sis, I want you to listen to the G-Time man. The money wasn't even the real point to all of this. It was more symbolic." He looked into her eyes. "You're upset because you didn't get to spend the entire $1,440 right?"

Amethyst nodded.

"And you feel cheated too--am I right?" He watched her nod again. "Little Sis, people blow 1,440 every...single...day. You want to know how?" He looked but she didn't respond. He continued. "Every single day we are granted 1,440 minutes to spend. And would you believe that people will waste it by sleeping in, dragging around, watching television all day long never moving from their comfortable little couches. Children get stuck on those video games, they lose all track of time, they don't read enough, and half do homework. But just like the $1,440 you received to spend in one day, you get the same 1,440--only it's allotted in time. And like the money you didn't get to spend you felt you lost, the same is true for the 1,440 minutes you get each day. What you don't spend is lost forever. It can't be rolled over to another day. It just can't be done!"

Amethyst looked up with tears.

He wiped a single tear away. "Sister, this may hurt, but if you learn anything from it, then I have done my job. Know this...whatever time you don't use wisely, is just lost. You can't save it up for retirement--it is only good for the time you are in at the time. And if you're fortunate enough to receive another 1,440 minutes on the next day, then all the better. But there will be no carryovers...ever. Oh and by the way, there is no such thing as living on borrowed time."

Amethyst smiled and gave him a hug.

"Aah, Sis. Now you've gone and ruined me. I can't believe you'd stoop so low as to actually hug me. Guess I'll just have to pass it on. The same way I hope you pass along what I have given--should you get the chance. Deal?"

She smiled. "Yes, Mr. G! It's a deal."

"Well, my time's up! Got to get you back to Ala-bam-a." The thunder and lightning began again...loud, clashing, and blinding. Amethyst covered her ears and closed her eyes as the wind blew--slapping and stinging her face.

## TWELVE

"Wake up there, Young Lady. Gardens don't plant themselves you know." A man with a thinly trimmed beard, and a hat topping his head shook Amethyst. "You can't expect to sleep all day long and get anything worth doing done now can you?"

Amethyst sat up and stretched. "Who are you?" she said yawning.

"The name's Countryman Full Of." He turned to leave. "You coming?"

"Do I have a choice?"

He looked back at her and laughed. "You do, but I don't think you'll like the consequences that come along with it."

She staggered behind him. "I had a feeling that's what you were going to say."

They walked out into a field as far and as wide as the eyes could see! A few chickens followed Countryman Full Of as he dropped chicken feed. He saw how Amethyst's eyes opened wide when she saw all that land. "Magnificent eh?"

"Not *quite* the word I was going to use, but I suppose you could say that. Just please tell me we're not going to have to work all of this."

"Not all at one time, but eventually. We'll get to each part, so don't you fret."

Amethyst couldn't believe this. He was serious; it was scrolled all over his face. "I'll never get home at this rate," she said hugging herself.

"Now you see. That's the problem. If you look at this and take it in all at once, it can be overwhelming. You start to believe you can't possibly get it all done. But if you just start out, one section at a time, heck...you'll have this knocked out before you even realize it." He picked up a hoe and handed it to her. "So, you ready to get started, Young Lady?" He smiled.

Amethyst took the hoe but refused to give up a smile. Work! She couldn't figure out what on earth she could possibly get out of working in the hot sun...digging in the dirt of all things. Worms wiggling around and stuff.

Countryman Full Of stepped up to her face. "Young Lady, half the battle is won with the right attitude. Yours needs a little adjusting, like some folk's spines, if you ask me."

"Well nobody asked you," she whispered, knowing full-well she never was allowed to talk back to grown folks.

"I heard that," he said walking towards an area tall with weeds. "I hadn't planned on starting here but maybe it's best we tear down a few weeds before we proceed to other areas. He found a swing blade near by. "I'll cut down, you dig up."

"You want *me* to dig up *these* weeds?" She stood looking.

"Yeah. And make sure you get down to the root, too. Otherwise we'll have the same problem cropping up again." He began swinging the blade away from where Amethyst was to be using the hoe.

"This doesn't make sense!" Amethyst said loud.

"I heard that, Young Lady. Seems like it makes plenty of sense as long as you keep up *that* attitude."

Amethyst continued until she had dug up all the weeds in the area. "I'm finished," she said, flinging down the hoe.

"And what did you learn?"

"Learn? I was suppose to be learning something?"

"Yes. What did you get out of this?"

### Destiny Unlimited

Amethyst thought for a second. "I learned weeds grow easier and better than the things you really want to grow. I learned that I'm going to dig them up by the roots and throw them as far away as possible so that I won't ever have to do this again!" She noticed he was smiling; she was only being comical.

"Go-on then, Young Lady! That was fan-tastic! There's hope for you after all. Yes...bad habits and attitudes are just like a bunch of weeds. They spring up, are easy to grow, and have no true value. You'll do well to find their roots, dig them up, and be careful of what's planted in place of them. All right, let's move to the next area." He shook his head and whispered, "Brilliant!"

"You mean now? You want to do some more work *right* now?"

He looked at her. "You have a better time than now for us to get it done?"

Amethyst decided it was in her best interest not to say anything smart here. No telling what he'd have her do! "No sir. Now is as good a time as any."

"As good my foot! Now is the only time you can grasp hold to. The rest is either *spent* or *speculation*!" He picked up small bags of seeds. "This I think you'll enjoy."

She rocked from side to side and smiled. "What is it?"

"We're going to plant seeds! Tell me...what are some of your favorite vegetables, Young Lady?"

"I like corn on the cob, peas...collard greens--"

"What about squash?"

She turned up her nose. "I don't like squash too hot."

He took off his hat and scratched the top of his head. "Hmmm, too bad. I do real well with squash seeds myself."

Amethyst smiled. "I'm not going to be here long enough for anything to grow. But I don't mind helping you plant," she said remembering the weeds she had worked so hard to dig up--her hands now scaled with calluses to remind her.

"Oh you'll be here long enough. I have some special soil in one area so some seeds do grow faster than normal." He held out his hand to Amethyst with four seeds cradled inside the middle line of the **M** etched in his palm. "Plant these over there; let's see what happens."

"What are they?"

"You tell me," he said as Amethyst grabbed them up.

She walked over to the area and squatted down. "I don't know," she said.

He stopped her just as she was about to drop the seeds into four prepared holes. "**Never** plant a seed unless you have full knowledge of what you are planting. How will you know what is to come up or what you should do to help it grow or feed it if you don't know what it is? What if you plant something you don't even desire? Imagine all the time and effort wasted. What if I were to tell you, these are talent seeds?"

"Talent seeds? I've never heard of talent seeds before."

"Well you have now! So pay attention. You hold in your hand four different talents. Do you want all of them to grow and prosper? Each requiring something from and out of you?"

"I don't know. What four talents are they?"

"One is a teacher, one is a violinist, one's a paratrooper, and the last one is something of a speaker."

"If I plant these, does that mean I have to take care of them...use them...harvest them later?"

"Yes, though no one can truly force you to use *or* take care of anything. Still, if you plant them, they will forever belong to you. Good, bad, or indifferent."

Amethyst stood and held all the seeds out to Mr. Full Of. "You can take back the violinist and the paratrooper seeds. I don't care to take care *or* use either of them--ever!"

# Destiny Unlimited

He looked in her hand...taking two seeds away. "Know what you're planting before you plant; then commit to take care and see that it grows and prospers." He pointed to the ground. "Commence to plant, Young Lady. There is more to attend to around here."

Amethyst planted the seeds and covered them. Countryman Full Of gave her a can of water and she showered the seeds--giving them all one good soaking.

"That's a special solution of water you're using. It has concentrated drops of success mixed throughout. Those talents should grow quite nicely now."

They walked to another row. "Plant these corn seeds and let's see what happens," he said as he pulled out a handful of yellow kernels.

Amethyst did as instructed, and the plants immediately began sprouting. First the blade...then stalks...then an ear...and finally full ears of corn. "Amazing!" Amethyst said as she rushed to get out of their way.

"Not really amazing. Time is relative. Now Young Lady, tell me what have you received back from one seed planted?"

Amethyst walked over to one of the plants. She examined the cornstalk from the ground to its brown tassels.

Mr. Full Of smiled. "Give me the short version if you don't mind."

Amethyst looked at him and then back at the corn. "The short of it is, I now have four full ears of corn on each stalk."

He plucked an ear from the stalk, grabbed the silk, and stripped it down before handing it to Amethyst. "Look deeper. Take your time. See beyond what is just on the surface."

Amethyst laughed. "Oh I get it. From only one seed sown, I have received many seeds in return?"

"Deeper," he said.

# Vanessa Davis Griggs

"I received enough seeds that I now can plant lots of rows, which in turn will produce even more corn, thereby giving me enough to eat...sell...give away, and still be able to plant more for my next harvest."

"All from one seed given, trusting that where it was placed, there would be a return. Young Lady, you are a seed. You already have inside, all you need to be who you already are. No one has to pull anything out, when you're in the right place--you just are. Like this seed, there's nothing to create. Stems, leaves, and other seeds are somehow hidden inside. It is, and has...it just needs to be. You decide the fate of your seeds harvested--whether eaten, used to create something else, or planted--the decision ultimately lies in your hands. Whatever you decide, realize that all decisions carry consequences--whether they be good or bad." He took a handful of seeds and began planting them. "Now--had you decided you didn't believe the earth would do what it was to do, and you kept the seed in a drawer...it could not have produced. You had to give, in order to get. You had to trust, in order to be entrusted. And what you received in return, was a multiplication of your seed sown. Fully realize though, when you plant corn...you don't get cucumbers. If you desire cucumbers, then you have to plant cucumber seeds. Everything produces after its kind."

"Mr. Full Of," Amethyst said, "then I'd like to plant some green peas."

He fished inside his pocket and took out a handful of seeds. "Go ahead, but this is regular dirt you're planting in now. It'll take the normal time to grow."

"That's fine," she said turning her shoes over on their sides and back up.

He smiled. "After you finish planting these, we'll go in and get a nice cool glass of fresh lemonade. Then we can come back out and work some more."

# Destiny Unlimited

Amethyst planted the peas and followed Mr. Full Of's footsteps to his simple little cabin. There was something about fresh squeezed lemons mixed with sugar and water that made Amethyst's mouth salivate and pucker up. She made herself comfortable in a wooden rocker, slowly sipping the cold tall glass of lemonade. But before she was ready...it was time to go back out into the field.

As Amethyst walked down the steps, she noticed two flower beds--one on each side. One was thriving while the opposite side was dead-looking and overgrown with weeds. "Mr. Full Of...why is this like this?"

"What Young Lady?"

"Your plants on this side are beautiful, while on this side they are straggly and almost dried up. This side doesn't have any weeds, while this side looks more like a weed garden."

Mr. Full Of looked. "You mean my children. You see that side flourishing, I gave them my full attention. I made sure they had what they needed, weeded out the place, and kept bugs away. But this side, I decided to just let be free-spirits...do whatever they wanted. I didn't try and train or direct them to be or do anything other than what they would be in my leaving them be. I decided whatever they did in life, was fine with me. I'd support and love them. I hadn't paid much attention to them until you pointed them out." He frowned.

"Well, I hope you know your free-spirits look sad."

"Maybe I made a mistake in just letting them be. I guess they needed some attention and direction after all." He smiled. "Do me a favor--run over to the side of the house and bring back my pick and shovel please. Brand new, never used."

Amethyst walked to the side of the house and looked at the tools that leaned against it. They were all rusty and the handles were broken and rotted. She came back with the tools. "These aren't any good!"

"Say what?"

"They're rusty. Falling apart. Look at them." She held them up.

He shook his head. "I guess that's what happens to things when they're just left to sit up and aren't used. And to think, they were brand new too. I'd rather things wear out than rust out. Live and learn they say." He flashed a suspicious-looking smile and shook his head. "Live and learn. "

He and Amethyst walked back to the row of green peas she had planted earlier. Mr. Full Of called her over, gave her a hand shovel, and pointed to where one of the seeds was. "Dig it up...let's see what it's doing," he said.

"Dig it up?" She looked at him with one hand on her hip. "I just planted these. They haven't had time to do anything. They haven't even begun to sprout. See?" she said pointing her finger towards the row of rich black dirt.

"Dig it up...let's see what it's doing! It's been down there long enough to be doing something. I want to know what it's doing...what's going on with it. The silence is just too loud."

Amethyst laughed until she saw he hadn't cracked a smile. He was waiting patiently for her to carry out his command. She squatted down and unearthed one of the seeds. Holding it up, she said, "See! It's still just a seed. It hasn't been there long enough to do anything. I told you."

He nodded and waved for her to follow to yet another area of the field. She covered the seed back, stomped dirt off her feet, and caught up with him.

"There's some money seeds planted over there," Mr. Full Of said pointing to his far right. "And next to it is some wisdom and knowledge to go with it. Over there, is plenty of love--you can never have too much of that you know!" He walked on. "On my left here is joy, peace, and forgiveness-- Will you look at those darn forget-me-nots. They're hard to get rid of once they

## Destiny Unlimited

take root. But I'm working on it...I plan to straighten this place out if it's the last thing I do."

He began stomping the ground. "Pesky bugs! They just won't quit! I've tried everything...sprayed them, relocated them elsewhere. It's the same with those pesky little rodents. But those foxes-- You know, it's those little foxes that usually spoil the whole vine. Between these weeds, bugs, and other pests; it's amazing anything produces like it should." He held his hoe in the air examining it. "Well let's get started. We need to knock down some of these weeds of hate, jealously, backbiting... there's bushes of doubt, fear, and procrastination trying to take over." He pulled a can of spray from his pocket and sprayed in a line on the ground. "Darn CAN'TS. There's a can't here, a can't there--the place is crawling with them! And when you see one can't...you know there's a whole line of them waiting for the scout to come back to give them marching orders to move in. I must admit though--I do admire their spirit! No matter how you try and stop 'em...they just won't quit! Killing them is about the only way to get rid of 'em."

Amethyst looked closer. "Those can'ts look like ants."

Countryman Full Of pointed to another spot as they walked back. "You see over there...those are *my* talents. I just wish I had a few more though."

"Then plant some more."

He stopped. "Young Lady, now that's an excellent suggestion." He reached inside his pocket and pulled out some seeds. "I've always wanted to play the violin, try my hand at being a paratrooper, and being a writer." He squatted down, dug three holes and dropped the seeds. "There! Shouldn't be long; I'll have to go out and buy me a violin now for sure."

As they walked past the green peas row, he glanced at Amethyst and smiled. "Dig it up, let's see what it's doing."

Amethyst looked at him. "Mr. Full Of, you know it hasn't done anything. If I keep digging it up, it's never going to grow. It'll never take root that way. I'll end up killing it."

"Is that right?" He rubbed his beard while he thought about her words.

"Yes! Things generally don't grow that fast. It takes time. You can kill your seeds if you go back, dig them up to see how and what they are doing."

"Hmmm. Then, I suppose those *dream* peas you just planted are going to have to take their time and fully ripen."

"What do you mean *dream* peas?"

"Those weren't *just* green peas you planted, Young Lady; they were *dreams,* desires. It's like you said--it's not good to plant and then continue to dig up what's been planted just to see what and how a thing is doing. It's best to plant and allow things to unfold at their own pace...trusting and believing that something is happening even when it looks like maybe it's not."

Amethyst whispered and smiled, "So **that's** what you were trying to prove."

Mr. Full Of and Amethyst walked over where the corn had grown so fast. In taking his hand out of his pocket, a napkin with seeds inside spilled onto the dirt. "Quick, help me get these up!" he said. "These are some lack of determination seeds Old Man Pessim down the road gave me out of his garden. I had them in this napkin intending to dispose 'em. Lack of determination is the *last* thing we need growing around here." And they rushed and picked all of them up.

Amethyst looked up at him. "You take this planting stuff seriously."

He smiled. "Just remember, should you ever plant something that you don't want to grow, dig it up before it takes root. Weeds, which suck nutrients from those things you desire, should be plucked up always by their roots. Remember also,

### Destiny Unlimited

what you sow is most assuredly what you will reap." He smiled. "Oh, and when it's your garden...you have final say so about what grows in it."

Lightning began flashing...thunder bellowed...the winds blew stronger causing the cornstalk to sway back and forth. Amethyst stood up and walked against the gale. The wind was carrying Mr. Full Of's words as she heard him shout, "One more thing, Young Lady! You can't control the weather! You just have to plan for those times and things. Control what you can, and what you have no control over, learn to still keep going!" Just then, lightning flashed, placing an exclamation mark at the end of his point.

## THIRTEEN

"Flo River, in the flesh!" A heavy set woman with flowing black hair tossed her long jet black mane from one side to the other. "Watch out now! I don't want to hurt nobody!" she said smiling. "Oooh! It's good to be so free!"

Amethyst stepped back one step.

Flo River moved closer and looked down at her. "Little Princess, I see you've made it this far. I certainly hope your journey has been a pleasant one."

Amethyst swallowed hard. "Yes ma'am. Fine."

Flo River reached out. "Let me see your hand," she said.

Amethyst slowly brought her hand up. Flo River jerked it closer. "I'm going to give it back! Gee, you act like somebody want to keep the old thing!" She turned it over. "Hmmm... calluses, huh? You've been to the garden I see."

"Yes ma'am."

"Good! Hard work never hurt nobody! Did you learn anything?"

"Yes ma'am. I did. Mr. Full Of has a lot going on in that field of his."

"Field of *his*? Why Little Princess, that wasn't his field. That field belongs to you!" She started to chuckle. "I sure hope you planted what you wanted to grow and pulled up what you didn't."

"But he said--"

"Aah, pay no mind to what that man said. After all, he is Full Of--" She laughed deep while stomping her foot. "Have

## Destiny Unlimited

you ever heard of cow manure?" she said. "Well Full Of uses more than is normally allotted to make things grow," she said.

Amethyst didn't like it here. She planned to hurry and get through with this one. Flo River wasn't the patient kind at all; she had a strange sense of humor. *What could possibly be so funny about cow manure?* she wondered.

"Well come on, Little Princess! We've got things to do. Might as well get to it!" She had such a rush about her... sashaying with grace as she moved. Amethyst couldn't resist mimicking her walk. Flo River turned and stared down at her. "Princess! If you gonna mock me at least have the decency to do it right!" She laughed in a bass-like voice as she jiggled like wild grape Jell-O.

Amethyst followed her to the bank of a great lake. The water was still, calm and relaxing. Flo River stooped over, not at all lady-like, and picked up a pebble. "Take this Little Princess and throw it into that water over there."

Amethyst took the pebble and hurled it. "Plip," it barely made a sound as it hit the water. She watched as the pebble made ripples--spreading continuously out from where the pebble had originally begun.

"Did you notice *that*, Little Princess?"

Amethyst smiled. "Yes, it was very pretty."

"Pretty? Pretty my foot! That was an awesome prayer if I *ever* saw one! That was a divine meditation. It was peace being still! That pebble represented your intentions--your desires in life. Did you notice how it silently, yet effectively touched the areas around it? First a tiny ripple, then larger and more reaching." She propped her hands on her hips. "Humph-- it was more than just *very pretty!*"

Amethyst looked back at the lake and noticed how angry the once calm lake was becoming. The winds beat against the waters causing them to wave. The waves began beating at each other. The water--choppy, full of passion and rage--then beat itself fiercely and unyielding against the rocks and the lakeside.

Flo River bent over and picked out a much larger stone than the pebble. "Okay, throw *this* one! Hard as you can now--not like a weakling!" she said.

Amethyst took the rock and drew back, putting as much force as she could muster behind the throw. She didn't hear when the stone landed, nor did she see any ripples.

"Not so pretty, huh? Still, that was a prayer. It was received, but there's so much turbulence, who knows what message you got back." Flo River started back up the hill. "Much better to receive in the stillness than in a rage. What do you think about that, Little Princess?" She turned and looked at Amethyst.

Amethyst blinked a few times. "Yes ma'am! I totally agree with you."

"Good! We can move on then!"

Amethyst began to shiver as they climbed up a snow-covered mountain. "Miss River, it's cold here. I need on a coat," Amethyst said.

"A coat? Stop being such a wimp! You don't see *me* frigid about this weather, do you? I'm the same warm person I always am. So stop whining like a baby!" She looked back and saw Amethyst a few feet behind her. "And if you lag behind me too much, I'm gonna leave you! I'm gonna tell you the truth. And the truth is going to make you free."

"Free?" Amethyst whispered under her breath. "Freeze is more like it." Flo River turned as though she had heard her. Amethyst smiled and hurried to catch up as they climbed higher. It had become more difficult for Amethyst to breathe, they were so high. She looked up--still a long way to go.

"You'd best watch your step around here," Flo River said. "Looks can be deceiving. I wouldn't want to lose you so soon. There's a lot more left than this."

Amethyst was careful where she placed her feet. The snow crunched like crackers underneath as she stepped lively and tried to keep up, but Flo River had already left her. Amethyst stopped to rest on a rock when she thought she heard voices like two people arguing. When she looked, there was no one.

"Hey you!" a voice said much louder, "Down here!"

Amethyst looked next to her feet and saw a smile in the fresh snow. "*What?*" she said hardly believing her own eyes. She looked closer.

"I'll tell you how to reach the top," the voice said.

She giggled. "Sorry, snow can't talk. So who are you?"

"My name is Grippo, but all my friends call me Grip!"

Amethyst laughed.

"Don't listen to him!" another voice said. She looked to her other side and saw a stepped on frown in the snow.

She laughed again. "And who are you? Slick?"

"Ha-ha. Not funny," he said. "I, dear lost mountain climber, am the great fun-filled Slippery, better known as Slip."

Amethyst couldn't believe she was having a conversation with snow. "So what do the two of you want with me?"

Grip cleared his throat. "Well I want to teach you how to climb the highest mountain," he said.

"And I," Slip sang, "...want to teach you the best way down from the mountain."

Amethyst laughed. "Well guys, Flo River is already showing me the way up--"

"Flo?" they said in harmony.

"Girlfriend, let me tell you one thing--Flo does not do well on mountains. Uh-unh. Not Miss Flo!" Grip said.

## Vanessa Davis Griggs

"I hate when this happens, but I must agree with my counterpart over there," Slip said. "Flo has been known to freeze up a time or two when it really counted."

Grip and Slip proceeded to tell Amethyst how it was better to step in fresh snow when climbing up because the roughness provided something to grip. But when it was time to come down--which she would invariably have to do--then a slippery smooth slope was the most fun mode...so long as the right equipment was used.

Amethyst made it to the top, but Flo River was still no where to be found. She appreciated the tips Grip and Slip had given her. Otherwise, she wouldn't have known *what* to do. After locating a sled, she slid down the smooth side of the mountain. She continued to searched for Flo River back at her ranch, but she wasn't there yet. As Amethyst walked past an elongated concrete planter, she smelled something awful. "P-U!" she said. "Man that stinks! Look at these mosquitoes...this thing is a regular breeding ground."

"Stinks, huh? Well if you're not going to help the situation, at least have the decency to shut up about it," the concrete planter said.

Amethyst looked closer at the planter. "Did you say something?"

"Yes, I said something! Over there talking about something stinks."

She grinned. "Well you do!"

"So you're short!"

"And you're ugly!" Amethyst laughed as she gazed at the planter with claw-like feet. "Wait a minute, I refuse to even argue with a piece of concrete."

"Make yourself useful then and commence to cleaning me out. This water is just sitting here encouraging all kinds of bad elements to come my way."

"Clean? You out? I don't *think* so."

"How about turning that handle on so some fresh water can make its way to me then. A grouchy old witch put that thing in to keep me from getting my fill."

"You're talking about this handle here?" she said, pointing to the wall.

"Yes, genius! If it's a handle then that's what I'm talking about."

She yanked her hand down. "Look, if you're going to be mean about it..."

He started to smile and speak softly. "I'm sorry. You're right. Here you are trying to help me, and I'm acting so bitter. I forget there are good decent people out there...like you." His voice then changed to a harsh tone. "Now hurry and do something before that witch comes back and zaps us both!"

Amethyst placed her hand back on the handle and started to turn it before stopping. "Are you sure it's okay for me to do this?"

"Sure I'm sure, kid! It's all right already! Now will you get to the turning before I've completed my decay process."

Amethyst turned the handle and heard the water sputter as it made its way through the pipe. The water gushed out, quickly filling up the planter.

"Aah!" the planter said. "You're a life-saver kid! Okay, you can leave now. What? You want thanks? Thanks! Now scram! Be gone. On your way!"

Amethyst watched with her mouth opened. The closer the water got to filling the planter and the water would begin to flow over, the higher and wider the planter became. The plants surrounding the planter all stretched--as if they were begging for just one drop of water while the planter snickered and continued to grow that much taller and that much larger.

Amethyst felt the ground tremble. She heard a rumbling sound as the water began to barely trickle into the planter.

"Just what do you think you're doing?" Flo River said to Amethyst. "Who told you to turn that on?"

"The planter asked me to--"

"You mean, Mr. Greedy-Don't-Circulate over there?" Flo River grabbed her by the hand and marched her out of the planter's earshot. "Do you see that body of water down there?" She pointed towards the lake.

"Yes." Amethyst nodded. Her hands were suddenly warm and sweaty. Flo River just seemed to make her nervous.

"That body does not hoard its waters. It knows there is plenty. It knows that which does not flow becomes stagnate and starts to stink. It knows that if it shares with others, eventually what was shared will return back to it. It knows the laws--both natural and spiritual." Flo River grabbed Amethyst by the arm and squeezed her muscles, dragging her back to stand before the planter.

"Now, on the other hand...Mr. Greedy-Don't-Circulate here, hoards every single drop he can get! He's so afraid there won't be enough, that he won't even share with these little plants around him. He doesn't care if everything else dries up or not, as long as his coffers are full and he has plenty. Mr. Greedy-Don't-Circulate has *yet* to learn the laws around this place. Therefore--he is cut off!"

"Oh give me a break Melodrama lama," the planter said.

"A break? A break! I'll give you a break all right! In fact, a crack might be one way to keep you from hoarding. Tell me, just how big were you planning on growing this time had I not gotten here to shut off the flow?" Flo River danced a tango with the planter, while Amethyst watched them go toe to toe.

"Eventually, dear Flo, I was *planning* to stop. You don't understand--I have low self-esteem. Don't you ever watch

## Destiny Unlimited

television? Besides, who knows what's going to pop up in life. Listen, when I feel secure, I'll be happy to share."

Flo River held up her hand like a policeman directing traffic to *Stop*. "Yeah? Well talk to the hand because the ears ain't listening!" she said.

"Look Madame Flo...you owe me! The world owes me! It's not my fault."

"Owe *you*? Who owes you? I owe you? The world owes you?" Flo River suddenly had a look of sympathy. Her voice became soft and sugary. "Oh Greedy...do you know what?"

"What?" Greedy-Don't-Circulate said strong but with a bashful smile.

"That's tough, ain't it! So why don't you just get over it and get on with your life!" she said. "I have!"

"Get over it? When I let things flow, I usually end up missing out on all the good stuff. My way ensures, at least I get to pick and choose what I want and desire to give away."

"Of course it does. And you can't wait to give up that slimy stagnate water you've held on to for ages. Now how right do you think that is, Greedy?"

"What's wrong with that? If I decide to share, then why can't I be the one to decide what I keep and what I give away?"

"Nothing would be wrong with that if you didn't mind receiving what you gave. But as it is, you have fits when you see a little green in your flow, yet you can't wait to give away that thick slimy junk you have!" Flo River said. Then she turned and glared down on Amethyst. "And *you*, Little Princess, before you start messing with stuff--calling yourself being all helpful and all--get yourself some knowledge about the situation first!"

"But you weren't around. And he seemed so...sincere," Amethyst said.

"Yeah? Well try explaining that to those poor little plants that were being deprived because of your actions. They are in need of constant mist. You came here, messed with this, and because you didn't know...you think that's some kind of a valid excuse. Well baby, let Flo River tell you...ignorance is no excuse! If you don't know, ask somebody who does! Have I made myself clear?" She thrust her fist in her sides, stared at Amethyst, and huffed to catch her breath.

Amethyst bent down and looked at the plants. "I'm sorry," she said as she touched their miniature leaves.

"I believe I just asked you a question, Little Princess."

Amethyst stood up. "Yes! I understand! I was wrong. I'm sorry, okay!"

"Being wrong and sorry about it is great. But if those plants die then wrong and sorry won't bring them back. And it sure won't change what you've done." Flo River stomped off.

The planter started singing. "Aah, alone at last. See kid, I told you there was a witch around here."

"And you were also wrong. When someone does something nice to help you, you need to learn how to pass it on. I gave you water, you should have passed something on to the others who needed it. That's only right."

"Yeah, yeah, yeah. And do *you* also have a broomstick, Witch Junior?"

"I'm not saying the way she talks to people is right, but you shouldn't be worried only about yourself either. Had I known, I would never have turned on that water for you."

"Oh well--I'm all right now. And another *jerk* who doesn't know any better will be along before too long. So you can save your drama for your mama!"

Amethyst was so upset, she ran away to an open field nearby. She noticed two brightly colored hot air balloons off a distance about fifty feet apart. Between them, lay a foot wide plank. She stood beside one of the balloons before deciding to walk across the plank. With arms extended, she easily kept her

## Destiny Unlimited

feet on the wood. A piece of cake! she thought with pride. She turned cartwheels without missing a step. Then she bowed for an imaginary audience.

Flo River walked up. "Great! I take it you're ready?"

"Ready? Ready for what?"

"To take to the skies...what else? That's your balloon there," Flo River said pointing to the balloon on the right, "...and this one's mine."

"But I've never flown in one of these before let alone flown by myself."

Flo River climbed into the basket. "And you never walked before you took your first steps but I see you're getting along fine now. So what's the problem?"

"No problem--"

"Are you saying you don't want to do this?"

"I really don't, but that's not what I'm saying."

Flo River smiled. "Then quit. I don't have time to baby-sit. It's only a silly game anyway. So you lose...what's the harm? Play again another day."

Amethyst pressed her lips together. She looked at Flo River before climbing into the balloon designated to her. "I'm ready! Now what?"

Flo River whipped out a remote and pressed a button. Both tie lines released from the stakes that held the baskets on the ground. Amethyst sighed...relieved to learn that the plank was attached to the bottom of both their baskets. Now there was no reason to worry about floating into never-never-land. And did they *ever* float! Over mountains, hills, trees, and valleys. Then the worst thing imaginable happened-- Amethyst's air valve began to malfunction.

Flo River yelled to her, "You're going to have to come over to mine now!"

Amethyst looked at her like she was crazy. "Excuse me? And how do you propose I do *that*?" she said.

"Can you fly?" Flo River said.

Amethyst frowned. "Of course not! You know I can't!"

"Then don't waste my time with silly questions! Seems to me your only option is going to be taking a trip across that plank there. It's secure."

Amethyst looked over the side--a long way down. "Say what?" she said.

"Walk the plank to this side! It's not like you haven't walked it already; I saw you earlier. In fact, you were turning cartwheels if my memory serves me correctly. Walking it now should be...*a piece of cake?*" Her hair flowed in the wind. "You can even moonwalk if you want to show off. I'm down with it."

Amethyst eyes widened. "Miss River, that was a whole different situation on the ground. I can't walk across this now! Not this high up anyway!"

"Now let me see if I got this straight. You can't fly, so that's out. And you say you can't walk across the plank now, although earlier, you did it to the point of turning little cartwheels. That sound about right?"

Amethyst began to breathe heavy while touching her chest. Her balloon was quickly losing steam. The two balloons would not remain level much longer. "Miss River...I'm scared! You've got to help me! Come get me."

"It's like this Little Princess, that plank is going to be breaking away soon. You see, I know I can't fly. So I'm *definitely* not going down with you. If you have plans that involve moving to this side, I'd suggest you take thirty seconds, get you and your plans together, and get yourself over here."

"Miss River, I can't. I'm scared. It's just not possible for me to do this."

### Destiny Unlimited

Flo River shook her head. "Okay then, let's see whether or not it's possible. Put one hand up close to your mouth and take in a deep breath." She waited. "Do it!" she said. Amethyst's hand went up to her face. "Now exhale, fast and hard." Amethyst did that. "Did you feel anything?" she said, searching Amethyst's face as though there was a certain sign she was looking for.

"Yes I felt something," Amethyst said. "My own breath! But what--"

"Breath you say? Breath? Then that means you're still breathing which means you passed the crucial test for possibilities. As information, any time you question whether a thing is possible for you to accomplish or to at least try, feel free to administer this test as needed. IF--however you should ever fail this all but important test, then and only then, will I agree it is highly unlikely a thing is possible for you." Amethyst's balloon began to make a hissing noise. "So are you coming over here with me...or are you planning to go down with your ship?"

Amethyst took a deep breath while looking over the side. If she took her chances and stayed with the balloon, her likelihood for survival would be slim and none. She decided her best out would be to walk across the plank. She hauled herself over the side and steadied her body; her heart pounded her chest like conga drums. Flo River managed to keep the balloons level. For Amethyst, this was frightening as thoughts of falling stayed uppermost in her mind.

"Don't think about falling, Little Princess. That's where your fears lie. Your thoughts are creating the wrong images. The only difference in now and when you walked it earlier, are the thoughts you have about it now."

"No," Amethyst said calmly as she balanced herself, looking straight ahead, refusing to glance down, "...the only difference in *now* and *then* is where this plank is *now*, and where it was *then*."

"I beg the differ Little Princess, but it *is* your thoughts. Your thoughts are creating your fears. Earlier you thought it was a cinch to walk this plank and it was. Now all you're thinking about is how hard it is...how you could fall...how--"

"I could die? if I make one wrong move," Amethyst said. "And this encouraging little pep talk you're giving, while enlightening as it might be, is not exactly helping matters any. That's IF...you don't mind my saying so, Miss River." Amethyst held her breath and took slow and careful steps.

Flo River reached out and grabbed her as soon as she was close enough to touch. Amethyst took quick breaths as she pressed tight her chest. Her heart fortunately was still beating-- albeit much faster and much harder. The plank began to make a creaking sound as it ripped away...plunging and whirling its way to the ground. Amethyst's balloon lost altitude and fell quickly out of sight.

"Miss River, I did it. I made it across! Look...I'm safe!"

"Yeah? Well you didn't even try to fly. But you walked; I guess that'll do."

They hovered back over the field as Flo River skillfully landed. Amethyst had never appreciated the ground so much as when her feet kissed it then.

"No time to stop and smell the grass. More business awaits us," Flo River said as she took long strides towards rolling pastures. She turned and glared. "Am I going to have to ask you every single time whether you're coming or not?"

Amethyst ran to catch up. "No. I'm coming. I didn't know."

"I was wondering. I figured you might be ready to quit after that last one."

## Destiny Unlimited

Amethyst shook her head. "No ma'am. I'm not. But thanks for being so concerned though."

Flo River stopped and smiled. "Is the Little Princess trying to make a joke? If so, your joking skills need attention: timings off. Otherwise, cute."

"It wasn't a joke. I'm just following you, Miss River. I'd just like to get this over with--if you don't mind."

"My sentiments exactly. I can certainly think of better things to do than spend time watching some whiny little kid."

They walked for what seemed like miles. Amethyst became tired, hungry, and thirsty. "How much farther is it?"

"Almost there! Don't tell me Little Princess is tired. Heck, you're suppose to be the youthful one of this little escapade."

"Well as you've already pointed out, I'm just a whiny little kid!"

"A child or an adult, life doesn't cut either of us much slack! You've got to learn to pull your own weight. From where I stand, you look to be about seventy...seventy-five pounds maybe sopping wet? Surely if I can pull my two-hundred plus pounds around, your little bitty self should be a day in the hay."

Amethyst decided to ignore Miss River's comments. What was the use anyway? This would all be a faint memory in just a little while. Then she could move on to the next "time of her life" adventure before getting on home.

"What's the matter Little Princess? Don't tell me you've lost your fight. And I was just warming up to you, too."

"I'm fine--a little thirsty maybe. But I'll be all right. So are we there yet?"

Flo River turned and looked at her. "You take all the fun out of a thing." She stopped, having topped the hill. "There! The old well and pump!"

Amethyst caught up with her. "A well and a pump? You mean we walked all this way to see an old well and a pump? There must be something else."

"No. You're thirsty aren't you? Well, we now have means of quenching that thirst. You have a need, here is the provision."

"Yes, but my need came from having walked so far for so long, apparently for a need I didn't even have at the time. Had we not walked all this way, I wouldn't be thirsty now, and I wouldn't have this need."

"Technicalities," Flo River said as she paraded down the hill to the well. But when she got there, she found the rope missing. Amethyst's mouth was so dry she felt like she had eaten a plate of white sand. Flo River tried getting the pump to give water, but it was no use--nothing came out of its mouth. She looked. "I know there's water down there somewhere. Interesting."

Amethyst couldn't believe they had walked all this way and now there was no water. She strolled over and sat on the steps of an old house nearby. As she looked around, there behind a plank, was a cool jar of water with a note: *Hello thirsty traveler. This jar of water is to be used to prime the pump. There is only enough water here to get the pump flowing. Please refill it for the next thirsty traveler who may come along later desiring a cool drink.* Amethyst couldn't believe it.

A miracle! She now had enough water to soothe her thirst. It was sealed in a jar and cool against her face. The note said the water should be used to prime the pump...to pour it somewhere? But what if the water was dried up? Or the pump doesn't work at all? All this water would be lost, serving no one's need or purpose.

Flo River stood by the pump talking to herself...loud enough for Amethyst to hear. "I can't get water from the well

## Destiny Unlimited

without a rope. And I can't get the pump to flow without giving it some of what it needs to give back what I need. I suppose we're in a bit of a jam since the only water anywhere close, is back on my place. If I had water to prime this pump, we'd have more water than we could possible handle. I guess we might as well hike on back. Come along, Princess."

Amethyst knew she had to make a decision. She *could* drink all this herself, maybe even share it with Miss River. Then again, she could follow the instructions on the jar...pouring good water down a pipe...believing that there would indeed be a return...taking a chance there would be. She walked over to Flo River. "Here's some water to prime the pump." She handed over the jar.

Flo River snatched it from her hands. "Oh! So you found the jar of water I left, huh? Great! This should just about get the water flowing. You just watch, we're going to have more than enough in little of no time."

She poured and began pumping. Nothing. She pumped harder, faster. Still, nothing. "Well I'll be," Flo River said. "I know this is *supposed* to work." She could see the look on Amethyst face. She pumped again and just as she had earlier declared--there was an overflow!

"Priming the pump is similar to paying yourself first. It starts the flow. One begets the other. It's also like giving tithes or just plain old giving...trusting enough to receive. It'll come back, pressed down, and running over unto you." Flo River splashed the excess water from the pump on Amethyst, and Amethyst kindly returned the favor. After a few minutes, Flo River handed an empty jar to Amethyst. "Fill this for the next one who might happen by."

Amethyst took the jar, filled it, and tightened the lid. It felt good knowing she was doing something that would help someone else--even if she didn't know who that someone else might be. She gently placed the jar back where she had found it. Flo River nodded with a smile. A warm cool smile. Amethyst couldn't ever recall seeing her smile that way before. Sure, she had laughed...but never a smile...warm like this. Amethyst returned the smile.

The sky darkened as thunder began making crashing sounds! The lightning flashed one behind another. Amethyst closed her eyes...it was again time to go.

## FOURTEEN

"Hello Mate, Captain Pye in the Sky at the helm! Come on aboard! This ship's about to cast off for buried treasures," said a one-eye-patched man dressed in a full pirate's suit.

Amethyst was starting to get accustomed to these sudden changes of scenery. The "ship" as he called it, was no more than a raggedy old boat that would barely hold more than fifteen people at one time.

"It's not the size of the ship that makes the difference, Mate. It's the size of the vision! And I see wealth and riches...treasure beyond your wildest imagination! So come on...we must be hurrying along."

Amethyst looked around to see who he was pointing to.

"No need to look for anyone else Mate. It's you I refer to. So get it in gear and let's get going. Treasure awaits us!"

Amethyst smiled and walked towards him. "Are you talking about real treasures?"

His eye widened as he rubbed his face with his hook. "As real as real gets Mate. There are many, many buried treasures out there. So--are you coming or are you just gonna stand there with those big brown eyes on me?"

Amethyst hopped on board. "Where's the rest of the crew?"

"The rest? Who needs rest! We have too much to do and not enough time to do it! Cast off, Mate! Let's be on our way!"

Amethyst kept watch. Two days, they sailed across the sea. When they finally docked, Amethyst couldn't help but laugh. "Captain Pye in the Sky, we're right back where we started from!" she said.

"Is that right?" He took out a pick and a shovel. "Well according to me map here, this is where it says we should begin looking for treasures. Now let's not waste any more time barking about it. Let's get to hunting!" He looked at the map. "It's yonder way, Mate!" He pointed the hook which doubled as his left hand to the right and took counted strides forward.

Amethyst followed him step for step...staying close as he continued to glance from the map to the ground.

He counted, "1, 2, 3, 4, 5!" before stopping to examine the map. "We're close, Mate!" he said. "I can feel it in me bones! I can smell it in the air."

Amethyst took a whiff. "All I smell are flowers. Honeysuckle, roses, gardenias maybe--"

"Shhh! We're almost there. Here," he turned around to her, "...make yourself useful and hold the shovel. I'll take care of the pick!" He held his black gloved finger into the air and smiled. "I'm about to show you one of the richest places on God's green earth. You wait and see! Captain Pye in the Sky, does not lie!"

Captain Pye in the Sky's steps lead them to a gate. "Aha! They have erected a gate to keep the treasures safe, Mate."

"Maybe they put up this gate to keep people out who shouldn't be in here," Amethyst said as she looked up at the brick and rod-iron gate. "And I don't believe buried treasures are in here either." She began to step backwards.

"Oh? And what makes you think you're so much smarter than Captain Pye in the Sky?" he said as he stepped behind to push her forward.

Amethyst looked up as they stopped at the entrance. She pointed to the sign above. "Well, for one thing, this is a cemetery! What are we doing in a cemetery searching for buried treasure?"

## Destiny Unlimited

Captain Pye in the Sky quickly checked the map. "It says it right here!" He popped the paper with his hook. "See! X marks the spot. Here is the X and this is the spot! So there! Now we know why *I* am the captain and *you* are only the..." he looked down at her and frowned, "...crew." He grinned.

Amethyst laughed. "Well were I the captain, I sure wouldn't be searching for buried treasures in some grave yard. *That's* for sure!"

"You've got a pretty sharp tongue on you there, Mate. I'd hate to have to force you to walk the plank." He fanned at a gnat buzzing around his face. "Dog-gone pests!" He continued through the gate. "Now are you coming? Or do I keep all the treasures for me own self?"

"Are you sure this is where the treasures are supposed to be? You didn't make a wrong turn or something like that?"

"Come and judge for yourself, Mate!"

Amethyst decided to follow him. "Captain Pye in the Sky, why would anybody bury their treasure in a grave yard? It just makes no sense."

"Aah, Mate. But it will make good sense soon enough. You still holding on to that little notebook I saw strapped to you earlier?" He sneaked a look at her. "I may need you to catalog our find."

"Yes," she said looking down at her note-pocketbook and giggling.

"Pretty neat idea there, Mate. You'd best be careful with those kind of ideas...someone is likely to *pirate* them." He began laughing. "Get it? Pirate them."

Amethyst shook her head. "Funny. It was so funny, I forgot to laugh."

"Then go ahead and laugh now. No harm done."

Amethyst shook her head again. If he's *really* real, this world is in more trouble than it knows!

"Look, Mate!" he said pointing. "There's the treasures now! Here's one, and another, and another." He laughed. "Why this place is full of buried treasures! Just like the map claims!"

Amethyst looked at the headstones and grave markers he had pointed to. Some were elaborate, but most were simple with the bare essentials inscribed. "What treasures? These aren't treasures! What kind of a captain are you anyway? It's no wonder you don't have a crew. You don't even know the difference between a grave chest and a treasure chest."

"Oh, but you're mistaken. I asked if you wanted to go treasure hunting did I *not*, Mate?"

"And I came! So where are the treasures, Captain Pye in the Sky? Look around! Does this *look* like a place full of buried treasures to you?" Amethyst stood with hands on hips. "Do you see signs of rubies, diamonds, sapphires?"

He smiled until it became a full grin. "Aah, but that is where you are mistaken Mate. There is in fact, too much treasure buried in this one place alone. And there are millions of places...just like this one all over the world! It is in places like these, that our greatest treasures can be found. Jewels that were to have been given to the world had they gotten that one break...had that one opportunity come their way...had time...had the money...had the nerve...had it to do all over again! Treasures the world never received because a life was cut down too soon...before its time...without having gotten the chance to share *their* unique gift. Treasures that would have improved the world...treasures that would have made others life that much better. Yet--most of the world's greatest treasures remain with those who could have bestowed them. And now, my little Mate--they are lost to us...buried forever," Captain Pye in the Sky said.

Amethyst read the headstone directly in front of her. *Our dear brother...a soul filled with songs the world will never hear.*

## Destiny Unlimited

*Rest in Peace.* She began to cry as she read the many headstones and grave markings one after another. She understood now what he meant by gifts the world would never know as she counted the many treasures buried here. She fell to her knees.

Captain Pye in the Sky came and helped her to her feet. "Don't cry for them--nothing said or done can bring *these* back. But cry, if you must, for the gifts that walk among the world each and every day, never ever realizing how rare...how special they truly are...how unique they have been fashioned."

Amethyst looked at him as his one eye twinkled. He smiled, showing off his gold tooth. "Do you know *you* are a priceless jewel, Amethyst?"

She wiped her eyes. "You mean because of my name?"

"No, Mate. Because you are a unique creation. Because there is not another exactly like you in this whole world over. And I should know...I've sailed it. You are beautifully, wondrously and gloriously made. Whether your name be Ame*thyst* or Ame*that*--you're priceless! You have purpose. And there is no other nor will there ever be anyone who can do what you do the way you were created to do it. Cry, if you must but cry for those who will never understand how much they should strive...with every fiber in their being...to make a difference...to live so their treasures will be shared for all to enjoy. Even if their gift is the gift of a smile, it should never be held on to--but passed on."

Amethyst continued to cry. "Treasures," she said. "We're all treasures."

"Hush now, Mate. I only wanted you to know real treasures--and to know the truth. It's important that you understand this in life--not in death. There is no way you, I, or anyone else, can ever mine *these* treasures that are buried here. Those that are already lost are already lost to us. Yet as your eyes now behold, here is evidence of untold wealth."

"I want to give my gift, but you don't understand what I have to deal with. I'm not even sure I matter...if what I'm to do is important. Maybe this is all an illusion! Maybe my efforts... my life won't make a difference. Does my life really matter—"

"Your...life...matters. Trust me...you're worth the effort necessary for you to succeed. Only *you* can leave your fingerprints, no one else can do it for you. Leave something with life...something that continues to live on even when you're not around. Leave something other than a grave marking. Build castles of cement or stone instead of sand. Then when the waves of time beat against it, it will not be so quick to wash away. Leave something so future generations will know without any doubt--You...Were...Here."

Amethyst dried her eyes.

"Aye Mate! Enough of the mushy stuff. Let's be off!" He pulled out his sword and raised it to the sky. When Amethyst looked down, her feet were on the edge of a board on his ship. "Sorry--time for you to walk the plank, Mate!"

Amethyst backed up as he laughed and charged towards her. The sound of a splash and the cold water surrounding her...convinced her she had fallen into the sea. In minutes, Captain Pye in the Sky was paddling over to her in a dingy. He rowed up next to her and extended his hand. Amethyst reached out; he pulled her up closer to the dingy. Then just as she was about to lift herself up, he took his hand and pushed her back down into the water.

"What are you doing?" she asked after the third time.

"Who me? Being myself, Mate. Now come on out of there so we can sail off into the clear blue yonder."

Amethyst tried again and again, but he continued to push her down. Twenty-five times he did, until she stopped even attempting to change her predicament entirely.

## Destiny Unlimited

"What's with you now, Mate?" Captain Pye in the Sky said as he took off his hat and scratched his head with his hook. "You're never going to get in here if you keep treading the waters like you're doing."

"Why try?" Amethyst said as she held tight to the dingy. "I'm tired. You get tired of trying when somebody's always there to keep or hold you down."

Captain Pye in the Sky began to laugh so hard he almost fell out of the dingy. He moved down to the other end and cast a fishing line into the water. Looking back at Amethyst, he began to laugh again. A fish tugged at his line, and he quickly reeled it in. "Look a-here, Mate! I caught one...on my first try at that. Man, what a beaut!" He held up the three feet tall red snapper for her to see.

Amethyst was confused. Here she was out in the cold waters while he was having the time of his life! How fair of a life was this?

He threw the fish into the boat, then scooted over to where Amethyst hung onto the sides. "You planning to hang there all day, Mate?"

"Why try? You're just going to push me back down anyway."

He had a frown like someone had squiggled it on his face with a marker. "Listen here, Mate," he said. "You might not be responsible for being pushed, held, or kept down, but you certainly are responsible for your getting up!"

Amethyst thought, then pulled herself up one more time--this time succeeding. Captain Pye in the Sky rowed towards the ship as Amethyst rolled her eyes; his face beamed. "Attitude Mate!" he said. "It's all about attitude."

They reached a rope ladder to climb aboard and Captain Pye in the Sky tapped Amethyst on her shoulders. "Remember Mate, when two wills oppose, the one who is the most persistent is the one who wins out. So no matter how many times you're knocked, pushed or held down...never wallow in it. Get up. And keep getting up until the other one gives up--but never you. Never you."

Amethyst started to climb the rope ladder.

Captain Pye in the Sky yelled up to her as he stood tall in the dingy being moved by the waves that beat against it. "Do you want to know what I found to be really hard, Mate? Climbing a ladder with both hands in your pockets. You must learn to use what you have, Mate, to accomplish things in life. Did you happen to note how much that ladder is like opportunity? When it shows up, you must be ready." His words began to sound more like streams of mini sermons.

"Persistence, now that's a good habit to form if you ask me. Notice how I didn't bring the ship down to your level so you're having to pull yourself up to its level. Had I pulled it down, then both you *and* the ship would have been sunk! Remember Mate...never ever give up! And do you want to know why...because your...life...matters," he yelled.

When Amethyst reached the top she looked down at him and smiled. He waved his left hook, and she waved back. Then the lightning and thunder began as the positive and negative electrons crystallized. The clouds billowed and rolled across the sky...the thunder rumbled, sounding like a bowling ball rolling down an alley played by professional bowlers. Streaks of lightning began to crisscross and decorate the sky.

# ᴅestiny 𝒰nlimited

## FIFTEEN

"What are you trying to do...get us killed?" said a man dressed in black overalls, a racing helmet and sitting to the right of Amethyst. His color had apparently drained from his now snow-white skin. "Keep your hands on the wheel! This is dead man's curve you're approaching! You *do* remember what you're suppose to do? Right?"

Amethyst looked down and saw dark brown gloves gripping tight a leather covered steering wheel. She could feel the car's vibration. "What?" she said.

"Look Champ! Don't start playing with me *now*! Do you remember?"

"Remember? Remember what?" she said keeping her eyes on the road.

"That if you start to skid and you feel you're about to lose control or hit the wall, don't look at the wall! Whatever you do, don't concentrate your energy on what you don't want! Set your sights only on where you desire to end up!" He pointed ahead. "There it is. Now whatever you do, don't panic!"

Amethyst rounded the curve and began to skid. The wall was rushing towards her and the car. All she could see *was* the wall! "Champ, focus your attention. *Now*! Don't see the wall! See victory! See yourself already where you desire to be!" In that instant, Amethyst forced her face in the direction she desired to go. She struggled with the steering wheel, and resisted the urge to look where the car was obviously heading despite her gallant efforts to steer it otherwise. She continued to concentrate only on where she wanted to be. The engine revved louder...she focused on her lane...she imagined the finish line. And in what seemed to take forever--but in reality only a few minutes--everything came to a crashing screeching halt! She sat in total darkness now. Then a laugh broke through the silence, and she realized...her eyes were still closed.

"Yahoo! You did it Champ! We made it!" the man sitting in the seat next to her said as his pink color came rushing back to his face.

Amethyst opened her eyes. She was sweating, trembling, nervous, and excited...all at the same time. "I did it!" she said. "We made it!"

"Yes you did! Now I see why they call you the champ, Champ. You are more than a conqueror! You are victorious!" He leaned over and hugged her before sliding out the opened window of the black and red race car. She tried opening the door but found she had to climb out as he had done.

He came around and extended her hand in victory for the roaring crowd as they cheered. Amethyst leaned over and had to yell in his ear in order for him to hear her. The sound of the crowd was deafening. "This is great! Now...who are you?" she said smiling.

He laughed and yelled back, "Mario Speedo--ready, willing, and definitely able! At your service!"

She smiled.

"Come on, Champ. We've got places to go!" He took her hand and whisked her away. They were now inside a quiet room with about twenty people all hobbling around on crutches. "Have you ever seen anything so sad-looking in all your days? Every one of them, still using their crutches."

"What happened to them? Were they in an accident or something?"

"Sort of. Max over there got hit by a truck filled with doubt. Tonya there, fell in a hole of fear. Pete got tripped up by a string of procrastination. Sandra was chasing blame and ended up running slap over unforgiveness, knocking it right on Rodney's foot. Then Rodney started hopping around and took out Bella, Troy, *and* Robin. Robin took bottles of anger and tossed them--she wasn't aiming at anyone in particular, and the bottles that didn't break on a foot, rolled like bowling balls, needless to say, taking out those eight you see pouting over there dealing mainly with the *'why me'* syndrome. The three in the corner--separate from everybody else--were attacked by severe strains of a crippling disease called *discriminated against*! One was attacked by racism, one sexism, and there's a new strain going around called societyism." He smiled. "That's society's perception of what is considered perfect, smart, beautiful, or right."

"Goodness!" Amethyst almost giggled. "I've never heard of such things."

"The pitiful thing is, they're all hobbling around on these crutches and missing out on the best party happening--life! Even worst is that everyone here could throw away these crutches of self-pity and move on...if they wanted to. Most of them continue to hold on in spite of that fact. It's been years, but they refuse to release the crutches that hold them back in moving forward."

"You're serious?"

"Yes I'm serious! I was thinking, perhaps you might speak to them. I mean, with you being the champ and all--"

"Me? You want *me* to talk to them?" She laughed. "But they're all older than me. What could I possibly say to them?"

"Just tell them what you know. Encourage them. They need to get past this, but we've run out of ways to help them see how important they really are."

Amethyst laughed. "They're not going to pay any attention to me! I mean, look at me--I'm just some young black child from--"

"What?" Mario Speedo said, jumping back. "How dare they do this to me! I have your file. It never said one thing about you being black or a child."

Amethyst put one hand on her hip. "Excuse me, but you can look at me and tell I'm black! And my height is a dead give away that I'm a child."

He smiled. "Oh, but you don't understand. You see, I'm colorblind. And on top of that, some of my best friends are little people. I'll tell you what I can do though; I *can* put in a call and get this mess straightened out like that..." he snapped his fingers, "...if you want me to."

Amethyst's curiosity was getting the best of her. She looked up at him. "Mr. Speedo, exactly what *did* your information say about me?"

He flashed her a smile. "It said...you were a human being, Champ. I figured...that was all I needed to know. But now if you like--"

Amethyst touched his arm. "Thanks Mr. Speedo."

Someone was yelling outside for help. Amethyst and Mario Speedo raced to the commotion. "What's wrong?" Mario Speedo said when he reached Tonya.

"It's Rodney! He fell into some water! He can't swim and he's going to drown if we don't hurry!"

Amethyst and Mario Speedo followed Tonya as she took long strides and hops, skillfully using her crutches. Amethyst and Mario Speedo exchanged looks when they finally did reach Rodney.

Mario Speedo shook his head. "Rodney, it's only two feet of water. Man...just stand up," he said loud enough for Rodney to hear.

Amethyst went over and helped Rodney as he stood to his feet.

# Destiny Unlimited

"I almost drowned!" Rodney said wiping the water off his face with his hand. "That water could have killed me! I don't believe this! If it's not one thing, it's another. Always something! I don't care how hard I seem to try, something always manages to pop up and get in my way. The devil is busy."

Mario Speedo put his hand on the left shoulder of a man now dripping wet. "Rodney...I don't know exactly how to say this, but that two feet of water would not have been the cause of your drowning had you drowned."

Rodney looked sideways at Mario Speedo. "Oh no?"

"No. You would have *drown* because you kept your face in the water. Man, you've got to learn to get up and stop wallowing in stuff once you fall in it!"

Rodney pulled Mario Speedo close and gave him a wet hug. "Wow! You *are* brilliant! Why didn't I see that? The water wasn't my problem but keeping my face stuck in it was!"

Mario Speedo looked at Amethyst--they both burst into a laugh. Mario turned and faced Rodney and Tonya. "Look guys, the Champ here has something to say to all of you. Why don't we go inside and see if we can't start a few miracles to happening around this place!"

The two started back to the building...hobbling on their crutches. Amethyst grabbed Mario by the arm. "I'm not sure *who* you think I am, but--"

"Think?" Mario pulled a mirror from his pocket. "Know," he said handing her the mirror. "Search your reflection in here, then tell me who *you* see."

Amethyst was reluctant. "I already know what I look like...and who I am--"

"Apparently not, Amethyst Destiny Price. What I and others see when we look at you, is obviously entirely different from what you see when you look at you. So take this mirror and tell me who and what you see."

*125*

Amethyst took it and a surge of energy traveled through her whole body in that instant. She quickly held the mirror down to her side, refusing to look. She thought about telling him there was a young black girl with sandy auburn hair and big brown eyes in the mirror, but then she remembered what he had said about being colorblind, so that wouldn't mean a thing to him. After all, how do you explain color to one who knows not color? Besides that, she liked what he had said about only seeing a human being.

"I'm challenging your spirit, Champ," he said. "Come on...give it your best shot." His stare was piercing and serious.

She sighed and held the mirror up to her face. Her mouth now seemed to have a mind of its own as it began... speaking things she didn't know was waiting inside to be said.

"I see a spiritual being in human clothing doing great and wonderful things. Things she is proud to own as her doings. I see a great teacher, writer, speaker...a person desiring to make a difference in the quality of people's lives. A being not giving away fishes, but teaching people how to build their own ponds, how to stock them with only the best, and how to cast their own lines and drag their own nets. A person of great influence...motivating others to good works, to knowing the true meaning of happiness. I see one burning with desire, filled with purpose. One who can--not only conceive--but achieve. I see a **Ph.D.**: Persistent, Hardworking, **period** plain old Determined. A being committed to *being* the best, regardless of background or origination...focused on intention and desire... daring not waste *any* energy on things that are not intended.

"I see a person with vision--passionate about what she does in life. A person who will forever thirst and drink from the fountain of knowledge. I see one who understands money...the importance of paying one's self first, of being one who *earns* interest instead of paying it. My wealth will be measured *not by*

## Destiny Unlimited

what I am able to earn, but what I'm able to retain...what I am able to ultimately do for others. I see one who realizes everything reproduces after its own kind, one who knows that attitude raises the altitude of a person." Amethyst handed the mirror to him and stumbled backwards. She rubbed her head. "Where did all *that* come from?" she said.

Mario Speedo nodded and smiled. "That was good, Champ. *'Twas blind but now I see.* Now let's go talk to those waiting inside with *their* crutches."

Amethyst followed him in and took a deep breath as she began explaining what she knew about the power of words. Mario Speedo stood in the back, smiling as she became stronger and more confident. She talked about being careful when naming feelings and things...about changing words used when describing negative feelings. She talked about being able to move on in life.

"You're a cute little thing, but don't you think you're a little *too* young to be calling yourself trying to tell **us** anything?" Robin said. "I mean, every one of us here is way older than you! Wisdom does have age privileges, I believe."

"Oh give the child a break!" Max said. "I doubt she'll be bugging us much longer. Just let her finish her little speech so we can get back to our lives."

Mario nodded. "Go on, Champ," he mouthed to Amethyst. He smiled and walked closer with legs that were slightly bowed. He winked and gestured for her to continue.

Amethyst smiled and took a deep breath. She continued by explaining the differences in simple words like *feeling a little down* versus *extremely depressed* and how just those words cause and create totally different feelings and reactions. She told them to examine the words that induced stress, and for them to work on finding a *lighter* version to use--especially when expressing negative emotions. "Your daily lives would take on whole new meanings if you only made this one adjustment," she said smiling. "I call this speaking light--similar to eating light, only with no calories. So instead of seeing something, for instance, as a rejection...try labeling it as your *motivational stepping stone*."

"I doubt that will work," Max said rolling his eyes towards the ceiling.

Mario Speedo stepped up and squared his six foot frame off with an even taller Max. "Why don't you try it Max? Let's see whether it works or not."

Max swallowed hard. "Okay Speedo," he said with a slight stutter. "Whatever you say. Like this? I look forward to this working." Max began to smile. "Hey--it's working! I didn't feel a twinge of doubt when I said that." He threw his crutches down and began to dance, laughing the whole while.

"See!" Amethyst said, surprised herself that it had worked. "See how even his tone changed as soon as he changed his words?" She looked in each of the other faces as she walked closer to them.

"Hey!" Sandra said almost scaring Amethyst. "I'm going to try it next!"

Bella turned her nose up at Sandra. "Of course *you* are! With your domineering bossy self!"

Sandra fired back. "Well it's people like you who cause me to be this way. It's the world's fault I'm the person I am today. Only the strong survive!"

Amethyst turned to Sandra. "Change the words she just spoke of you."

"What?"

"I said change the words *domineering* and *bossy* to something else. Find a lighter word or phrase to use instead." Amethyst was suddenly starting to feel grown up...like a person with something to offer. These people were actually listening and paying attention to what she was saying.

### ~Destiny ~Unlimited

Sandra looked around as all eyes were on her. "Okay," she said frowning. "Here goes. I'm a quality conscious, get-it-done, take charge kind of person." She turned and smiled. "Wow! That felt great!" She looked back at Amethyst. "So whom should I blame for my having gone through all these negative feelings for so long?"

Max was still dancing around the room. "Sandra, why don't you throw away your crutches girl. Stop blaming other folks for what goes on in your life! Come, dance with me." He stood with opened arms and a smile.

"Why Maxie...aren't *you* just the little charmer!" she said with a Southern drawl as she flung down her crutches.

"You see! See the difference!" Amethyst said to the others. "The feelings attached to words can cause distress, but by changing those words, you can get a different feeling altogether. You no longer feel so beaten down when you find a lighter word for what's going on. Transform by transforming your words. Come on, try it. Throw away your crutches everyone! Release them and free yourself! Dance, I say! Dance the dance of life!" Amethyst laughed and pranced around the room. "You've been missing the party for far too long."

The others began changing their words and when all was said and done, everyone in the room was dancing and not one crutch was left still standing.

Mario walked over to Amethyst and raised her hand. "You did good, Champ. You did good. Even I was able to come up with another word to replace the word failure. The feelings attached to that one word alone has grieved many a souls. So instead of feeling like one has failed, one should just think of it as having eliminated one way that *doesn't* work. You know, I love your phrase for rejection too," he said with a short laugh. "Anyone can take a *motivational stepping stone*, evaluate it to see if there's anything of value to be extracted from it--then promptly pack it under their feet, moving on up a little higher." He smiled. "You're a good speaker. Got a lot of fire and spunk about you. Continue this, and you're bound to only get better."

"Well thank you for the encouragement, Mr. Speedo. I've always admired those who speak like I just did today. Now that I've had this opportunity, it was really great! Seeing people dancing, happy and carefree...that's what I want to do with my life. Whatever I end up becoming, I want to help others know the truth and to set people free."

The lightning and thunder began. Mario blew Amethyst a kiss as he opened the door. It was hard to believe this one could be over so soon. And this time, she had helped someone. Cast and broken a few spells by using spells of her own: fondly referred to and known as *spelling*. Words! That's all she had used. Words. Yet, she was now a witness of the tremendous power of words. The power to hurt, to hinder, to motivate...to heal. Word power. Power to the people!

## SIXTEEN

Amethyst looked around. This was a dark room, except for the fireplace's dancing orange light.

"Kid! You're late," a man in a shining armor suit bellowed as he held up a matching shining sword.

"What?" Amethyst said, scooting further down to the end of the couch.

"I said," he pulled the helmet off his head, "...you...are...late! What are you...hard of hearing?"

Amethyst laughed. "No. My hearing's fine. And who are *you* suppose to be? And what are you planning to do with that sword?"

He sat his helmet down on the sofa table and walked over to the fireplace. "The name's...Don In Lieu! Defender of the weak! I was just about off to fight for the release of one held captive, when I received word of your pending arrival. And of course, getting in and out of this tin can suit is not half as easy as one may think. Trips to the bathroom require a major act of congress and takes equally as long getting it done."

The telephone rang. He glanced at the distance it would take to reach it. "One moment, kid. Let me see who this could be calling." After taking slightly bent, giant clanking steps, he finally made it to the telephone. "Hello," he said putting his sword back into its holder.

Amethyst wiggled with nervous energy and looked around his castle.

"That was my friend Misery," Don In Lieu said, having slipped the receiver back onto its hook. "She lives in a *cute* little castle out of the way. She was calling to see if you and I--me mainly--might care to stop over tonight. You know, to sit around and chew the fat, play games--stuff like that. I hope you don't mind, but I told her we would pass, though that woman will hardly ever take *no* for an answer. I declare if Misery doesn't *love* company!"

Amethyst smiled. "So we're going to visit Misery?"

"Oh no. You and I have far too much to accomplish to do that." He beat his chest once and stumbled several steps backwards. "I'm ready now. I've got my truth girt about me," he said tightening a leather belt, "...my breastplate of righteousness, my feet are covered with high tech peace...nothing shoddy about this! And here's my shield of faith, my helmet which has been most of my salvation as it continues to protect those vital portions. Then...my sword..." He pulled the sword out and raised it in the air. "...the sword of the Spirit. Word."

She laughed.

"What are you laughing about? I am well-prepared...well-trained. When things happen, I don't have to call anybody and ask what I should do. In a crisis situation...in the heat of the battle--I have been so well trained, I simply react with what I have already been taught. There is a great difference in having knowledge...and using it!"

He escorted Amethyst out of the castle. Amethyst noticed a weird 'L' shaped looking object in the grass and picked it up. "What's this, Mr. Lieu?"

"Kid--whatever you do, just don't throw it," Don In Lieu said as he turned back around, licked his index finger, stuck it in the air...testing the wind.

Amethyst looked at the object, then back at him. He wasn't even paying attention. Drawing back with all her might, she threw it as hard as she could muster...watching it spin

## ᴅestiny 𝒰nlimited

clumsily in the air. It flew farther and farther out-of-sight. "Now that made a lot of sense!" she said. "What a useless item!"

Don In Lieu began to count as he struggled to get to the ground.

"Get down, kid," he said as he put his face in the grass. "Five, four, three, two, one...incoming!" he shouted.

Amethyst stood laughing and watching him, wondering if he was just eccentric or plain old crazy. She heard a whirling sound in the air before an object whacked her upside the left of her head. "Ouch!" she said holding the place she was hit. She looked around and saw it was the 'L' shaped object she had thrown just a minute earlier. "Who threw this?" she yelled as she continued massaging her head. "Come on out you coward! Why don't you show your face!"

Don In Lieu struggled to stand back up. "That is one of Misery's toys. She calls it a boomerang. But that thing is full of judgment, unforgiveness, envy, strife, and resentment if you want to know the truth about it. You'd do well, kid, not to play around with it--unless you're prepared to catch it one way or the other when it comes back. You know what they say, the same might with which it is thrown, the same might will be used when it returns to you."

Amethyst rubbed the spot on her head. She felt a bump rising fast. "That *really* hurt!" She felt like crying.

He laughed. "Yep, that's how it works. The one throwing it is usually the one who ends up feeling the most pain from its wrath. Just let it go, kid. Learn to let some things go."

Don In Lieu and Amethyst walked a few blocks before coming upon an even bigger castle than his castle was. He pushed the gate open, drew his sword, and walked slowly up the overgrown path. "This is the place," he said looking at the expression on Amethyst's face. "You must *always* be prepared!"

*133*

They walked inside, Amethyst *careful* to stay close behind Don In Lieu. A huge ball made of a smooth glass surface clutched inside a claw-like hand base, rested in the foyer of the house. Don In Lieu stopped and took notice of how the ball reacted. Amethyst raised her hand to point, when a set of unchained lightning bolts began to crackled inside the glass ball. She moved, and it seemed to surge with power.

"Look at that!" Amethyst said as the swirling formation of lightning began to pulsate with her voice.

"Yes, that ball is used to harness energy flow. It receives its power from all kinds of negative sources. My desire is to shut the source down completely, but at present, my efforts have been more reaction than action."

"What is its source?" Amethyst whispered.

"Blame is one. You know, when people blame others for their lot and misfortunes in life instead of realizing that *they* are responsible for what is happening now, and that *they* are making the choice to continue to be miserable. Now did you see how the lightning danced around that time in the ball? That was hate and misunderstanding doing the tango. If you pay real close attention, you might even see...there! Did you see those sharp quick subtle flicks of light? That was hidden racism and sexism if I've ever seen them. Look there! There's enough ego and complaining in that one charge alone to power New York City. If we had time to just stand here and watch, you would see all kinds of doubt, fear, procrastination, set limitations, and mistrust, flashing like lightning bugs."

"So the stronger the negative forces, the stronger the power surge?"

"Whether it be thoughts, actions, or simply reactions--" Don in Lieu said as he nodded.

"The stronger the force, the greater the power exhibits?"

### Destiny Unlimited

"Yes! And had this ball not been constructed, there would be destruction all around. I always check the ball to ensure it is still continuing to hold, before I proceed with my duties. I wish I could shut off these negative forces entirely."

"Is it possible to do that?"

Don in Lieu retrieved his sword. "Not with a sword unfortunately. If only it *were* that easy I would have cut them down long ago and been able to retire this garbage can suit. It takes unconditional love. But egos won't let that happen!"

"What would happen if you got the negative to stop flowing?"

"For one thing, all that energy being used could be directed to many more positive things, like joy, happiness, peace, getting along...things like that."

They continued quietly around the side of the hall and walked down a narrow flight of stairs, passing a door chained from the outside with a sign nailed on it. Don In Lieu turned and whispered to Amethyst. "Those in there were so negative, we had to quarantine them. An outbreak would have been deadly. We later found out they were negative carriers and spreading negatrons like wild fire. But they're under control...for now."

Don In Lieu slinked alongside the wall, but his armored suit squealed each time he planted a foot down. He handed Amethyst his shield before kicking in the door. With his sword held high, he yelled, "Unhand Giselle, you creeps! Anger!...I should have known you were somehow behind this!"

Amethyst watched as the two fought with their swords. She heard metal hit metal. It was iron sharpening iron. Steel sharpening steel.

Anger tripped Don In Lieu up and looked down at him as he drew back his sword. "I'm not the one holding on to her, she's been holding on to me!" he said, pointing to a mousy-looking woman gagged and tied in a chair.

Don In Lieu kicked Anger against the wall. He quickly looked towards Amethyst. "Untie her, kid! Help her get free!"

Amethyst wondered what he thought *she* could do. Four other strong gigantic forces entered the room as Don In Lieu fought from one to the other. He saw Amethyst still standing at the entrance. "Hurry, kid! Untie Giselle so we can get out of here! I'm not sure how much longer I'll be able to hold them off."

Amethyst ran to the chair and tried to untie the rope. "I can't!" she said.

"Can't? What do you mean, *can't?*" He continued to fight as he talked.

"It's too thick! And it's tied too tight!"

"Then stand back. Let Amer I can do it!" Don In Lieu said as he sliced through the rope. "Did you get that? American... Amer I can!" He backed up while holding the forces up against the wall. "Hurry you two! I'll be all right!"

Amethyst and Giselle ran out the door and waited for Don In Lieu.

"He is so brave...and courageous!" Giselle said. "They tortured me in there. One held me down and replayed hurtful scenes, while the others stabbed me constantly to ensure I not only relived, but felt the actual pain of it."

Amethyst looked at the wounds--the most being near her head and heart.

Giselle, seeing Amethyst's concern, proceeded with the details. "You see, I had helped this friend in her desperate time of need...her marriage was on the rocks, she was always depressed. But now that things are going fine for her, she treats me like dirt...won't even speak to me. She goes as far as to turn her head when she sees me coming. I've tried to forgive, but it's hard when someone mistreats you like that. Whenever I tell Don In Lieu that I *am* trying, he says, 'In these cases, there's no such thing as *trying*, either you do, or you don't!' He keeps telling me that whatever anyone does or has done to me, will go against their ledger...and that they will have to balance their own account in the end as I, mine. He says I should send out thoughts of love, not for the actions done against me, but for the being who obviously doesn't know any better."

"Being?" Amethyst said as she peeked over at the door...still hearing the clashing and clanking of the swords meeting each other.

"Yes, *being*. He says, 'People who hurt and do wrong to others are still a being. They're just lost and in need of pure love.' Don In Lieu says, 'Love never fails!' Well I *was* doing fine about this person...sending out love whenever I saw her anywhere, but then unforgiveness showed up the other day, and dragged me right back, starting things all over again! It's just so hard. But Don In Lieu maintains I can beat it! 'Love shatters all negative forces!'...that's what he keeps telling me. I know he's right. The only one experiencing pain from this now it seems, is me. I have to care enough about myself to stop it. And then there are my parents, responsible for my having grown up so poor...having to do without as a child. I *still* haven't gotten over that! I'm mad and upset about it, too."

"So how do your parents feel about it?" Amethyst asked. "About your still being so upset?"

"My parents? Oh heck, they've been dead ten years now."

Amethyst frowned. "And you're still causing yourself grief about it?"

Giselle laughed. "Ridiculous, isn't it? But it's just so hard to let it go."

## Vanessa Davis Griggs

Don In Lieu was close to the door now. He began to shout with a loud voice at the negative forces, "And when I have done all I can to stand do you know what I do?"

They giggled and shook their heads. "No, Don In Lieu...what do you do?"

"Why, I stand of course!" Don In Lieu then began singing it like a song. "And when you've done all you can to stand--Stand, stand, stand I say!" He struck another blow as he jumped outside to the hall and shut the door. He smiled at Amethyst and Giselle. "Quick, let's go!" And they all ran up the steps.

Amethyst looked at the ball; it was much quieter now. Then the ball burst into a thousand pieces as the lightning filled the entire house. "Love never fails!" Don In Lieu said. The thunder boomed and rumbled louder. Over the thunder, the cries of those locked inside the quarantined dungeon filled the house. Amethyst checked to ensure her notebook was still hanging across her body--it was. She then heard a familiar voice. "If you don't let the negative go, it will continue to grow," the voice said. "So let it go." Then a bright light flashed.

## SEVENTEEN

"I am the great Miss Christen Listen. The master of illusions. Come one, come all. I make the blind see," proclaimed an average height woman with a charm-like voice. She looked to be about twenty-five.

Amethyst watched her before stepping forward, bold like a lion. "What you're doing isn't real," she said. "You're a trickster...tricking folks with the slight of your hands!" A hush quickly swept over the crowd as Christen Listen cut a path, slinking her way towards Amethyst--her red cape flapping in the breeze.

"And who are *you* to speak of *me* and my gifts in such manner?"

"Since you know so much and are suppose to be so great and wonderful, *you* tell me!" Amethyst said, putting one hand on her hip and staring back.

"Aah--a challenge." Christen Listen rubbed her hands together and grinned. "I love challenges! So! How many guesses do I get for your name?"

Amethyst smiled. "Three. But you'll never guess."

Christen Listen looked somber. "Hmmm, you *do* have me on that one. You are correct my little young friend. I will never guess."

Amethyst's face was now smug as delight began to dance in her voice. "See, I knew you were a phony."

Christen Listen smiled and ticked her index finger back and forth in Amethyst's face. "I *will* never guess--Amethyst Destiny Price!"

Amethyst pulled back in fear and sheer amazement.

"Now...come with me! I have things to show you. Then we shall *see* who is phony and who is *Too legit to quit*."

Amethyst was transported immediately to a high school basketball gym. There, a young black boy with a close-to-the-head kept afro, attempted to dribble the ball and then shoot.

"He's awful," Amethyst said.

"Awful is a pretty strong word, my Little Friend."

"Okay...then he's not very good. Is that better?"

"Better," Christen Listen said smiling. "True, he is not the best player I've ever witnessed...he's not a great shooter...and his feet seem to be made of lead, but he does have potential--and a strong desire to play for the NBA one day."

"Then he'd better get himself another dream because that's *never* going to happen!" Amethyst watched him shoot and miss again and again. "He's failed to hit the basket enough times. He's about got that missing down pat, I'd say." She giggled. "Potential? Ha! He'd best read the handwriting on the wall and give this up. Basketball is, obviously, not his game nor his claim to fame."

"Well, as it turns out...he did all right for himself. Come, let me show you what this '*failure*' as you say, became later in life." In a blink, Amethyst and Christen Listen were sitting in front row seats at an NBA finals. Christen Listen leaned over and whispered, "These seats are the perks of my profession."

Amethyst smiled. She couldn't believe she was *here*. "Look, there's number 23!" The ball rolled from his finger tips and swooshed through the basket from the three point line... nothing but net! Amethyst kept her eyes glued to the court and whispered, "Christen Listen, look! That's Michael Jordan!!!"

Christen Listen turned and smiled. "Great. I see you picked him out on your first try."

Amethyst stopped cheering and looked at her. "Picked him out? Who *doesn't* know Michael Jordan?!!!" Just then

### ᴅestiny Unlimited

Number 23 leaped through the air with the greatest of ease, his signature tongue hanging out. He delivered the ball to the basket like it was fine china on a silver platter. Amethyst began cheering again. She turned to finish her conversation with Christen Listen. "What do you mean 'picked him out' on the first try? He's retired, not forgotten."

Christen Listen smiled. "Oh, my error. Apparently, you *didn't* pick him out. This Number 23...Michael Jordan you cheer so loudly for, I take it you think him a good player?"

"Good? What planet are you from? He was fantastic! Still awesome."

"Oh--from *awful* to *awesome*. Quite a leap!" Christen Listen said smiling.

Amethyst looked at her with a scowling face. "Awful? Who in their right mind *ever* called Michael Jordan awful?"

"You did. Allow me to quote your exact words--'He's awful...he's not very good!' " Christen Listen said.

"Are you saying that kid we saw was actually *Michael Jordan*? Now you must be out of your mind! There's no way that kid we just left could have ever been Michael Jordan. At least, not *THE* Michael Jordan."

Christen Listen continued to watch the game. "You didn't truly believe he was born flying, dunking, shooting, and dribbling like this, did you? Well maybe a little dribble in that baby phase of life, but nothing like he does out there." She began to laugh. "Little Friend, most people are not born prodigies! It takes a lot of commitment, hard work, and determination to get to a place of *awesomeness*. Give the man credit. He paid some *dues* to fly as high as he does!"

And in a blink, they were standing on a sidewalk near a noisy neighborhood. "Let's try again."

Amethyst saw two young black boys rolling on the ground in a tight grip. "Why did you bring me to see this?"

"Just be quiet and pay attention." She looked over at Amethyst. "You'll see soon enough."

Amethyst watched as two teenage boys fought. One of the boys drew a knife on the other. "Aren't you going to stop them? He's going to hurt him!" Amethyst grabbed Christen Listen's hand as fear masked her face.

"We can't stop what has already transpired; all we can do is learn from it."

The teenager with the knife drew back, plunging the knife hard into the other teen's stomach. Amethyst flinched... closing her eyes tight...unwilling to watch the bloody outcome. When she opened her eyes, the teen was gazing at his knife now with a broken-off tip. The other teen's belt buckle had stopped the knife...saving his life! In another blink of an eye, Amethyst found herself behind a large glass window observing someone's surgery.

A doctor sitting behind them whispered to a second doctor, "He is such a skilled surgeon...black, white, red, yellow, or brown...he's just good! We are fortunate he became a doctor. I can't *imagine* the loss were he not doing this."

The other doctor whispered back, "Yeah, but I'll never let *him* know how good I think he is! Yet, look at the many lives this one life has saved alone! A sure case of the *one life touching another* concept. The circle of life, they call it."

Amethyst grinned and whispered to Christen Listen, "That's the boy whose belt buckle stopped that knife, isn't it?"

Christen Listen smiled back. "No. *That* is the boy *with* the knife. He was smart enough to put it down back then, and brilliant enough to pick it up in here. Dr. Ben Carson--a man who worked *hard* to get where he is today." She looked at Amethyst. "Let's try another."

Amethyst and Christen Listen watched as two older women stood around a little black girl. She was tall for her age,

### Destiny Unlimited

that much Amethyst was able to determine from the two women's private conversation.

"Why doesn't she talk?" one of the women said to the other. She turned to the little girl. "Open your mouth and speak girl!" But the little girl remained silent, not even looking up as they spoke. "I don't understand why she doesn't talk. She used to, didn't she?"

The other woman nodded. "But every since she told on that man that violated her, and then later he got killed, she hasn't uttered a sound."

Amethyst leaned over and whispered, "Is she deaf and dumb or something? I mean, can she really not talk? Will she ever speak again?"

Christen Listen smiled and began to spin slowly in a circle with her cape opened to the wind. When she stopped, she and Amethyst were sitting down at the 1992 Inaugural Address. A tall, finely dressed black woman stepped up to the microphone and reeled a powerful nation with one powerful poem she had written especially for this occasion.

Amethyst felt chill bumps crawl up and down her arms. She whispered to Christen Listen, "I remember this! I was much younger, but I know who that is. That's Maya Angelou! And that's the poem she wrote for President Clinton's Inaugural Address–" Amethyst stopped. "Do you mean to tell me *that* little girl, is the girl we saw? The little girl who couldn't or wouldn't speak?"

Christen Listen smiled and cocked her head to one side.

"Well I'll be! Who would have thought?" Amethyst said.

Christen Listen showed her many more people. Some she knew of, some she had only recently heard of, some she had never heard of before, and some she now wanted to learn even more about.

# Vanessa Davis Griggs

"A black man winning the Masters," Amethyst said. "A young black man at that! My daddy says most black folks don't care much for golf. He says, 'Who wants to hit a ball then chase behind it to hit it again?' But I'll let you in on a secret...even my daddy watches golf when Tiger Woods is playing."

Amethyst was shown slaves that worked to free other slaves. Even one former slave who eventually headed a college--Booker T. Washington. She saw Jackie Robinson, Madam C. J. Walker, Fannie Lou Hamer, Toni Morrison, Muhammed Ali, Bill Russell, Arthur Ashe, Wilma Rudolph, Jesse Owens, Ken Griffey Sr. and Ken Griffey Jr. There was Charles Alfred...a black pilot who taught himself how to fly...people called him *Chief* Anderson. Amethyst heard Chief say, "Performance is the measure of merit" and wrote that statement down in her notebook. There were the Tuskegee Airmen--"Oh the people *could* fly!" Thurgood Marshall, George Washington Carver--he wasn't even allowed to sleep in most of the places he was asked to speak although he was helping to educate the agricultural world. There was a black female neuro-surgeon named Deborah Hyde, the self-made millionaire Dr. A. G. Gaston..."A part of all you earn is yours to keep!" Dr. Martin Luther King, Jr., "Let freedom ring!"

She saw many more that she definitely had heard of! Stevie Wonder, The Jacksons--especially Michael and Janet, Tina Turner, Spike Lee, Jackie Joyner-Kersee, Jerry Rice, Oprah Winfrey, Face, Kirk Franklin, Salt-n-Peppa, Danny Glover, Louis Gossett Jr., Samuel L. Jackson, Patti Labelle, Sinbad, Bill Cosby, the actress Miss Tyson, Whitney Houston, Prince--or the artist formerly known as Prince. Jamie Foxx with a great talent to be a concert pianist had he chosen to be. Will Smith...MIT material before MIB was even a thought in anybody's mind.

Lena Horne, Diahnn Carroll, Brandy, TLC, Mahalia Jackson, Ella Fitzgerald, Duke Ellington, Eddie Murphy, Cuba

## Destiny Unlimited

Gooding, Jr., Mario Van Peebles, The Wayans. She saw Kasi Lemmons--actress...writer...director. "Keep your eyes on her," Christen Listen had said with a wink. "You talk about not giving up and working hard for what one desires!" There was Debbie Allen--told she had the wrong body for dance--Phylicia Rashad, Colin Powell, Spike Lee, Jay-Z...a tremendous long list.

The last two they visited were Amethyst's own mother and father as young children, then as the adults she knew them to be. And Amethyst couldn't have been prouder to add any other names to her list of those who had worked hard to get where they were. She saw how much her folks had to overcome. Her mother, scrubbing floors...barely making enough to live off to now responsible for the health and welfare of those who entered the doors of the United Care Hospital. Her father, respected for being fair, fixing things and treasures people already cherished. Amethyst understood more than ever, how truly special the two of them were. She couldn't have chosen any better parents.

\* \* \*

"Wake up, my Little Friend! We have arts and crafts today. I hear you really like being creative, so let's move it."

Amethyst sat straight up. Christen Listen stood before her with an I Dream of Jeanie costume on. "Who are you pretending to be today?"

"Pretending? I have no need to pretend. I am who I am. The question is...who are *you*?"

She grunted to this senseless exchange. "I am Amethyst Destiny Price."

"Oh yeah? And who, pray tell...is *that*?"

Amethyst stopped and thought for a minute.

"Come on, my Little Friend. You can think about it on the way." Just then a gigantic bald eagle landed. "Perfect timing. Our ride's here, Amethyst."

"We're riding on an eagle?"

"You have something better?" She looked at Amethyst who just shook her head. "I didn't think so. Well, if you're riding with me, you had best get on. Otherwise, get there the best way you can just as long as you're not late. Being late is the same as quitting according to the rules. And I hate when people are late. It's so disrespectful of another's time which is such a valuable commodity in this day and age." Christen Listen mounted the eagle. "So...you coming?"

Amethyst mumbled under her breath, "I guess *you* aimed for the stars."

Christen Listen turned and looked. "Excuse me? What did you say?"

Amethyst smiled. "I said...where should I sit?"

Christen Listen looked her up and down. "If you want something bad enough, find a way to make it happen."

Amethyst sat on the other side of the eagle as it soared. It wasn't long before they landed. Amethyst found herself standing in front of a huge block of gray marble. Christen Listen pulled out a hammer and chisel and turned to her. "Here you are, Little Friend. Now free the lady from within."

Amethyst looked at Christen Listen. "Do what?"

"I said, Free the Lady."

"What Lady?" Amethyst stepped back from the marble.

Christen Listen stepped closer to her, holding up the hammer and chisel. "There's a lady concealed inside. See if you can find her."

Amethyst laughed. "Are you serious?" She took the hammer and chisel. "You think there's a lady in all this junk?"

"You can find her. You can do anything if you set your mind to it! You must see it, before you can see it! So get to it. I look forward to seeing what you see."

"You know what you said makes no sense, right?"

### Destiny Unlimited

"Yeah, well just free the lady, and we'll see about that. I'll be back soon."

Amethyst worked what felt like all day and night--banging and chipping away at the stone. Sweat poured from her face, but she kept knocking and chipping away. When she finished, she stood back and examined her handiwork. Amethyst then heard a single applause behind her.

"Great job, my Little Friend. I see you *were* able to find the lady after all."

"Sure. After I got rid of all the stuff that *wasn't* her, there she stood!"

Christen Listen trotted down the hill. "Come on, Amethyst. No time to rest now. There's still much left to be done."

When they reached the bottom, they passed a group of people who were gathering for some kind of auction. Amethyst stopped to watch.

"What is your bid for this wonderful talent? It was owned by a little old lady in Pittsburgh who used it only on Sundays!" the fast talking auctioneer said.

People began bidding until the man banged the gavel and announced, "Sold, to the young man in the red shirt!"

One thing after another was auctioned--persistence, determination, trust, greater spirituality, a Spirit of Excellence--until finally the man looked directly in Amethyst's face and said, "What are *you* willing to pay for success?"

Christen Listen grabbed Amethyst and pulled her along. Amethyst continued to look back at the man who smiled and winked at her. "Come on now! Quit dragging your feet! There are flowers--blossoms, stems, and leaves that require your immediate attention. Look at this, we're going to be late!"

Amethyst thought they were going to look at a garden, but instead they stood outside a place with a sign over the front entrance door that read: *Success--Push!*

"Go ahead, Little Friend. Push."

Amethyst pushed the door. She looked at all the people inside the room working. "I thought we were going to look at flowers," Amethyst said.

Christen Listen laughed. "Look at? No Amethyst. You're going to be making flowers...assembling, painting, things like that...for others to behold."

"Make them? You're talking about artificial flowers--"

"Oh no. Nothing artificial about these. Angelica there will show you all you need to know. Enjoy!"

"Wait a minute! This is getting weirder by the moment."

"Does this mean you don't desire to do this?"

"No, I didn't say that! In fact, I'll make a bouquet while I'm at it."

Christen Listen softly pinched Amethyst's cheek. "You are so cute! I'll be back for you soon." She then gestured for Angelica, who promptly came over.

Amethyst sat with Angelica as they painted petal after petal. Leaf after leaf. Stem after Stem. Amethyst was surprised at the level of attention to detail each flower was given. The undersides were apportioned just as much care as the topsides that would always be seen. The stems were not allowed to have even a slight drip. She had never before considered the amount of work and effort that actually went into something as unpretentious as a flower.

"No one's going to look under this leaf," one woman said. "So why do we have to waste our time and effort painting it?"

"Because," Angelica said, "success is awarded to those who close that hairline of a fracture between good and best. A flower painted extremely well on the topside but half-done on the underside, is not a mark of quality. Even if no one sees all that was done, your efforts should always be one of excellence."

## Destiny Unlimited

Amethyst thought as she finished her assigned flowers, of the many flowers she'd picked. She was unable to recall ever a time when she'd found even one half-done flower--they all had been exquisite. Created with the Spirit of Excellence, even those destined only to blossom for a day.

When Christen Listen returned, Amethyst handed her one perfect red rose. Christen Listen turned it in her hand. "Impressive, my Little Friend. Impressive," she said with a smile as her words were quickly being drown out by blasts of thunder and the room lit by unflagging streaks of lightning.

Amethyst took a deep breath as she rolled the stem of a half-white, half-red rose she had made--but didn't get to finish painting--between her two fingers. Carefully, she stuck the stem in the spine of her notebook as she smiled and heard the words of yet another who had also founded a college--Mary McLeod Bethune. "Faith in God is the greatest power, but great, too, is faith in oneself."

## EIGHTEEN

"Hear Ye! Hear Ye!" A young boy with a loudspeaker for a voice, short sandy brown hair--much like Amethyst's--with matching sandy brown skin rang a bell as he strolled down the street. "Before anything is...I am!" he said.

Amethyst snickered. He must have heard her because he turned quickly and searched the crowd.

"You!" he said pointing her out. "Come!"

Amethyst looked around to see who he was possibly talking to.

He put the bell in his pant's pocket. "You! I said come!"

Amethyst pointed at herself as if to say, "Me?"

He yelled this time. "Come...now!"

Amethyst pretended like he was causing her to tremble. "Oh please. Don't tell on me. I'm so scared!"

He glared at her. "Truly you do not realize the truth of which you speak."

"So who are you suppose to be?"

He grinned. "I am Brother Mic!"

"As in Microphone?" she said pressing her hands tight over her ears. "Must you be so loud when you speak?"

"I'm much like a loudspeaker...so yes! I must be so loud when I speak!"

"Then could you possibly tone it down, at least while I still have some hearing left."

"Everyone wants to be a comedian!" he said as he pretended to turn a button over his heart. "I am Brother Mic, the well-known Thought Master."

### ᴅestiny 𝒰nlimited

"You must not be that well-known, I've never heard of you before."

"Hearing *of* me and hearing *me*...is entirely *two* different things!"

"My, so prim and proper. All dressed up in your little white tux with tails, top hat...and sporting a cane too. Are you always this uptight?"

"Someone has to hold things together. Tell me, you ever seen thoughts run wild?"

Amethyst smiled as he continued to wait patiently. "Oh. You were actually expecting an answer to that? I thought it was rhetorical." She smiled. "No, I must admit, I can't say that I've had the pleasure."

"Then today is your day! Today I become a Dream Master as well--making dreams come true. So come, let's get to it." He started back down the street ringing his bell. "Hear Ye! Hear Ye! Before anything is...I am!"

"Now you wait a minute you little Fantasy-Island-wannabe! I'm not--" And for some unexplained reason, her lips would not part again for her to speak.

He began to laugh. "See how well thoughts work? Just thinking your lips ought to zip because your tongue was starting to slip, and *Whomp!--There it is!*" he sang while laughing that much more.

When they arrived at a mansion--Amethyst's lips returned to working order--Brother Mic smiled at her. "You might want to close your mouth...before a fly mistakes it for a hanger and lands in it." He took his hand and made like an airplane headed for her mouth.

Amethyst closed her mouth but continued to stare. "Wow! Does all this...this...this belong to your folks?"

He smiled as his little short legs made long strides to climb the concrete semi-circular steps leading to the entrance of the front door. "All this," he said, "belongs to me. A vacation cottage actually. It's nothing compared to my place in LA."

They stepped inside; he carefully placed his hat and cane on top of the glass of the cherry wood table in the foyer. He then directed Amethyst to a room off from the kitchen, walked over to a large gray box and pulled out a clump of soft form-less material. "Here," he said dropping it on a nearby work table in the room. "You *do* know what this is, right?"

She smiled and made a face at him...sticking her tongue out part-way and crossing her eyes. "Yes, I *know* what *that* is," she said mocking him. "Clay."

"Oh it is, huh?" He smiled and sat down on a swerving stool, gesturing for her to come join him. "How about we sit and just talk for a while--if that's okay with you."

Amethyst sat down and spun a 360 degree revolution on the padded stool. "Fine with me little man. It's your show."

"You know, I'm starting to feel some resentment and hostility on your part. Is there something about me you don't care for? Have I done something maybe I am not aware of?"

She laughed. "I don't know exactly what it is. Except, you do remind me a little of my baby brother. I guess I expect any minute for you to run tell on me."

He smiled. "Well, you and I both know that I am *no* brother of yours. Yet, the sins of your brother are being visited upon me."

Amethyst began to relax and before she realized it, she had broken off a large piece of the clay and was now rolling and kneading it.

Brother Mic took a brief second to glance down at her hands and smiled. "So what's that you're making?"

She looked down and noticed that she had relaxed and was pressing her fist into the middle of the clay while pushing up its sides. "A bowl I think."

## Destiny Unlimited

"A bowl, huh." He twitched his mouth and gently stroked the right side of his face. "That must be a hard thing to do."

She grinned. *So maybe he's not so smart after all.* "Oh it's not hard."

"If you don't mind, could you explain to me how you're able to work such magic out of such a useless piece of clay."

Amethyst's hands continued to shape and smooth as her eyes glanced between the clay and Brother Mic. "Well the first thing I do, is get the clay to loosen up a bit. Then I think about what I want--"

"When you say *think about*, what exactly do you mean?"

"I mean, Brother Before-Anything-Is-I-am, that I picture it in my mind. I see what the finished thing should resemble...what it will or *should* do. Then I use that thought--the image--as a pattern, and things proceed...working at making it happen." She put the finishing touches on the bowl and proudly held it up for him to see. "The results...like what you see here," Amethyst said.

"So let me make sure I've gotten this right. You see in your mind what you desire, then by following that, you see it?"

"Yes. You see, this is what I saw...or at least, close enough to it, and now we *both* are able to see what I saw."

"Okay, so you have to *see* it first, before you can *see* it?"

"Yes! How many times do I have to say it. I *saw* this first in my mind, and now I *see* it here!"

"So--you have to *see* it, before you can *see* it, and then you can *see* it?"

"Yes, yes, a million times...yes! You know, you're starting to get on my nerves again. Kind of the way fingernails on a chalk board or a knife being sharpened on a rock does. *Those* nerves. I see...I saw; you see...you saw."

He smiled. "I am sorry. I'm only trying to understand. So tell me, is this the way all things are or were created? I mean, using the **see-saw** method."

Amethyst sighed and leaned back, holding herself on the stool with the muscles in her abdomen. "I would *t-h-i-n-k*!"

"Now are you sure? Has there ever been anything...anything at all that you can think of that was created, before it was first a thought?"

Amethyst looked around the room. She got up and looked out of the window. There was a tennis court, swimming pool, cars...she then looked at the grass and the trees. "Well, I'm not God, but I can't come up with anything."

"Nothing?"

"Nothing! Even God must have thought about what he wanted before he called it forth! Indeed *we* are said to have been created in His image."

Brother Mic laughed. "Then I guess that means you agree with me."

"Agree with you?" She came and sat back down. "What are you talking about, agree with you?"

"You agree that if I am the Thought Master and thoughts come before things can even manifest, then before anything was or is...I am!"

Amethyst started laughing. "You really are living on Fantasy Island!"

"I'll prove it. You say that is a bowl, correct? Well what if I say it is a hat? Think about that thought for just one second. Then show me the picture that comes to your mind."

Amethyst stopped laughing and picked up the bowl that had already begun to harden slightly. She turned it upside down and placed it on his head. "Okay--it's a hat." She giggled.

He directed his eyes upward. "Sure. Now, take this *hat* and make a ball."

## Destiny Unlimited

She took the bowl off his head, closed it, and made it tight and round.

"Now make a baseball bat." And Brother Mic continued from one thing to another until Amethyst started making something he had not called out. "What are you doing? That doesn't look anything like a giraffe! It's too flat! Whoever heard of a flat giraffe? Amethyst, what are you doing? Earth to Amethyst!"

Amethyst stood up and walked around him. Taking her new invention, she placed it teasingly over his mouth. "What a coincidence—this is a muzzle, so now *you* can shut up!"

They both laughed. Brother Mic put down the clay.

"A coincidence?" he said. "Tell me, does something show up because you were thinking about it or were you thinking about it and caused it to show up, or are you just more aware of the two at the time?" Brother Mic stood and walked over to the doorway. "Let's go down to my theater. I have a movie I'd like you to see. There are more lessons to be learned...and time surfs these days. This movie was created expressly to speed this process along."

Amethyst stood admiring his cute little round face. "Hey, little man. How old are you anyway? I mean, you look to be about nine or ten, but you act more like my old grandpa."

He smiled. "Let's just say I'm old enough to accomplish what needs to be done. After all, isn't that what truly matters?"

The theater was large and equipped with real theater seats. The scent of fresh hot buttered popcorn filled the room.

"Wow! You really *are* living large!" Amethyst said.

"No, not really. Just living. My thoughts, visions, and dreams are what's large. Anybody can do this; they just have to stick with it long enough to see it come to pass. Thoughts *do* go a long way, but thoughts isolated from action generally go nowhere. People must realize desires must be worked if they are to become more. And working them doesn't always mean those dreams will magically appear overnight."

"Brother Mic, do you ever pray?"

He stopped and looked as he fumbled with the equipment. "What?"

"Do you pray? You believe in thoughts, dreams, visions, and work; I was just curious what you thought about prayer."

"I do pray, but I believe like this: if a shark is eyeing you for lunch, you'd do well to swim like the breeze for the ship ahead! I believe God helps those who learn to help themselves."

"So you don't believe God gave you these things because of Divine Will? That he favors some folks over others?"

Deep lines formed across his forehead. "I really had no intentions of discussing spiritual beliefs with you...but I will say this much--my God does not *have* or *play* favorites. I believe we are all given the same measure in the beginning--all that is ever needed has been safely tucked inside us. However, it is up to each individual from that point, to work, increase, pump up, plant, develop, and make what was given, to grow."

He put his fingers together, matching finger to finger at the tips and became quiet. Walking over to a glowing flame on the bar, he said, "If this light is covered by my hand, does it truly exist?" And Amethyst--lost for words--could only reflect.

"*Does God have favorites?* Brother Mic said. "Have you ever read Genesis where it states...*In the beginning God created*?"

"Yes," Amethyst said attentive to his every word now.

"Well, if you'll notice in the middle of the second verse it says *and the Spirit of God moved*. In some bibles *Spirit* is capitalized...a proper noun. Well, I like that--the *Spirit* moved. Action...doing something." He looked at the puzzled look etched on her face. "Observe my feeble attempt to explain."

And in a matter of seconds, Amethyst and Brother Mic were sitting inside a fine restaurant with a lovely window view

## Destiny Unlimited

and handed fancy menus of which to make their selections. The menu had entrees and side dishes like Grace, Love, Mercy, Peace, Joy, Patience, Freedom from Debt, Free from Anger, Freedom from Fear, Freedom from Lack, Deliverance out of Poverty, Deliverance from Sickness. Then Amethyst turned it over and saw more things like Money, Jobs, Houses, Cars, Furnishings, Clothing, Knowledge, Wisdom. She giggled.

"What kind of a place *is* this?" Amethyst asked.

"A place where desires are made known and catered to. Observe." Brother Mic beckoned the waiter, who came swiftly. "Spirit...we'd like to order now. I'd like some Grace, a helping of Mercy...tell me, is the Mercy fresh today?"

Spirit with a slightly French accent said, "Brand new every single day."

"Wonderful! And bring me a deluxe platter of Peace--" he looked at Amethyst and smiled, "...and a side order of Money--a nice juicy T-Bill, if you will."

The waiter called Spirit smiled. "On that order of Peace, Monsieur...did you want it like the world prepares it--"

"Oh no, no, no. *Not* like the world; heavenly please. I want something that's going to stick to my ribs, not leave me two minutes later. Oh, and Spirit...could you cover that Peace with the House's *finest* dressing. Please."

"Sure, Monsieur," Spirit said, jotting down his desires. "Now, on your order of T-Bill, would you prefer it seasoned with the *cash* or the *check*?"

Brother Mic smiled. "Check is fine. You know both are still *tender*."

"And would you prefer it prepared for you rare, medium or well done?"

Brother Mic leaned over and whispered to Amethyst. "Rare is faster, but rare. Medium is, so-so." He rocked his hand from side to side. "With well done, it some times takes a little longer, but it's certainly healthier and well worth the wait." He looked back to Spirit. "Well done, please. Well done."

"Monsieur is correct that well-done may take a little while longer, but with all the reports going on these days about these type things causing problems, your long-term well-being is always our utmost priority." He turned to Amethyst and smiled. "And for you, Mademoiselle?"

"I'll have the same," Amethyst said grinning, hardly believing this place!

"And to drink?" Spirit said to them both.

"A tall cold glass of Living Waters is perfect for me," Brother Mic said.

Spirit wrote and turned to Amethyst. "Mademoiselle?"

She bit down on her bottom lip as she thought a second. "Do you happen to have..." she looked over at Brother Mic and smiled, "...Ginger Ale?"

Spirit smiled. "Is that Mademoiselle's desire?" Amethyst smiled and nodded. He grinned. "Then may you have *your* heart's desire."

Then just as suddenly, Amethyst and Brother Mic were back in their seats at his home's theater room. However, Amethyst still didn't know what Brother Mic thought when it came to God.

"So you don't believe God likes one person or one group better than the other?" she said. "Is that what you're saying?"

He laughed. "I don't know what kind of God you have, but if anything, I can say my God is just. Justice to Him is not based on external things. He has a way of seeing right through people...getting to the heart of the matter." Brother Mic stopped, and then added one more thing. "When I am told I can have, do, or be...and then I mix my belief with it, all that is left, as far as I'm concerned, is the doing of *my* part."

### Destiny Unlimited

Amethyst sighed. "You know...I like the way you put that. Maybe I was wrong about you earlier."

Brother Mic turned to her. "Look, I just believe since everything else God made does not *try* to be or do, they just are...so should we be. A flower doesn't try to bloom, it blooms. Grass doesn't try to grow, it just grows. An eagle doesn't try to fly, it just spreads its wings and takes to the sky! When you know *who* you are and your glorious purpose, all that is left is to be and do." He pressed the start button on the remote control. "Now, can we watch the movie already?"

Amethyst sat and watched clip after clip of failings and failures. There were babies learning to walk. Baseball players striking out. Golfers missing putts. Football players missing passes, missing catches, missing tackles. Basketball players missing baskets. Track runners tripping over hurdles, running out of steam. Television reporters getting fired or demoted. Writers receiving rejection after rejection. Singers receiving lukewarm applause. Comedians getting no laughs. Actors never getting a call. Inventors with inventions that didn't work. The clip rolled on and on, one right after another.

Brother Mic turned to Amethyst and pressed the pause button. "Pretty good, huh? So what do you think thus far?"

"What do I think? I think failing is a bummer, even when it's not your own. No offense, but I could have sat this show out!" She put a handful of popcorn in her mouth. "This is great movie theater popcorn. Orville Redenbacher's?"

"Amethyst, do you believe any of them will ever succeed?"

"Succeed? You mean be great someday?"

"Yes."

Amethyst recalled her time with Christen Listen. "I'm sure *some* will. Who can really say?"

He smiled and without a word, pressed the play button. She then saw home-runs, holes in one, three point baskets, gold-silver-and-bronze medalists, top rated talk show hosts, best-selling authors, sold out concerts, Superbowl Champions, World Series Champions, million dollar inventions, even Orville Redenbacher...popping popcorn. There was no end to the parade of success.

Brother Mic looked at Amethyst and smiled. "There is no such thing as true failure. There's only success in discovering what *not* to do and successfully finding out what doesn't work--a process of elimination to getting the answers sought. If a baby never attempted to walk, that baby would never know, first off, that traveling by way of the knees is a slow way to go and second, what else can be accomplished. To attempt, is to find where success is hiding. It takes failing sometimes to succeed. But one has to be *committed* to making a thing happen. It is in practicing what you do, that separates those with whims, from those who are truly committed to making it happen. The only true failure I've found, is the one who never makes an attempt. You try, you fall, you get back up, you go at it again! Like a stand-up punching bag with sand in its bottom, you get knocked down, you bounce back up. Even when you don't feel like it, you bounce right back. And occasionally, you may even get to punch back!"

"I just think people worry about--"

"Worry? Worry is only good for draining energy! What has worry ever accomplished? Does it have potential to change a thing? Does worry make a thing move along any faster? No. You have to do what you can, and that which you can't, *worrying* won't help it. Worry is energy that could and should be used for those things you *can* affect."

When the lights were turned off in the theater room, Amethyst felt this was not the end of her visit with Brother Mic.

## Destiny Unlimited

She was right. It only took a few minutes for her to discover what he had next on his little agenda.

Amethyst now found herself standing before a huge boulder...five-feet high by four-feet wide. Brother Mic handed her a short-handled sledge hammer.

"Go ahead--a stake has already been driven in it. Split the rock."

She laughed so hard at him she almost hurt her sides. "Now I know you have too much free time on your hand if you think I can split *that* rock."

"What? Think it can't be done?"

"No it can't be done! At least not by me! This rock is big; it's too hard."

"Nothing is *too* hard when you set your mind to getting it done. If you make up in your mind you can do it, you can. So go ahead...split it."

Amethyst held the hammer and lined it up with the large spike nailed in the middle of the boulder. She hit the steel stake hard, "Clank! Clank!" about ten times. "Clank! Clank!" it said. Brother Mic leaned against the side of the boulder while she banged away.

"This thing is never going to split! Why am I having to waste my time?"

"Waste? Nothing is a waste if you search deep enough. Do you believe my having you do this serves no purpose?"

"I don't know. But I do know I'm not going to be able to split this rock!"

"What if I were to tell you it is possible...that things have been lined up in your favor to do it?"

"Then I would tell you I appreciate your confidence, but I don't see it."

Brother Mic stood up and said, "Whatever you do, do it with all your might. Commit yourself to seeing it done. If you can't see it before you see it then you will never see it." He took the hammer from Amethyst and hit the spike. Then he turned back to her. "What if I were to tell you that this boulder is only a few strikes from breaking wide open? Would you continue striking it then?"

"If it were only a few more? Sure."

"Why is that?"

"Because I'd hate to be so close and learn that I quit just one short of it happening."

"Then I'll tell you. With everything you truly commit to do, you are only a few strikes away from making it happen."

Amethyst smiled. "Yeah okay." She took back the hammer and struck it ten times, then looked hateful at Brother Mic. "A few, huh?" Twenty more times...still nothing! But in the back of her mind, she couldn't help but wonder if the next blow would be that deciding one. So she continued. After 1,000 strikes--her hands hurt, sweat dripped down her face--she took all her might and hit it one more time. And the rock did not break! "This is ridiculous! What's the use? I'm not quitting but I see no reason to continue wasting time and energy."

A little girl about eight-years-old was walking nearby. Brother Mic yelled down to her and her mother to come up to the rock for a minute.

"Dear little child," Brother Mic said, "...do you think you could possibly split this rock with this hammer?"

The little girl turned to her mother who nodded her okay for the child to answer him. The little girl, grinning from ear to ear said, "Yes, I think I can."

Brother Mic took the hammer from Amethyst. "Then show me, please."

The little girl hit it once, twice, three times. "I'm going to try it again, okay?" she said. "I know I can do it. I just know I can." She hit it once, twice more and the boulder split wide open--straight down the middle! "Mother! Mother!" she said, "...look! I did it...I did it! I actually did it! I knew I could do it, and I did it! Wait till I tell everyone!"

Amethyst looked at the split boulder. Then she glanced over at Brother Mic who looked back at her and smiled.

After the mother and daughter left, Brother Mic started to leave, too.

"Wait a minute!" Amethyst said stomping both feet. "Why did you let that little girl think *she* was the one who did that?" She ran and caught up with him. "You know I hit that boulder over 1,000 times. She came along and hit it only five! It split because of the 1,000 times I hit it! Mine! Not her little five!"

Brother Mic tried to control his giggles. "Aah, what you say is part true. But because you stopped hitting five short of what it took to actually split it, that little girl gets the satisfaction of having done it!"

"But it was *my* efforts." Amethyst held out her throbbing hands. "Look at my hands! I worked at this! It's not fair..." she stomped her right foot down hard. "Why should she get credit for what I worked so hard to accomplish?"

"Not fair? Not fair you say? If you had known how many times it would have taken, then you never would have stopped, right? Well, here's a tip. Fair or not, if you can't believe and stick with a thing until it is manifest, then you're liable to lose out. No one knows the exact number a thing will take, but you must know this, it takes only one and you should not stop until you have found that one." He touched her hand. "That's as fair and as simple as it gets. Interpret setbacks and failings to mean you're apparently on to something great. After all, who wastes time and effort to discourage someone who doesn't stand a chance of succeeding? No intelligent being I know!" He smiled. "So if something or someone is trying to discourage you--encourage you to quit--there must be something happening there you don't see." He handed her her notebook. "Don't forget this." He reached into his coat pocket and pulled out a withered half-painted rose, "...and this also."

Saddened, she took them both, her gaze fixed on her feet. "Thanks," she said sticking the rose between two pages.

He smiled. "You know I *thought* you would say that. And you did. Thoughts then words...what an explosive combination!" He waved good-bye and strolled away. "Hear Ye! Hear Ye! Before anything is...I am!" Lightning began to flash, strong this time. Thunder rocked the earth underneath her feet like an atomic blast. A strong funneled cloud hovered over Amethyst as a gust of wind sucked her up like a piece of crumpled paper.

*Destiny Unlimited*

## NINETEEN

Amethyst fell from the funnel and landed in a kitchen very much like Miss Jamahri's. A woman with long pressed hair stood at the table kneading and beating dough. Her long sweeping skirt was similar to what Miss Jamahri wore, yet her hair showed no signs of gray and she stood much taller...no, straighter than the kind old woman. Amethyst tip-toed over to look at her face...easily Miss Jamahri's daughter...clearly a younger version. The woman didn't look up.

"Hi. I'm Amethyst."

The woman spoke without looking up. "How did you get in here?"

"I sort of dropped in, I think," Amethyst said. She continued to stare. "It's amazing how much you and Miss Jamahri favor. Are you her daughter?"

"I don't know a Miss Jamahri, Child. Never heard of such a name either." She wiped her hands on the dish towel. "Folks call me Fair Share," she said shaking Amethyst's hand. She then washed her hands off in the sink, dried them on a towel tied to the handle of the stove, and started back to beating the dough.

"Fair Share?"

"Yes, Fair Share. I believe in folks doing and receiving their fair share."

"You look so much like Miss Jamahri. Are you sure you're not any kin to her?" Amethyst watched Fair Share beat, pound, and push away the dough.

"No kin I know of. Sorry I'm not the person you're expecting me to be."

Amethyst smiled. "Oh it's not that." She looked around. "This house looks like Miss Jamahri's house too. I'm just surprised you two aren't related. That's all."

"You and this woman—big time buddies or something?"

"I guess you could say that. I just need to find her. I know my folks are worried sick about me. I've been gone it feels like forever." Amethyst walked around the kitchen table. The table was the same size and a reddish speckled color like Miss Jamahri's except this table was obviously new. "But if all that's happened to me in the last—however long it's been—is only a dream, then I suppose it won't matter. If this is real, I need to let someone know I'm okay."

Fair Share flipped the dough over and began shaping it into a loaf. "I wish this was my house. I'm renting it for now. It'll be a while before I can afford anything like this." She put the dough in a bowl and covered it. "Don't get me wrong now, I am working on it. I'm doing all I can to make it happen."

Amethyst sat with elbows resting on the tabletop. "What's that you're making?"

"Bread—for you I guess. Call it, your daily bread." She laughed.

Amethyst smiled. "I love fresh bread. The way it smells when it comes out of the oven...spread a little margarine on top. I can hardly wait," Amethyst said as she sat all the way down in the chair.

Fair Share rinsed and wiped her hands—leaving the bread to rise. "A little leaven will make it double in size. I used to forget the leaven all the time and ended up with the flattest heaviest loaves!"

"I know all about yeast. During the winter holidays—Thanksgiving, Christmas, New Year's Day—and of course, every Sunday, my mama makes homemade bread. She told me all about yeast making things rise."

## Destiny Unlimited

"Child...you don't say?" Fair Share pulled out a chair and sat down.

Amethyst leaned forward again. "How long before it's ready to go into the oven?"

"About thirty or forty minutes. Baked at 350 degrees for about an hour should just about do it." Fair Share stood up. "Excuse me a minute, I'll be right back." She left and came back with a book.

Amethyst pulled the notebook from across her body and began writing many of the things she hadn't had a chance to jot down. Thirty minutes would be plenty of time to catch up. Man, was she ever hungry too! All that zipping and zapping from one place to the other and no one thinking much about stopping for a bite to eat. At least Fair Share was seeing to it that she got fed. And right too.

Two hours passed and Fair Share's eyes were still buried in her book.

Amethyst stood up and looked at the bread in the bowl. It had definitely doubled. Fair Share continued to stay buried in the pages of her book. Amethyst started fidgeting and humming a song. Fair Share continued reading.

After four hours, Fair Share closed the book and stretched. She looked over at Amethyst and smiled. "There's the bread, Child. Why are you just sitting there looking at me?"

"But it's not done," Amethyst said. She glanced over at it so Fair Share would do the same.

"Well I've *done* my part. I made it. Now it's time for you to do something." Then Fair Share got up and left.

Amethyst couldn't believe this. She was never told she needed to do anything. Had she known, she would have been through. Fair Share had taken care of everything...after all, Amethyst was only a visitor.

Amethyst put the bread in the oven. Fair Share came back and sat at the kitchen table again. She had two books this time and a black Bible much like the one Miss Jamahri had handed to Amethyst. This Bible was new...nothing worn about it. Amethyst noticed how Fair Share would read from one book then turn to various pages in the Bible and mark passages of scriptures. Fair Share wrote inside a spiral notebook Amethyst hadn't noticed until just then.

The whole day, Fair Share sat reading: book after book after book. Amethyst tried to find something to do. She went outside for a while. There was nothing there worth her time or energy. When she came back inside, she stood next to Fair Share then cleared her throat.

Fair Share didn't look up. "Yes, Child. You want something?"

"I'm bored. I'd like something to do."

Fair Share stuck a marker between the pages and closed the book. "Bored? How can you be bored when there is so much going on around you?"

"Because I'm just here. People need something to keep themselves busy. There's no television. No radio. No telephone. You don't even have a computer. Nothing! There's nothing here but you and your books."

"Why don't you go outside—"

"I just came from outside. I watched a caterpillar stuck on a leaf. I was out there so long, I saw it shed its green skin and crawl out with a black velvet one. Had I stayed and waited for you to finish reading, I might have gotten to see it metamorphose into a butterfly! They do that, you know. I've never seen it, but you don't always have to see a thing to know it is so!"

## Destiny Unlimited

"Why are you so angry?" Fair Share stood up. "I have a library in the back. Come see if I have anything you might be interested in. Wouldn't you like to read one of my books?"

Amethyst rolled her eyes. "No," she said, then added, "Maybe some other time."

"Okay. You say you're bored?"

"Out of my mind!" Amethyst said pacing.

"All right. Let's go for a drive then."

Amethyst stopped pacing. "You mean in a real car? I mean a *real* car?"

"Yes, a *real* car. Not brand new, mind you, but it beats walking. It takes me where I need to go."

"If it will get me out of here, I don't care if we have to hold it up and power it with our feet!" Amethyst said.

Fair Share laughed. "The Flintstones. You know that was one of my favorite shows when I was a little girl."

"Mine too!" Amethyst said. "Only, I guess I'm still considered to be little."

Fair Share took keys off a hook near the back door. "Let's see what we can do about my little pupil being so bored."

"Pupil? I don't mean anything by this...you seem really nice and all, but how can I possibly be your pupil when you're not teaching me anything."

"Oh my mistake. If you don't want me to refer to you like that, then I won't. I just thought we could pretend I was the teacher and you, my student. But if you don't want to play--"

"Okay! I'll play already! You be the teacher and I'll be your little pupil."

Fair Share and Amethyst got in the car and started down the road. "Pay attention while we travel. I have a few things I'd like to share with you."

"Like what? I already know what trees look like; I've seen *them* before."

Fair Share's glances alternated between Amethyst and the road. "Seeing and appreciating are two different things. The problem with most folks is, they travel the same road so often, they get used to it. Before long, they're just traveling along without even thinking about where they are or where they're going. They start out on one end and without being able to tell you how they got there, they end up 'there.' On the other hand, when people travel unfamiliar roads, they tend to pay more attention to everything...hardly missing even minute details. That is what's called *being* in the moment.

"The problem comes from wandering mindlessly from one state of being to another without ever *being* there. No kind of appreciation is there and most times we end up missing out on some grand moments. So never take a thing for granted. Receive everything as though it has never been before. In truth, every moment granted us is new. Taking things or people for granted is just wrong. It shows a lack of respect, and worse, a lack of appreciation towards the giver."

"You got all that from these trees?" Amethyst said pointing to the colossal of trees lining the road like soldiers with moss veils draping from their helmets.

"I travel this same road every time, and every time, I see it in the light of true appreciation...as if it were my very first...and very last time. In truth, every moment *is* new, and then it's gone. I desire all to know--without a doubt--how glad I am for the gift of new moments with them. There's just something special about the way a family member smiles, or a friend who does a thing in only the way they can do it. And should there ever come a time when I no longer can experience any more moments with them, my desire is no regrets. I want to be sure that all know how much I appreciated each and every moment." She looked at Amethyst. "That Child, is what I call...living loving moments."

## Destiny Unlimited

"Fair Share, I really miss my family. I miss things I thought got on my nerves. I appreciate them now more than ever. I did take many things for granted--feeling like they and I would always be there. Except...," Amethyst looked out the window, "...they're not. And I miss them. I can't wait till I see them again...even my brother, Michael." She turned to Fair Share. "This game is taking too long. Yet, I'm afraid of what would happen if I would dare quit."

Fair Share stopped the car. She and Amethyst got out and stood on a cliff above a large body of still water. A cool breeze blew on their faces.

"Take this," Fair Share said picking up a small rock, "and throw it into that water down there."

Amethyst laughed. "Been there, done that already. If this is about hearing God, the Spirit moving, meditating, being at peace--"

"Throw the rock already," Fair Share said without smiling. "Then listen and watch."

Amethyst threw it. "Ker-plip," she heard as the water rippled.

Fair Share smiled. "You hear that...see that?" Fair Share said and Amethyst nodded. "Well..." Fair Share said while looking at her, "...so did God."

Fair Share lifted a rock twenty times larger than the first and handed it to her. "Okay Child, now I want you to take this one and throw it." Amethyst did and the water said, "Ker-plunk!" while making a huge splash. Fair Share turned to look at Amethyst again. "Did you hear and see that?"

"Yes," Amethyst said, wondering how Fair Share could not know that this was just as boring as watching her read.

Fair Share raised one finger to her lips. "Well," she said, "so did God."

She then reached and picked up an even larger rock than the last one and handed it to Amethyst. As she waved her hand, she began to shout and rage at the water until it suddenly became turbulent and seemed to roar back. "Now throw that one. And be careful not to strain yourself." Amethyst threw the rock hard though it didn't travel as far as the others. Fair Share turned and smiled at her. "Did you hear and see that as well?" she said.

"Hear and see what? There was too much going on down there to hear or see anything! Waves beating against the rocks, beating against each other. How could you expect *anybody* to see or hear anything?"

Fair Share clapped her hands in delight. "You're such an excellent pupil, Child. So much potential! You have the ability to do much--I trust you will."

Amethyst and Fair Share rode back in silence. Amethyst realized how much more enjoyable her journey was when she paid attention to where she was at that moment. She could actually experience the deep hues of the trees. Squirrels seemed to scurry more playfully. Birds soared more gracefully, and flocks of birds made interesting geometric patterns and shapes. A rainbow on the right side of the road arched across the sky with beautiful calm pastel colors.

There was something special about being in the moment. Something magical...spiritual about living that way. Had she not been paying attention--were her mind on memories already lived or speculating and contemplating on possibilities of what was yet to come--she utterly would miss what is to be received in the present.

"The past is spent," Fair Share said. "The future...what may or may not ever be. But the now...now the now is now."

## Destiny Unlimited

Amethyst knew if she missed the now, it would be left to join the ranks of the past--revisited in reflection but never again to be fully experienced.

"Now is eternal," Fair Share said. "It is always and forever now."

Amethyst looked at Fair Share who smiled as she stopped the car. "We're home," Fair Share said before looking down at Amethyst. Seeing the look on her face, she said, "Home for me anyway. Just remember the rocks; those cast into calmer waters and those cast into the turbulence. Remember Child, which could be seen and heard the best."

## TWENTY

Amethyst and Fair Share sat at the kitchen table again. "Amethyst, you must think I'm rude in my reading so much with you around. There's just so much knowledge and wisdom out there. And most of it is free...for the asking and taking. It's like I'm cramming for an exam."

"You're in school?"

"The school of life. And it never takes a break. Knowledge is power. It's the key to whatever door you wish to go through. There's no excuse for not knowing. There are too many books available with the answers. I'm just trying to get all the knowledge I can. The sooner, the better. I don't have time to waste. So I read and read and then I get it and I move on to the next one. Remain teachable, you're never too old to learn. Never think you have all the answers or that there's nothing left for you to learn. Imagine life and live." Fair Share stood and stretched. "I discovered a secret about the word Imagine."

"A secret? I love secrets!" Amethyst said, her eyes wide with anticipation.

"Imagine gives rise to thoughts, visions, pictures and personifies them in the mind. I decide what I want to see...and imagination works out the rest. Like a genie in a magic lamp, *Your wish is my command*--no matter the size, no matter the difficulty, no matter the normal nature of things--it is granted. The word Imagine let's me know that a genie inside a lamp is not so much a fairy tale as I grew up believing. It became evident when I broke down the word Imagine and the words...I'm a genie leapt out for my attention. See it? Im a gine. I am the lamp--the genie lives inside of me. I speak my desires,

## Destiny Unlimited

believe, and my *gine* goes about to make things happen. Too simple, huh? Imagine with all detail...in color...with all sights and senses. The mind cannot tell the difference. It merely desires a blueprint. Mind over matter...and even your body is matter. Your mind will not say, 'this is not real', because what is real to it, are images. And whether by **eye**sight or **in**sight, all it knows are images and that its job is to take the blueprint and create--to make manifest. It's the power of imagination."

"So if you want more talent in an area--"

Fair Share sat down. "Then you say to your gine, '*I wish for more talent to...*', add the what, and things begin to happen."

"I wonder why no one else ever found that message before?" Amethyst leaned her body against the table's edge.

"All I know is when you break the word *Imagine* down into parts, you end up with *I'm a genie*. Now grant it, it does take some imagination to see genie in the word *g-i-n-e*, but that's the beauty of the mind. See. Imagine...Im a gine."

"Miss Jamahri said something about that. You know, you're pretty smart. I don't think I ever would have seen that."

Fair Share looked solemn. "It's funny, some have tried to label me stupid and slow." She looked in Amethyst's eyes. "Never let anyone label you. *You* tell them who you are." She smiled. "But back to imagine. Granted, things don't always happen as quickly--at least not like the genies in those Aladdin tales...you know, you wish, he blinks, it's done. But at least the *gine* inside you is real. Do you know how I know?" Fair Share smiled as Amethyst shook her head. "Because *you're* real!"

"But does it work?" Amethyst said. "Can you really cause things to happen?"

"Yeah. Let's say I want to learn to play the piano. I think about it, say it, then go about getting the knowledge I need to do it. I work at it. Practice it. And before you know anything, my *gine* has caused it to come to pass."

Amethyst sat back in the chair. "But why does it take so long for things to happen? And why do you have to work so hard at it? Why can't the *gine* just make it happen, just like that." Amethyst snapped her fingers.

Fair Share smiled. "Because, Child, you don't appreciate a thing as much when you haven't put your own interest in it. There must be effort on your part. Questions to be answered before anything can happen are: What is your contribution? What's your vested interest? What are *you* willing to give in order to receive it?" Fair Share began to flip the pages of the book that rested under her hands. "Bums wait with open hands for a handout. Those who *would* have are those willing to work at it...for it. Once these questions have been satisfied, things will begin to happen. And don't dare think you can fool those unseen forces working on your behalf with lip service either. They have ways of weeding out those who are sincere and those who attempt to scam their way up Mount Success."

Amethyst leaned forward again. "They do? How?"

"Those who truly believe, don't quit. No matter what, come what may. Even when it looks like they're losing, they still believe. When it looks like nothing is happening--like it will never happen--they *still* believe. They walk, talk, act, and breathe like they believe. Time. Oh yes, G-Time has his own way of discovering who are true daisies and who...dandelions."

"I met Mr. G..." Amethyst said, "he's tight."

"Tight are not, G-Time gets the job done. So if you're still believing and working at it--even years after it hasn't happened--that's commitment. If after six months it hasn't manifested and let's say you decide maybe this wasn't meant for you...maybe you even think someone somewhere else has decided you don't need it--and then you quit..." Fair Share slammed the book closed and sat back against her chair, "...then you break the powers that were out there working on your

## Destiny Unlimited

behalf. Can you imagine the hurt felt by those invisible forces that have been busting there behinds...diligently working to make things happen, and they learn you no longer believe? And once you stop believing, they immediately get marching orders. Laid off...that's what they call it! They might be one step away from completion, but once you stop believing, they have no more say so in the matter. The shop is closed, then and there, no arguments...no stay...no explanation. And you'll never even know just how close you were."

"Well what if I imagine I'm a six feet tall basketball player?" Amethyst said with a smile.

"There *is* a such thing as knowing your limitations. Before you begin anything, know yours."

Amethyst quit smiling. She reached and picked up one of Fair Share's books as disappointment loomed over her.

"But--" Fair Share said as she lifted Amethyst's drooping face to look into her eyes. "...when you know something is possible for you to do, you *can* imagine that! If you're a five-feet-five guy who believes you're good enough to play for the NBA, then you work at it, Child! Work...at...it! Work for it! Learn your craft. Practice what you do. Know all there is to know--and then some. Study and show thyself approved."

"You really remind me of Miss Jamahri. What both of you said about Imagine, and believe it or not...she has her own library just like you."

"Now what is this name you keep referring to? Miss *Shamari*?"

"No, it's Miss Ja-mah-ri. And--"

"Does Miss Jamahri have a first name?"

Amethyst thought about it. Miss Jamahri had told her, but what had she said? "A-lure...A-lurie--no wait...Alura! Alura Jamahri! That's it!"

"Interesting name. Has a certain something-something about it. By chance, would you know what her name means?"

"Heck, I don't even know what my name means," Amethyst said.

"Let's go to my library and look it up? I have a book of names in there." Fair Share got up and gestured for Amethyst to follow. "Hurry Child, we have too much to do—"

"And not much time to do it!" Amethyst said.

"Pray tell, how could you have possibly known I was going to say that?" Fair Share said. "Not Miss Jamahri again?"

Amethyst nodded and grinned. "Only she says '*Come along Child. We have much to do but not much time to do it!*' " Amethyst mimicked Miss Jamahri.

"Sounds like my kind of woman. I hope to meet her some day—soon. Even her name starts to grow on you after a while. It's kind of...tight."

Amethyst followed Fair Share down a short hall. Miss Jamahri's hall was longer and this house was smaller although certain areas were almost identical.

Fair Share walked in, then turned to Amethyst. "It doubles as my den. And over there..." she pointed to a corner, "...is my library!" Amethyst's mouth fell open. Her library consisted of a three-feet by three-feet wooden bookcase!

"This is your library?" Amethyst said.

"Yes. Isn't it the greatest!" Fair Share pulled out a book. "I hope to have a bigger library someday, but everyone has to start somewhere." She turned the pages then handed Amethyst the book, marking the page with her thumb.

"Alura—Old English: Divine Counselor." Amethyst smiled and nodded. "Yep, sounds like her!"

Fair Share retrieved the book and turned the pages. "Amethyst..." she said, "Greek: Wine-color. A jewel." She smiled and nodded. "Yep, sounds like you!" They both laughed.

## ᗯestiny ᑌnlimited

Amethyst and Fair Share went back into the kitchen and read. Reading was fun. Especially with someone else to share and exchange thoughts, concepts, and ideals. Amethyst noticed Fair Share writing inside a notebook.

"What are you doing?" Amethyst said.

"Jotting down a couple of things. Thoughts, stuff I learn, things I run across that I don't won't to lose in a sea of other knowledge."

Amethyst noticed how large her notebook was--much larger than the one she carried. "You sure do have a lot in there," she said.

"That's because I've been doing this for a long time. Every since I was about...twelve. Yeah. I started then, and I've not quit yet. This is my tenth notebook. I seem to get better with age." She noticed Amethyst attempting to read it upside down. "Would you like to read a page or two? There's nothing personal in *this one*."

"You don't mind?"

"Of course not. What's the point of having knowledge and wisdom if you *can't* and *don't* share it with others?"

Amethyst took the notebook and anxiously read page after page. "This is great! You're good. You know...you really should publish this."

"It may be good, but anything can always be better. I'm still learning my craft...working at it. Between me and you, I hope to write a book some day. Maybe speak across the country, though it's still hard for me to imagine anyone would really care to read or actually hear my thoughts." She smiled. "Let alone pay me to do it. But that's what I'm working towards. You know--Imagine--Im a gine. And I also want to learn more about other cultures...firsthand. To see just how different and similar we all truly are."

"Where do you want to go?" Amethyst said.

## Vanessa Davis Griggs

Fair Share's eyes lit up. "I'd love to visit the West Indies, Trinidad, any of the islands...even Jamaica! *Hello Mon!*" she said with a simulated accent.

"Well if this is any example of your work to come, then I can't wait to see all you'll accomplish. You're definitely going to be somebody great one of these days! And I'll tell everybody, *I knew her when...*"

"Is that right, little pupil?" Fair Share laughed. "Well--I would like to thank you, Miss Amethyst, for your unwavering encouragement. I did so need to hear that from you."

Lightning began flashing...filling the entire room. The thunder began to clash like tin pans crashing from the sky. The wind blew Fair Share's hair and Amethyst held on as she grabbed for her notebook, but it was too late. It got caught up in the whirlwind...spiraling quickly away and out of her reach. She searched desperately for it as the lightning and thunder continued to clash with one another. Then out of the winds, Amethyst heard a soft voice say, "My people are destroyed for the lack of knowledge." And straightway the wind sucked her through and out of the kitchen doorway.

## TWENTY-ONE

"Oh Amethyst dear...you've done it! You played the tenth card and now you're finished."

"Miss Jamahri?" Amethyst said as she stood in a clearing in the jungle. "Is that you?"

"Why yes, dear. Of course it's me. Though I admit to not feeling so well at the moment. Won't you please come and help this feeble old soul?"

"What do you mean the tenth card? I counted nine."

"Dear, I assure you it was ten. Come on and quit now. Come help your old friend Alura. You understand how difficult it is for me to get around. Otherwise, I'd come to you. Old age is causing my steps to grow shorter with time."

Something didn't feel right. "Miss Jamahri, if the game is over, then why are you saying *quit*? I counted nine cards if what Mother Earth said was correct."

"Now dear, I'm sure if Mother Earth told you something, she told you right. The problem may be in the way you counted. Now, what was your first card?"

"*Creating Your Own World*," Amethyst said as she watched the old woman move slowly towards her.

"Y-e-s, yes, that's right. Creating your own world. And the second one?"

"The second was *Gardening--Tending To Your Own*."

"Oh now I see where you got off track. You see dear, the second card was actually *Time*. You remember Father Time."

"G-Time," Amethyst corrected her, confused now. "That was the second one? But there was no lightning and thunder..."

"Sure there was lightning. Oh I distinctly recall lightning streaking across the sky. Don't you remember? How it came across so beautifully?"

Amethyst batted her eyes quickly trying to recall. "I suppose I do."

"See, that was a sign of a new card. Your second card. Add that to the nine you already have, and you have ten! See?"

Amethyst was getting a sinking feeling in the pit of her stomach. It was an unsettling-type feeling. The woman who stood before her was so unlike the Miss Jamahri she had met. "Are you *sure* about this Miss Jamahri?"

"Am I sure? Dear, I'm positive! Nine plus one is ten. Always was, always will be." She saw the hesitation on Amethyst's face. "Amethyst, I'm feeling faint. Please hurry to me dear. Amethyst...I need you," the old woman said.

Amethyst's feet wouldn't budge. She tried to go, but she couldn't move.

"Quit all this foolishness and come here and help me!" the old woman said almost in anger. Then she spoke softer. "We can go back to my place. I need to get you home as soon as possible. You've been away too long."

Something just wasn't right. Amethyst wasn't sure what to do now. True, Miss Jamahri had been a great help to her. She had shown her much kindness. How could she possibly ignore her cry for help? But Miss Jamahri had also warned her, "no matter what, no matter who." She had specifically admonished her not to quit. Yet now she was continually using the word quit. Also--Miss Jamahri had seemingly gotten around quite well--until now.

"Okay," Amethyst said, "if you're *really* Miss Jamahri, then what are the words I am supposed to repeat?"

"I'm an old woman, dear--a harmless old woman who's never hurt a soul. I confess I don't remember things like I used to. Please Amethyst...help a feeble old being. I don't want to die out here all alone. I want to get you home. Your mother's worried sick about you. Quit this grand-standing and let's go home!" Amethyst didn't move. "I'll tell you what...if you'll come a little closer so I won't have to use so much strength, I'll tell you," she said. Then she collapsed.

Amethyst instantly ran to her. "Miss Jamahri! Miss Jamahri, are you all right?" She was running as fast as her short legs would carry her. Then it happened. A soft squishy substance. "Quicksand!" she said. "Help! Miss Jamahri! It's quicksand!"

Miss Jamahri quickly stood to her feet, and Amethyst stretched out her hands to her. "Hurry! I'm being sucked down! Miss Jamahri! Help me!"

The old woman brushed herself off and began to mimic Amethyst. "Miss Jamahri...help me!" she said. "Miss Jamahri...Miss Jamahri! Help me!" She walked closer to Amethyst's outstretched hands and looked down at her. "Help yourself--dear!" Then she changed into a much younger woman. "Madame Deck don't help nobody but herself!" she said. "And I'd suggest you learn real *quick* how to do the same...dear! Otherwise, there will be nothing left to help." She began to laugh bending and slapping both thighs.

Amethyst couldn't believe it--it was a trick! She should have known. Miss Jamahri didn't call her Amethyst. "Am," she had said, "for short!" Now what was she going to do? This *was* the tenth card. She hadn't quit, but swimming to reach the side when stuck in quicksand was impossible. Then she saw another figure standing before her.

"Hello, Amethyst. Nice swimming pool you have there!" A young girl had stepped from behind a tree as she laughed and pointed. "I don't suppose *your* daddy cares what his little peach dips in, does he?" She looked at Madame Deck.

"Mommie, she didn't honestly think it would be that easy did she? She should have known there was no way we would sit by and allow her to win."

"Eerie...baby...now don't be such a lousy sport." Madame Deck turned back to Amethyst. "Amethyst...dear...I do want you to know it was nothing personal against you. There's just a lot more at stake than you realize. It's kind of like I say all the time...some folks are and some folks aren't."

"There are those who have and those who have not," Eerie added. "We just happen to have!" She looked at Madame Deck. "Isn't that right Mommie?"

Madame Deck reached down and picked a lotus flower and twirled it in her hand. "I love my daughter, dear. I do hope you understand." Then she tossed the flower to Amethyst. Don't worry, it won't be long now. Try not to struggle; it might go quicker. I really wish there was another way."

"Mommie, I will miss Amethyst. We were kind of getting close. Especially in those days before that *thing* happened." Eerie laughed. "Bye Amethyst. Oh, did I tell you? I got promoted to the ninth grade! Wish me success! I plan to be as popular in high school as I was in middle school. And I *was* popular! So many, many...awards. What's that...you want me to have your trophies? Okay."

Amethyst struggled for something solid, yet the more she struggled, the faster she seemed to sink. She decided to stop resisting...just to detach herself from what was happening and try to come up with a way out.

"Child...what are you doing in there? All you'll find in there is doubt, unbelief, fear, worry, hate, jealously, disharmony, strife, bitterness, and a whole lot of trouble mixed together to create one sorrowful mess," the old woman said.

"Miss Jamahri? Is it really you this time?"

"None other, Child."

## Destiny Unlimited

"I don't mean to doubt you, but could you say something to let me know it's you for real."

"Am, we don't have a lot of time to play games. We have much to do but not much time to do it."

Amethyst smiled. That was all she needed to hear. "It really is you! Hurry and get me out. There's a twine on top of this tree above me." The quicksand was up about her waist now. "If you'll grab a stick and push the twine off, I can pull myself out—"

"Child, I am so sorry but I can't do that."

"What do you mean, you can't? You're kidding right? Take the can'ts out of your vocabulary and replace them with some cans! I'm in trouble here—"

"I'm not allowed. This is your tenth card. Helping you now—would in the end—not help either one of us."

"Miss Jamahri this isn't funny. It's a silly game. Okay, so I lose it. So what! If you like, I'll play again another time. I'll come back and visit with you and we can play as long as you like—"

"No other time. If you stop now, you won't have to worry ever again about playing any games whatsoever."

Amethyst was quickly going under. "So you're just going to stand there and let me die?"

"Remember the rules, Child. Remember the words." Miss Jamahri began to back away and then just as suddenly as she had appeared, she was gone.

Amethyst was tired. What was the use in fighting anymore? She had been through a lot and the one person who could have helped her, had stood by and not even stretched out a hand to save her. "Remember the words," she had said. What good were words *now*? *How can thinking, saying, or believing anything help me out of this?* she wondered.

Amethyst took a deep breath. What would be lost in saying them? She began. "Imagine. Im a gine...make things happen." She thought about the words and said them again. "Imagine. Im a gine...make things happen." She suddenly remembered the belt double-looped in her pants--her father's belt, a good size forty to circle his waist. She reached in the muck and undid the buckle, pulling the belt from her "no-name" jeans. Throwing the buckle upward, she hoped to knock the twine off the limb herself.

The quicksand--up to her armpits--sucked harder as she continued with her only shot at surviving. "Focus," she heard a voice say. "Never give up. You only need one...find the one."

Amethyst threw again and again...the quicksand at her chin. She knew it wouldn't be long now...history, another piece of buried treasure never to glisten in the light. Was that music? Oh yes...music. But from where was it coming? No matter, she was tired now. She closed her eyes. Sweet, sweet...music.

# Destiny Unlimited

## TWENTY-TWO

Nature's Symphony played a concerto for Amethyst. Birds flying south in assent for winter. Leaves of gold, orange, and burnt crimson twirling gracefully to the ground. The sun shining, the moon glistening, the stars twinkling, the thunder clashing, the lightning flashing. Stars falling elegantly from the sky. The ground slowly pushing up daisies, flowers bursting to bloom. Darkness to day, a sunrise a sunset resting on the water before sinking to dusk. "Code Blue! Code Blue!" Snow falls, snow flakes, snow balls, snow wo--and men. "Dr. Stanton to ICU. Stat! Dr. Stanton...to ICU, stat!" Winds chiming, leaves flying, trees bowing, clouds sailing quietly across an ocean sky. "Nurse, give her 4 ml's of..." Thunder, lightning, raindrops falling on a rusted tin roof. "We're losing her!" Floods, deserts, droughts, blizzards. Birds singing, bees buzzing, frogs croaking, crickets chirping, a line of ants...thousands working constantly, as they march...silently by. "No! Not my baby! N-o-o-o! Please Lord! Not *my* baby!"

Finally the rain ceases: colors tightly bowed around His shoulders...a token of an old covenant *that the waters shall no more become a flood ever again to destroy the earth.* A tear, a smile, then warm kisses from the sun. Words, familiar voices...words.

A merry-go-round is too much like worrying...it gives you something to do but it doesn't take you anywhere. A swing has its own ups and downs. A see-saw needs balance. You become what you see you are what you saw. The brain needs a blueprint in order to create. *You will always get what you've always gotten, when you always think like you've always thought.*

*You have purpose*! Find your true purpose. *Know* your purpose. Know why you do what you do. If someone has done it, then why *not* you? If no one has done it, then why not *you*? Speak of things as though they were...not will be...but is. I *am*, already is. And that...is *that*. Saying 'I will' recreates itself and will forever keep a thing in future tense. Whether it be spiritual or natural, the law is the law. And a law is no respecter of person--it cares not who you are.

The genie is inside you. You hold the key to every problem, question, and desire of your heart. Think only the highest thoughts. Speak grand things. Do what need be done.

Your todays are created by thoughts, words, and actions of yesterday. Cheerfully circulated money comes back. Flow is a current. Money was created to flow. Money is a creative energy itself. Energy not allowed to flow, explodes. Be excited when you move energy. When paying for things or services--imagine the many people your circulating helps support. Between you and money there can be only one master; the other will always be slave.

"Breathe! Come on...breathe!"

Choices embody consequences--whether they be good or bad. All decisions carry within it a seed of consequence--whether they be good or bad. Whatsoever you say, believe you receive. Invest in yourself--the returns far outweigh any charges! Accept responsibility. Stop blaming others. Forgive, if not to release another then to release yourself.

It takes as much time and effort to wash a cheap dish as it does to wash a fine piece of china. Life was created for living! Give attention to what you intend and watch things flow. Release the fixation as to *how* a particular thing will come to pass and believe however it does...it *will* be done. Say I love you in your mind when you meet and greet others--the air around you has a tendency to reflect thoughts. The only

## ᗪestiny ᘻnlimited

difference in those who have and those who have not is their decision--one decided they would have, while the other decided they would not. Anything worth having is worth fighting for--fight for your dreams. Fight for your own visions.
"Fight, Child. Don't you quit! You must believe!"
    Prejudice and discrimination can be rendered unconscious when tightly squeezed with the powerful arms of the Spirit of Excellence. Raise your standards and your standards will raise you. Iron sharpens iron. Steel...steel.
"Miss Jamahri. Help me. Help me, Miss Jamahri."
    Extract the seeds of opportunity that hide inside all adversity. It takes courage to persist. Never quench your thirst for knowledge or information. Whatever you desire to be--study *that*. Learn new things...unlearn the old that holds you back. Remain forever teachable. Develop a need to must know.
    "Erica! N-o! Oh my God! What have I done?" ..."Amethyst, would you mind doing me a favor?"..."Oh my God--what have I done?"..."Mommie, but if she's dead, then no one would know who did it."..."Please don't be dead!"..."But Mommie, I'm the spitting image of you."..."Oh my God--"..."Why wasn't Amethyst still with you? I trusted you to keep my child safe!"..."It wasn't my fault!..."Mrs. Price, I can't believe all this happened so fast! She should have known better than to talk to strangers."..."Erica and I weren't even gone that long."..."Amethyst and I were just really getting to be good friends, too. She wanted me to have her two trophies...I couldn't possibly take them though."
    "Erica? Where's my locket?...my Prayer Box locket with my parent's picture inside? I know you took it! Where is it?"..."But Mommie, I'm the spitting image of you."..."Doctor?...what is it? Oh my God, no. Not my child. Not my baby girl!"..."Mama, don't cry! Please Mama, don't cry."..."Amethyst? Baby come back."..."What is it,

Doctor?"..."Mommie, she didn't really think it would be that easy, did she?"..."Oh my God--what have I done?"

True power is within. Persevere. Demand the best from yourself: settle for nothing less. Careful who you associate with.

"I am A-lura Ja-mah-ri."

To transfer the invisible to the visible pray and then work. Faith without works is dead. You will never rise higher than what you believe. You activate forces and powers already working in the universe when you believe, then you and your goals are drawn closer to each other.

*And the Lord God said, Behold, the man is become as one of us, to know good and evil: and now, lest he put forth his hand, and take also of the tree of life, and eat, and live...*

"Say *yes* to life and life will say *yes* back to you! Child, set forth your hands...take of the tree of life...eat...and live. Remember your tongue, Child. It is the pen of a ready writer."

"Miss Jamahri?"

"Here, Child. Use your mouth. There is so much to do."

Amethyst began to mumble, "Imagine. Im a gine...I make things happen. Imagine. Im a gine...I make things happen." She took the belt and threw it one last time as she struggled to hold her head above the quicksand. The buckle flew in slow motion as she said with power, "Imagine, Im a gine. I make things happen!" The buckle landed, too far from the twine and time had almost run out. "I have to try one more time," she said. "I just have to. I don't know the number, but I do know, it only takes one." Only now the buckle was caught on something. She jerked and jerked, but it wouldn't turn loose. She then took a deep breath, closed her eyes again, and waited to be swallowed whole. It would be impossible to hold her breath forever...she knew that. But at least she would have tried. She had not quit, and still...this was how it would be. Suddenly, there was silence...nothing but a deafening silence.

*Destiny Unlimited*

## TWENTY-THREE

Amethyst--inside a miry pit--was drowning in its united forces. Sucked in by doubt and fear, she was being suffocated by hate, ignorance, anger, and unforgiveness; overtaken by bigotry, poverty, and procrastination; blinded by a lack of vision, the blaming of others, lack of commitment, the twins...no and low expectations. It was all in there--mixed together--as she was left to wallow unwillingly in its clutches. She *had* tried, what else was there left for her to do. Not even Miss Jamahri had reached out a hand to help her.

She had believed in the "genie" inside, but when it had really mattered, nothing had happened. She had done her part; believed, confessed, and thrown the belt as she focused on desired intent. And what had it gotten her? Nothing.

Her breath was almost spent. How much longer? Inside, she heard her mother's voice. "Come back baby," she said. Then, she heard laughter nearby. Madame Deck? Miss Jamahri? What was the difference whichever one it was?

"Child," Miss Jamahri said, "exactly *what* do you think you're doing?"

Amethyst couldn't speak...she was afraid to move. Opening her eyes wider now, she hadn't noticed until then that her stillness had caused her to stay afloat--sinking no more. "What do you care?" Amethyst said. "You won't--oh, I'm sorry--*can't* help me. Now, I'm just about out of time...and options--"

"And there is *still* much to do, Child!"

"Then help me, Miss Jamahri."

"I told you the rules. If you need help, help yourself."

"All right. I'll just die then. Why even try anymore?"

Miss Jamahri shook her head. "Die then. Your choice."

"Choice? What choice? I choose to get out of this nasty mess! But it doesn't look like *that's* going to happen, does it?!"

"Use what you got, Child," Miss Jamahri said. "Use what you got!"

"I *got* nothing, Miss Jamahri."

"Then what is that still in your hand?"

Amethyst glanced at her hand. It was the belt. She had somehow held on to it after having thrown it that last time. Maybe that's why she hadn't gone under. "My belt. But don't you get it? I keep missing the twine. If I can get the twine out of that tree, then I could pull myself out. But I keep missing it."

"And--"

"And? And what? Now the belt is stuck--"

"Am, listen to yourself. Hear what you're saying. You have your mind so set on *how* a thing is suppose to happen that you're missing your intention of getting out. There are more ways a thing can come to pass other than what you've decided and locked on. You want out, the belt is stuck, it won't let go." Miss Jamahri laughed. "Must I spell it out for you?"

Amethyst couldn't believe she hadn't seen it before. She pulled hard, it held tight. She pulled with all her might until her body pressed against solid dry land. Gasping deep breaths of fresh air, she lay near the feet of Miss Jamahri. *Air, how wonderful being able to breathe freely was!* She flipped onto her knees and raised up. "I did it," she said. "Imagine that. I really did it. Me and my *gine* made it happen."

Miss Jamahri didn't say a word, only bowed her head slightly. Lightning began flashing again and thunder began to roar. And for the first time since all this began, a heavy rain poured down on her. Amethyst spun around like a caterpillar spinning its way out of its cocoon. She twirled like a ballerina as the rain cleansed her from head to toe. It felt like shedding an old skin and crawling out with a brand new velvet one. Just as quickly, the rain stopped, the sun burst forth...bright and bold...drying her completely. Amethyst smiled at Miss Jamahri.

Miss Jamahri stretched out her hand returning Amethyst's notebook and pen to her. "I found these and saved them for you." She smiled. "Well--looks like you've done it, Child. Looks like you won this round...head and hands up! I am so very, very proud of you, too...my Child. And now, you are free to soar."

Amethyst looked up. "It's time for me to go, isn't it?"

Miss Jamahri nodded and smiled.

"Will I ever see you again?"

"Rest assured, one day in the not-so-distant-future, you will gaze into this old woman's face again. That's a promise."

"But what do I do if I want to talk to you again? Before we happen upon each other again, I mean. You know...like if I need your advice, guidance, direction, or maybe just want to talk about absolutely nothing anyone else would consider important?" Amethyst fought back the tears that came anyway.

Miss Jamahri reached out and gently brushed her tears away. "No tears today, okay. Save those dew drops for another watering, but not this one. I would hate for you to mess up your pretty little face over this. Trust me, this is a joyous time. And your folks are going to be so happy to see you."

"But I'm going to miss you, Miss Jamahri! Can't you come home with me? You understand me better than anyone. Life is just not fair--"

"Child! Who told you life was supposed to be fair?" Miss Jamahri looked into her face as she smiled down upon her. "Believe me, Child...Am, life is a lot fairer than you'll ever know. Not many are granted the opportunity you and I just had. Trust me on this one. Occasionally, life has been known to cheat and grant the tiniest of favors." Miss Jamahri smiled and stepped back. "Remember, if you ever need me, I'll always be close by. By the wings of soul, I'll hear when you call. Be still, learn to listen, feel my presence and suffer no limit to destiny."

Amethyst desperately wanted to believe. "You promise, Miss Jamahri?"

Miss Jamahri was being drawn farther away from where Amethyst stood. "I promise." She waved and blew her a kiss. "Now, repeat those important words I taught you." Miss Jamahri was fast beginning to look younger the more she seemed to drift from Amethyst.

"Imagine, Im a gine, I make things happen," she said.

"Again," a thirty-year old looking Miss Jamahri said.

"Imagine. Im a gine...I make things happen."

"Good," a twenty-year old woman the spitting image of Fair Share said as she grinned. "Once more Child. And let the world hear you!"

Amethyst smiled. She couldn't believe her eyes as a mirror image of herself stood reciting the words in concert with her. "Imagine, Im a gine...I make things happen!" Then, like magic, the young girl on the other side of the mirror...was...no...more! The word **ENIG**, in big bold letters, was now reflecting in the mirror. When Amethyst turned to see where the image was reflecting from, she saw an amazing thing. **ENIG** was actually **GINE** spelled backwards!

Amethyst began to feel like a butterfly, spreading her wings, preparing to fly. Facing the sun, her body quietly lifted off the ground as she twirled and basked in the brilliance of the sun. Warm, light, free. High above the trees she soared. Closer and closer to a bright and morning star. Gently, she flapped her new coat of fine colors. Warm, light, free. Destiny...Unlimited, laden with knowledge and purpose, and now...*Free to Soar*. "Imagine," she whispered, "I'm a genie, I make things happen."

## TWENTY-FOUR

"Imagine. I'm a genie. I make things happen," Amethyst whispered as she slowly began to stir.

"Nurse! Page the doctor...she's coming to," Amethyst's mother shouted down the hall toward the nurse's station from the opened door. "She's trying to speak. Hurry!" She then ran back and stood beside her daughter. "Glory to God, my baby girl is finally waking up!"

Amethyst was groggy as she tossed and turned. "Miss Jamahri?"

Her mother rubbed her hand while blinking back tears. "Baby, it's Mama."

Amethyst struggled as she finally opened her eyes. "Mama?"

"Yes baby! I'm here. You're going to be all right. You're going to be *just* fine." She laughed through her sniffling.

Amethyst pressed her teeth against a dry bottom lip. "But Mama, what are you doing here? I got out of the quicksand all by myself. I won, Mama. I won the game. I didn't quit. I played all the way to the end, and I made it back home. I'm finally home."

"Yes baby, you're home. And no, you didn't quit. You won. We all did." She leaned down and kissed Amethyst on her bandaged head just as the doctor walked in. "Doctor, she's talking. She's going to be all right."

The doctor smiled. "Well...let's have a look and see." He leaned over and began to shine a pen light in Amethyst's eyes.

"Why hello there, young lady. You gave us quite a scare there for a while."

"Ouch!" She touched her head where the boomerang had whacked her when she was visiting with Don In Lieu. "You're Dr. Stanton aren't you?"

Dr. Stanton looked puzzled at Mrs. Price. "She just woke up you say?"

"Yes, Doctor."

He smiled and looked back at Amethyst. "And how is it you already know my name?" He remembered his name tag. "Oh-h-h. I bet you read it on my jacket."

"No sir. That's not how." She looked at his coat. "Your tag's missing anyway." He looked down; she was right. "I just remember your voice and some nurses calling your name."

"Oh? And *when* might this have been?" he said, continuing her examine.

Amethyst thought about it while following his every movement. "I'm not exactly sure. I just remember the voice...it's so deep and all. You told one of the nurses to give somebody 4 ml's of tri something or other."

He looked over at Mrs. Price and mouthed the word Amethyst had referred to. Mrs. Price smiled and nodded back. "So you heard me say *that* did you? Interesting. Interesting indeed." He smiled and shook his head.

"Yes sir," Amethyst said as she started to close her eyes. "I'm tired. Miss Jamahri was right...that game was more serious than I ever figured it would be. But don't you think putting me in the hospital because I got hit in the head by a boomerang is going a bit overboard?" She began drifting back to sleep.

Dr. Stanton shook his head and walked Mrs. Price to the door. "Who's Miss Jamahri?"

"I don't know."

"She's not a relative...one of Amethyst's friends maybe?"

### Destiny Unlimited

"No. My first time hearing the name Miss Jamahri, was when Amethyst woke up."

"I wonder who she could be talking about then. Well, not to worry. She *has* been through a lot these past few weeks. It's probably effects left over from the medication. In a day or two, I'm sure she'll be back to her normal self again."

"She was repeating something when she first woke up...it was about being a genie and making things happen."

"A genie, huh? Well, like I said--she'll be back to normal in a few days."

Mrs. Price laughed. "Doctor, my baby made it! If this is all I have to be worried about, then everything's fine. I need to call the rest of my family and tell them the news. Oh--and I really should call Mrs. Dexter as well. She has either called or come by every single day since this tragedy, checking on our Amethyst. She asked if I would let her know if--when-- Amethyst regained conscious. She and her daughter have been so great through all of this...never have I witnessed such *genuine* concern. Who would have ever imagined--they hadn't even known Amethyst for that long. I just know they're both going to be so relieved! Mrs. Dexter will finally be able to rest now, knowing Amethyst indeed pulled through!"

Amethyst was sitting up in the bed looking out at people's comings and goings below her perched window, when a nurse--a rather large woman with jet black hair and a certain playful demeanor about her--quietly waltzed in.

"Well, well. It's my Little Princess! So, how are you getting along?"

Amethyst laid back against the flatten pillows while getting her blood pressure checked. "I'm fine," she said, staring up at the familiar-looking woman.

The nurse took out a thermometer and stuck it in Amethyst's mouth as she held onto her limp wrist. "I'm Florene, but everybody calls me Flo. You had us worried there for a while. I don't know if you realize just how serious you were. But I took one look at you and said...'*Now Flo, that's a strong little warrior there. If anybody will pull through, she will!*' " She took the thermometer out and stared. "Yeah, you're doing fine. Just fine!" Flo shook the thermometer, wrote on Amethyst's chart, and smiled. "You need anything? Juice maybe?" she said.

Amethyst nodded, but then the picture of a toy with a spring for its neck made her stop, and instead she said, "Yes, ma'am."

"What kind? Apple, grape, cranberry--"

"Grape."

"Grape it is then! I'll be back in a few primes of the pump." Then she left and came back five minutes later with two cans of juice and a pitcher of ice.

Mrs. Dexter and Erica rushed through the door bearing a bouquet of flowers, not five minutes after Flo left. "Oh, Amethyst, dear...you're okay! We are so glad you're all right," Mrs. Dexter said. Erica shadowed her mother's every move. Mrs. Dexter put the flowers on a stand and pulled up a chair close to Amethyst's bed. "The nurse said it was okay to come in. Mind if I sit?"

Amethyst rolled her eyes and continued to stare out of the window.

"Now listen, dear...I don't know exactly what all you remember or think you remember, but I'm going to tell you what actually happened that night at the park." Mrs. Dexter looked at Erica who was also staring down at the people's comings and goings. Mrs. Dexter continued. "Erica and I were standing next to my car talking as we prepared to get in. It was

## Destiny Unlimited

dark...with the exception of the street light a few spaces down from where I was parked. We heard someone coming towards us, I pulled out my gun believing we were in danger--"

"But you saw me," Amethyst said looking in her face for the first time...her eyes, full of pain. "You looked me dead in my face, Mrs. Dexter. I saw you! You stared right at me as I *walked* up only a few feet in front of you..."

Mrs. Dexter was surprised at the words coming from such a young child's mouth. She stuttered as she spoke. "Yes Amethyst...that is true. Give me a break. Everything happened so quick; there wasn't much time to do or to think--"

"What are you talking about Mrs. Dexter...I'm the one who got shot!"

"Now dear, don't be rash with your thoughts. That's not what happened. I mean, it is what happened, but it was all an accident...plain and simple."

"No, Mrs. Dexter! It was not plain and simple! Erica took that gun from you intent on shooting me. You saw her. She stood square in front of me. She took aim and tried to pull the trigger...except the safety was still on."

"Yes dear...the safety was on...I believe a safe gun is a good gun--"

"But then she fumbled and hurried to take the safety off." Amethyst looked in Mrs. Dexter's face as tears filled her large brown eyes. "Then you..." Amethyst stared at her...hard. She refused to allow even one tear to fall. "But why, Mrs. Dexter? Why?"

"Dear, I am *so* sorry. But please believe me. It was purely an accident. An accident that never should have happened."

"Erica was pointing the gun at me, except this time, the safety was off."

Mrs. Dexter turned away as she wiped tears that rolled down her face. "Amethyst," she said as she turned back to look at her, "I am sorry. So sorry."

Amethyst blinked, and tears rolled down her face one after another on to the crisp white sheets as she recalled everything as it happened.

Mrs. Dexter had run to Erica and demanded she give her the gun. Erica held her stance, and Mrs. Dexter stepped between the gun and Amethyst--becoming literally a human shield.

"Move Mommie! I want Amethyst out of my way! Those awards were mine. They belonged to me! And they would have been awarded to me had it not been for her. She has no legal right to keep what should be mine!"

"Erica...baby...what is wrong with you? Now I want you to give me that gun this instant." She held out her hand. "Erica? I'm talking to you girl!"

"I said, move *Mother* dear!"

Amethyst began taking small slow steps backwards.

"Erica, I'm not going to just let you shoot her. Now you know that. I don't know where I've gone wrong, but this is not the appropriate behavior for you."

Erica was hard and unmoveable. "I want what belongs to me, Mommie! Tell her to give me my trophies and I'll forget all this. I want what's mine, and I want it now!"

"Oh my God! What have I done?" Mrs. Dexter said as she walked closer to Erica. "You ungrateful, spoiled brat!"

Erica tried going around her mother while Amethyst continued walking backwards...afraid any sudden movement might panic Erica. Mrs. Dexter grabbed Erica's extended arm. "Erica! N-o!" And in the struggle, the gun fired.

"Oh no, Mommie! What have we done?" Erica released the gun into her mother's hand. "I didn't mean to do it. Is she dead? Oh, Mommie, why did she force us have to do something like this?"

Amethyst lay motionless on the ground. Mrs. Dexter hurried over to her body to see if she was still breathing.

"Is she dead?" Erica asked as her mother looked at her with a look that could have knocked her to her knees. "I didn't mean to do it, Mommie! You've got to fix this. You've just go to!"

Amethyst remembered it all. She wiped the tears from her eyes and turned again to the window.

Mrs. Dexter put her hand on the bed, touching Amethyst's shin through the covers. "Amethyst, what are you going to do? What will you tell people when they ask?"

Amethyst turned and with a burning look she said, "I always tell the truth!"

Erica walked over to Amethyst's bed. "If you do, no one's going to believe you. It will be your word against ours. We'll tell them it was an accident...that we didn't even know it was you. It was dark, we never saw you. We didn't see anyone." Erica smiled as she looked at both Amethyst's and her mother's tear stained faces. "Frankly, I'm rather fond of *my* version. We never saw you, Amethyst! Didn't even know you had been hit. Why, had we known, we would have called for help immediately! Even after we heard about the shooting, we didn't realize it was Mommie's gun's stray bullet that was the cause of it." Erica began to laugh. "You're a loser Amethyst. I know it, you know it...everyone knows it. So face it, losers never prosper."

At that moment, as if by cue, a man in a dark blue suit entered Amethyst's room. "Oh...I'm sorry. Am I interrupting something?" He smiled. "Hello Mrs. Dexter...Erica. There's only one problem I see with your version of the story." He walked in front of Mrs. Dexter who had stood up to leave. "Oh excuse me," he said holding a locket up, "might this cute little trinket belong to you, Mrs. Dexter?"

"My locket. But where--"

He smiled as he closed it up in his fist. "Found in Amethyst's balled-up hand that night in the park. Appears she was bringing it back to its *rightful* owner."

"Then she must have stolen it!" Erica said. "She's a little thief! She must have stolen it when she visited our house that day." Erica turned and looked at Amethyst with hate and disgust. "Why you little ungrateful thief! So this is how you repay our kindness? Stealing from us when we invite you into our home! Mommie, I thought she was a liar, but I didn't know she was a thief or I never--"

"Stolen, huh? Well now, let...me...see. The only problem with *that* scenario is a young man named Aljuwon--an exceptional student, active member of his church...a young man clearly headed somewhere in life. Well, it seems this young man came forth with an entirely *different* story. He claims to have seen your little girl drop this locket from a bracelet. He said he tried to get it back to you only, Mrs. Dexter..." he looked into her eyes, "you pulled a gun on him and his friends?" The man shook his head and grunted with a slight laugh. "A gun, Mrs. Dexter...which coincidentally, seemed to be the same type weapon of choice used on this young thing here. According to this young man--Aljuwon--and his three friends, Amethyst was being nice...doing a favor by *returning* this item to you after his failed attempt."

The man opened his fist and took the sterling silver charm out, dangling it by the ring in Mrs. Dexter's face. "Now, I'll admit this locket may not be worth much in the money department, but I'd be willing to bet the value of the picture inside of a mother, father, and their baby girl must be priceless!"

## ~Destiny ~Unlimited

Mrs. Dexter put her hand up near her chest and pressed down firmly. "You mean...those boys were only trying to return this locket?" Mrs. Dexter said.

"Yes ma'am, that's what it looks like."

Mrs. Dexter stumbled back against the wall.

Two police officers came in. "Mrs. Dexter," the man in the blue suit said. "...you are under arrest! Read them their rights and get them out of here."

"What about my lawyer?" Mrs. Dexter said.

"You'll be allowed to call your lawyer from the station." He looked over at Erica who was backed up against the window now. "You've got to go too little lady," he said as he shook his head.

"You *can't* prove any of this," Erica said. "It's all circumstantial--"

The man in blue began to laugh. "Television. Makes folks say and think the darndest things! Little lady, we have a warrant for your mother's gun, and I am sure, once we request your mother's cellular phone records, there will be a call to 911 just around the time someone left this little one here at that park for dead. Oh, and one more tiny little evidence that's sure to cinch this case...we happen to have a living, eye witness, to the *alleged* crime." He retrieved a small tape recorder from the night drawer and clicked it off. Then he motioned to the two officers to take them away.

He turned to Amethyst. "Well little lady, looks like everything's going to be all right after all." He slipped the tape recorder inside his jacket pocket.

Amethyst gazed down at her hands. "I told you they were going to try something," she said.

"*That* you did. But I want you to know...you done good. Real good."

"You know, they're really not bad people. They're just lost beings who made some really bad decisions. And Erica is just spoiled to the core. She's like a garden that never got the proper attention. Her mother...well, at least in the end she did try to stop Erica. It was just too late, the monster was already too large and out of control."

"Yeah. Well, they had better be glad you didn't die. All the evidence we had would have pointed to murder. And we were convinced it was the mother that did the shooting. Who would ever have figured that innocent-acting child could be so heartless and devious? I don't know what's going on with the young people these days, but we'd better find out and fix it. Both that mother and that child need some serious help if you ask me. And I mean in a hurry."

"Thank you, Officer Hunt," Amethyst said extending her hand.

"No, thank you. It took a lot of guts to pull through like you did. And then to stand up to them so soon after regaining consciousness. You're just a real paratrooper! And smart too. Telling your parents, who in turn, alerted us before the Dexters could get to you." He opened the door. "There's a crowd out here waiting to see you. I'll send your parents in okay?"

Amethyst nodded, took a long deep breath...then exhaled. Air...it tasted so good!

## TWENTY-FIVE

Mr. Fuller and Mr. Lewis both stuck their heads inside the half-opened doorway. "Is it okay if we come in?" Mr. Fuller asked as he grinned at Amethyst.

Her eyes sparkled. "Mr. Fuller! Mr. Lewis! What are you two doing here?" She looked around; the room was full. Her parents, two sisters, brother Michael, and now Mr. Fuller and Mr. Lewis were all there.

"I take it you're glad to see us then?" Mr. Lewis said. "We're not infringing on family time are we?" Mr. Lewis said to Mr. Price.

"Oh not at all," Mr. Price said, "the more, the merrier." He turned to Amethyst. "These two gentlemen have been almost religious in coming to check on you since you've been here. I hear, they were struck by your magic dust."

Michael walked up to the bed. "Am, guess what I brought you?" He pulled out a round key holder. "Keys, Am. I brought you keys."

"Keys? Michael, where did you get so many keys from?" She thought a second. "And since when did you start calling me Am?"

"I got the keys from different folks. They're spares...about thirty here. I wanted you to see that I did believe you." He held up the keys. "See, the keys to success and making things happen, Am. Just like you always say."

Amethyst hugged Michael. "Well Michael, we won't be needing these keys any longer. You see, I found the real keys to success and making things happen," she whispered. "I ended up in this place called Enig. And there was this woman there named Miss Jamahri...she was the cause of me finding them. I saw the earth...it's a she. She was all balled up, then she stretched and started talking and everything. Michael, Earth talked. And there I was, standing out there on nothing." Amethyst grinned and fell back against her pillow.

Amethyst's mother and father exchanged glances as did both Christine and Charlene. Mr. Fuller and Mr. Lewis looked at Mrs. Price who only nodded for everyone to go along with Amethyst as she recanted her "adventures."

Mr. Fuller and Mr. Lewis told Amethyst how they had formed a partnership thanks to her, but Amethyst was more interested in telling them all about her quest. How she had wanted to call home and tell her parents she was all right, but there wasn't a phone to be found. How she won the game simply by finishing it. (She decided it best not to cause them worry, so she skipped the part about almost not finishing it and what that would have meant.)

Everybody smiled as they wondered where she had inherited such a vivid imagination. Dr. Stanton did say she would be back to normal, though in truth, this *was* normal for her. Her mother figured since her tales really weren't hurting anybody--in fact they were quite entertaining--to just let her have at it.

"You know, Am..." Michael said, "...your story would make a great book. A movie even! I like it, and I'm young. It looks like Mr. Fuller and Mr. Lewis like it too, and they're old--"

"Michael!" his mother said. "Now that wasn't nice."

Mr. Lewis and Mr. Fuller laughed. "Oh, but the boy speaks the truth," Mr. Lewis said. "We like the story and we're not nearly as young as we claim to be."

"Michael's exaggerating," Amethyst said. "Who'd be interested in reading my adventures anyway? It's not like I'm somebody famous or anything like that."

# Destiny Unlimited

"Not yet," Michael said. "But someday...right Am? So that makes it already true right now."

Amethyst smiled. "Sure Michael." She recalled the lessons she had learned. "I am...right now."

They began leaving so she could get some rest. All in all, it had been a pretty good day. Yesterday, she hadn't been conscious to *this* world, and today, she was back.

Amethyst's mother was the last to leave. She smiled as she planted a kiss on her daughter's bandaged head. "You get some rest now, okay. I'll get everyone settled at home, then come back and sit with you some more."

Amethyst smiled. "You believe me...don't you, Mama?"

Her mother blinked several times. "I'll tell you what I believe...I believe that you believe it. And that's all that matters."

Amethyst's smile all but disappeared. If her mother had believed her, she would have said so. Seems no one really believed what happened. Proof. She needed proof. Unless it really *didn't* happen...was only a product of her "over-active" imagination. The notebook. Why of course!

"Mama?" she said, "would you mind seeing if you can find my notebook. It's purple and blue with fancy designs on the front. About this tall," she gestured with her hands, "...and this wide. I can't say where it is now for sure, but I had it...at one time."

"Your backpack is at home. I'll look for the notebook in there and bring it when I come back. Is there anything else you need or would like? A book to read maybe?"

"Oh yes ma'am! A book would be wonderful."

"Any particular one?"

"My teacher gave me three...I *know* they're in my backpack. Any one of them would be fine. The doctor says I'll be going home in a few days. One should be enough to hold me."

She laughed. "Mama, it's the strangest thing. Suddenly, I'm having an incredible desire to sign-up for violin lessons."

Her mother stood up and smiled. "A violin, huh? Sure baby. Well, the doctor also says you'll be back to your old self in a few days. But I'll bring your notebook and one of the books in your backpack." She leaned down and kissed Amethyst on her head. "It's good to have you back, baby."

Amethyst slipped off to sleep, and there stood Miss Jamahri in a dream.

"I know who you are," Amethyst said.

"You *do* now?" Miss Jamahri laughed. "Then let's keep some things between ourselves, shall we?"

"If you like."

"So what's up?" Miss Jamahri said as she climbed on a tall bar stool and folded her arms. "Why did you summon me?"

"I wanted you to know how much I appreciate everything you did. Nobody believes me, though. They think I made it up. I see how they look when I tell them about all the places and things I experienced. They don't say it, but I can tell. They think...*She's fantasizing again.*"

"Oh Child, never mind what people think. Have you not gotten it *yet*? You don't have to prove any thing to any one--not now or ever. You know, I know, and through your life's true work, others will some day come to know the truth. Just hold the wheel of the ship on course and the rest of the ship will ultimately have to follow. Understand?"

"Yes," Amethyst said. "Now tell me...do you have any idea why Michael suddenly began calling me Am? If I recall, only you called me that."

"Well now, Amethyst *is* a long name you know."

"Miss Jamahri..."

## Destiny Unlimited

"Oh all right! Maybe I did have a *teensy* little something to do with it. A whisper maybe. I just want you to remember who you are and the power of *Am*."

Amethyst smiled. "Well, I appreciate...all that you are and have been."

"I know. Now, I must be going Child. There is much to do, but not much time..."

"...to do it!" Amethyst said laughing.

Miss Jamahri smiled as she climbed down and started to walk away. The beads on her skirt beat with the rhythm of her stride. Turning back to Amethyst, she said, "Am...I'll see what I can do about that fantasizing stigma you've seemed to have acquired. By the wings of soul, until we meet again."

Then the screen went to black.

Outside of Amethyst's door stood an old woman with a large, old raggedy bag. She had a long braid that trailed down the spine of her back. Judith Price returned just in time to see her rub--almost prayerfully--the closed wooden door.

"Ma'am? Are you lost?" Judith said.

"Me? Lost? No, Child. I was looking for a girl named Am...Am...Am--"

"Amethyst?"

"Yes, that's it. The nurse told me she was in here. Such a sweet child. She and I played together in the park a few weeks ago. I'll never forget her spirit. I heard something horrible happened to her. Would you know if they've caught the ones who did it yet?"

"Yes ma'am. They were picked up today." Judith looked closer at her. "Forgive me for staring, but you look so familiar. Where do I know you from?"

"Familiar? It's possible. I've been told I have one of those type-faces."

"It's so strange. I've heard other people say things like that and I always thought it corny. I suppose now I see how they feel."

"Possibly, it will come to you some day. And if not, no harm done."

"I'm Judith Price," she said extending her hand, "Amethyst's mother."

"Oh yes...I saw the resemblance immediately. She definitely has your eyes, but I bet she gets told that all the time. I'm Alice Josephine Morrison, but everybody calls me *O My, Alice Jo*." She held tight to Judith's hand.

"Nice to meet you Ms. Morrison--"

"Please...call me *O My Alice Jo* like everyone else Child."

Judith smiled. It would have been much simpler and less words to say Ms. Morrison, she thought. "All right, O My Alice Jo. Would you like to come in and speak to Amethyst? I'm sure she'll be delighted to see you."

"I just peeped in on the little angel; she's fast asleep. I don't want to disturb her. But I would like to leave something with you to give to her when she wakes up." O My reached into her old bag. "This belongs to her I believe. I'm sure I saw her writing in it that day in the park. Quite fancy...couldn't help but remember it. Not like those plain ones of my day, but then, that's a whole nother story altogether." O My smiled as she handed the notebook to Judith.

Judith looked nervous...almost like she was afraid of it.

"I found it earlier today," O My said, "as luck would have it, under the merry-go-round of all places! Must have gotten there *by the wings of soul*. Did you know merry-go-rounds are like rocking chairs and worry?" She smiled. "They all give you something to do but take you nowhere. Worry... worry...hurry...hurry. Hurry...worry. Round and round. *Faster*."

Judith tried not to laugh.

### Destiny Unlimited

"Anyway, I had dropped my bag near the merry-go-round, and when I got down on the ground...low and behold, there was the notebook with a lovely pen stuck in the spiral part. It writes good too." She looked down. "I don't usually go on and on like this, but your daughter impacted me so profoundly. She made me feel...special. Talked to me like I was a person instead of something somebody threw out with the trash. If you'd just see to her getting this, I'd be much obliged." *O My* touched Judith's hand, then walked--practically strolled--away.

Judith smiled as she watched the spry little woman looking more like somebody in her twenties. "She gets around better than I do," Judith said out loud as she pushed opened the door to her daughter's room.

She was glad Amethyst's notebook had been located, having searched everywhere she could think of without luck.

Amethyst was still asleep. Judith smiled and sat in a chair next to her daughter's bed. Pulling the pen from the spiral of the notebook, she began to flip through the many handwritten pages. A pressed, still moist rose fell to the floor. She leaned down and picked it up.

"How *odd*; half-white and half-red," she whispered to the unusual created rose. Sitting back in the chair, her eyes began to scan the contents of her little girl's thoughts.

"Amazing," Judith said. "Simply amazing."

## TWENTY-SIX

Mrs. Price couldn't believe what she was reading. So much wisdom inside these pages--on every single page. It was too much, too advanced for an eleven-year-old to have written. There were things she herself hadn't known or considered. Had the penmanship not been Amethyst's, she would have believed someone else had done it entirely.

Only now did she better understand the confusion of Amethyst's "real" adventures. Apparently she had written all this before the shooting and her mind used it to create a fantasy world to help bring her back to the real world.

Mrs. Price sat forward when Amethyst began to stir. Amethyst opened her eyes and smiled. "Mama, you're back."

"Yes baby. Just like I promised."

A bird landed on the ledge outside the window. They couldn't hear her all that well, but *she* seemed to be singing just to them. When she finished, she flew away, having performed grand melodies. Watching her, one would have believed she never even noticed her audience consisted of only two people.

Amethyst sat up and noticed the beaten-up notebook in her mother's lap. "You found it?"

"A little worn for wear, it looks like it's been through a storm," her mother said smiling. "It took cover under a merry-go-round in the park. An old woman found it, in fact, you just missed seeing her...a woman named Ms. Morrison?"

Amethyst frowned. "Who?"

"*O My* Alice Josephine Morrison, I believe that's what she said anyway."

## Destiny Unlimited

"*O My* was here?" Amethyst said. "She's gone already?"

"She peeped in on you, but you were asleep. Calls you a little angel, and I must confess, I agree. She wanted to make sure you got your notebook back." Her mother kept her hand on a page, before placing the pen inside and closing it. "Amethyst, I brought you one of the books from your backpack. But did you realize there were actually four books in there, not three?"

"Four?"

"Yes, there was this one," she pulled out a black Bible. "It's not one of ours."

Amethyst smiled. "Oh that's Miss Ja--" She stopped. *What was the use? Nobody believed her anyway.* "Just one somebody let me have...it was an old one they weren't using anymore." She cradled the Bible, finding it nearly impossible to contain or conceal her joy.

"Baby, I have a new Bible at home. If you like--"

"No, this one is perfect. It has all these wonderful passages marked," she said continuing to grin from ear to ear.

"Well I brought you this book to read." She retrieved a small book from her purse--*To Kill A Mocking Bird*. "I hope you like it. You know, Harper Lee is also from Alabama?"

Amethyst smiled. "Oh really." She tried to hide her grin. *Miss Jamahri's old Bible! I have Miss Jamahri's old Bible!* Proof--at least to herself--that this really did happen.

Her mother looked down at the notebook as she began to caress its cover. "Amethyst, there are some powerful words in here. You truly do have a gift."

Amethyst stopped smiling. "Really Mama? You *really* think so?"

Her mother nodded, then read from a few of the pages. Amethyst smiled, remembering each lesson that had prompted those words.

Turning the notebook to the back page, Amethyst's mother suddenly became quiet.

"Mama? What's the matter?" Amethyst said, following minutes of stillness and silence.

Her mother looked up at her with tears in her eyes. "It's a letter. To you. Dated today."

"From whom?"

Her mother then turned a page and gently pulled out a golden parchment.

"Mama? Who is the letter from?"

Her mother handed her the notebook as she sat reading the golden paper that was now trembling in her hand. Amethyst anxiously read the letter addressed to her.

*Am,*
*I am Shaman...you are Shaman. Before I am, you were. Knowledge Child...an all important key that will unlock many doors. "Sticks and stones may break my bones but words can never hurt me?" No Child, words have power to cast many spells. Words are powerful tools. Able to hurt as well as heal. To cause pain as well as joy. "I hate you!" Only words, but oh, feel the pain. "I love you." Words of joy and assurance. Yes, only words—yet full of power. Learn to use your power for good. Realize that words in and of themselves are neither good nor bad; the possessor and/or the receiver determines that. I pray you know that in the saving of yourself, you saved me. And I shall always and forever be a thought away...*

*Always,*
*Alura Jamahri*

*P. S. Here's the original recipe for my famous soup—The ABCs of Success and Making Things Happen. Add your*

# Destiny Unlimited

*own special spices; you're the salt of the earth...season as well as preserve. As usual, we have much to do but not much time to do it! In the stillness...I still Am. Take care Child. Always remember this:* **Even the Sky truly Knows No Limits.**

Amethyst couldn't believe it; Miss Jamahri had written her a letter! Then her mother handed her the worn gold parchment paper. *Alphabet Soup For Success* was penned across its top. Such a flowing handwriting. Amethyst traced the letters of success with her finger, then read the twenty-six ingredients with its one line of direction: *Add equal parts, adjust to individual taste, and remember–stir constantly.* "If you're hungry," it said, "then open up a can of Chunky Chicken Soup. *Bon appetit!*"

**A**ccept Responsibility
**B**e who You Are called to be
**C**ommit to your Dreams and Goals
**D**on't ever quit!
**E**xpect what you Desire
**F**aith without Works is Dead
**G**ratitude Magnetizes that much more
**H**ave Faith when you Believe
**I** am adds power to both written and spoken words
**J**ust because it appears you're losing, doesn't mean you are
**K**nowledge is the key to otherwise Locked Doors
**L**et there be! always causes things to Happen
**M**aking a living is not as divine as making a Difference
**N**othing outside yourself is greater than *Who* is within
**O**pportunity, at times, must be snatched from Adversity
**P**urpose is both Persistent and Determined!
**Q**uiet time equals a Guided Mind

# Vanessa Davis Griggs

**R**emain "Forever Reachable and Teachable"
**S**uccess is knowing your Purpose and working to Fulfill it
**T**hings are *Thoughts made Manifest*
**U**nderstand first what Needs to be Done, then Do it!
**V**ision is "Sight" before "Things" are physically seen
**W**hat you Sow is what you will Reap
**X**-ray Vision is no match for "Clandestine" Vision
**Y**ou can never Rise Higher than what you Believe
**Z**ip your Lips when your Tongue starts to Slip

Amethyst looked at her mother and smiled. It didn't matter if anyone believed her or not. Like her mother said, *she* believed...and in this world, that is all that truly counts.

"Keys," Amethyst said holding up the recipe.

Her mother smiled then squeezed her hand. "Yes baby..." she said looking down at the golden paper, the notebook, then back at her daughter. "*They*, most certainly are."

**THE END**

Order Form (Copy as Needed)

Knowledge is power [Nam et ipsa scientia potestas est].
Francis Bacon

We encourage you to check with your favorite bookstore for this book if you don't already have your own personal copy. If they don't have it in stock, please request that they order a few copies (for the next person looking for it).

This book may also be ordered directly as instructed below. It is available to organizations, corporations and other associations at quantity discounts. For more information, please contact us. Our e-mail address is: FreeSoar2@aol.com

Telephone Orders: Monday - Friday 8am - 5pm CST (Credit Cards Only)
Toll Free: (877) 5TO SOAR (586-7627) In Alabama: (205) 956-2889

Postal Orders: Free To Soar, Vanessa Griggs, Dept. G,
P. O. Box 101328, Birmingham, Alabama 35210-1328

Please Print
The following book is being requested: Destiny Unlimited

Number of Copies _____ Would you like it Autographed? _____

If so, whose name(s) _____

_____
_____

Your Name: _____

Address: _____
_____

Telephone: _____

____ Number of Copies @ $15.95 each        $ _____
     Alabama residents must add 8% Sales Tax  $ _____

     Shipping and Handling $4.00 for (1) Book   $ _____
     for each additional book add $1.00.
     Be a Blessing! Order 6 or more books here
     (yours, family, friends, an eager child's),
     and We'll pay your Shipping & Handling!

     TOTAL AMOUNT ENCLOSED              $ _____
Payment: ____ Check or Money Order (Payable To: Free To Soar)

       ____ Credit card (Complete below)
            ____ Visa   ____ MasterCard   ____ Discover

Card number: _____

Name on Card: _____

Exp. date: _____ / _____   Signature: _____